The Lighthouse Keeper

by

Liv Rancourt

Liv Rancourt

This is a work of fiction. Names, characters, places, businesses and incidents either are the product of the author's imagination or are used fictitiously. Any resemblance to actual persons, living or dead, events, or locales is entirely coincidental.

The Lighthouse Keeper
© 2023 by Amy Dunn Caldwell

Cover Art: Kanaxa
Editor: Angela James
Copyedits/proofreader: Meg DesCamps

ISBN: 978-1-7368520-9-5

Dedication

To KB, for taking me out on the water and showing me the lighthouse, and to KSC, for putting up with my obsessions.

Liv Rancourt

Table of Contents

The Lighthouse Keeper

...And as the evening darkens, lo! how bright,

Through the deep purple of the twilight air,

Beams forth the sudden radiance of its light

With strange, unearthly splendor in the glare!

From The Lighthouse by Henry Wadsworth Longfellow

Liv Rancourt

Chapter One

My name is Vincent Fairchild, and I'm too pretty for my own good. At least that's what my mother always said. "Those lying eyes," she'd say, "are someday going to make you tell the truth."

She may have been right, but it hasn't happened yet.

Besides, in my experience, eyes don't lie nearly as often as lips do. That simple fact might have led to my present condition: coming to wakefulness in a strange bed with my eyelids gummed together with sleep and my mouth a foul desert. My heartbeat rose in tandem with my consciousness until it came near to bounding out of my chest. I was alone, likely the only positive to take from this unfortunate circumstance. The grey light through the window suggested I'd risen with the sun.

Before moving, I attempted to recreate the events that led me here, using logic to stem the tide of fear. I'd finished work last night and met up with Rutger. We'd gone to our neighborhood watering hole. Ran into others of our kind and drank some more. Got dinner from a street vendor, first a packet of fried oysters and later on a tamale. Gah. Food. My stomach roiled and I sat up fast enough to make my head spin.

I didn't want to puke on a stranger's bed. I'd been raised better than that.

Sitting up proved that I still wore my trousers, a minor reassurance. My lower lip throbbed and a light touch showed it to be tender and swollen. Either I'd been smacked in the mouth with a fist or hit with a very large prick.

I didn't want to wait around for the owner of either of those anatomical gifts to return. Rutger's was the only prick I knew well, and his never left a mark no matter where he put it.

My undershirt had been rucked up, exposing my nipples, and my wrists felt strangely raw. A silk necktie had been wrapped around one, a tie with an I Magnin label. *Strange.* Rutger shopped at I Magnin. I let the striped silk slip through my fingers. *Had someone used his tie to bind my wrists?*

The Lighthouse Keeper

Blushing at what I couldn't remember, I began buttoning my shirt with shaky fingers. My own necktie and one boot were visible on the floor. With luck, my waistcoat, jacket and the other boot would appear.

How much had I drunk? My head whirled and I clenched my jaw. I had a vague memory of laughter, a dark alley, and... absinthe?

Jesus, what had I done? This kind of thing hadn't happened to me in months. Where was I? If I'd been in this room before, I had no memory of it. And where was Rutger? We were much more likely to go home together than to go off on our own. Of all the witches I'd come to know, Rutger Smit was my closest friend, my sometimes-lover, and my protector. If I had ended up under questionable circumstances, he must be in even worse trouble.

Footsteps sounded overhead, inspiring me to find my missing things. As quickly as possible, given my state, I dressed. My jacket pocket jingled with coins. *Good.* I hadn't spent everything. I even found my hat, a dapper bowler which disguised the bird's nest on my head. Stifling my growing sense of foreboding, I buttoned my jacket and made ready to leave.

The door opened to an anonymous hallway, grubby and stinking of piss. My stomach nearly rebelled, but I managed to avoid adding to the stench.

It wasn't until I'd shambled down three flights of stairs that I recognized anything at all. *Recognized* might be an exaggeration. I'd come out on a street near the waterfront. A few deep inhalations of the salt-and-fish-scented air cleared my head and helped settle my stomach. There must be a reasonable explanation for this situation, and I would find it.

My first step would be to locate Rutger. He had to be in trouble.

Fog blunted the harsh details of my surroundings, but despite the early hour, stevedores and fishermen were at work. Their shouts and the clanging of metal landed like spikes in my head, though they were too far away to notice me. Grateful for small favors, I put my back to the water.

Home was a boardinghouse on the edge of downtown. I took a moment to orient myself. "Chestnut?" The nearest street sign made my spirits sag. "How the hell did I end up here?"

No one answered me. Heaving a sigh, I started off, girding my loins for the hills I'd have to climb. San Francisco had many good points, but topography was not one of them. They say the city has seven hills, though those seven multiplied whenever I had to walk somewhere. With luck, I'd find a streetcar on Market.

And Fate owed me a bit of luck.

A block or so later I passed a woman and a child, sleeping rough. The mother shrank away from me, as if even in her sleep she meant to protect her little one. If Fate owed me luck, it owed this mother even more.

4

The Lighthouse Keeper

I took a quarter from my pocket and tossed it in her direction, an act of defiance more than generosity.

The clink of silver woke her and she clutched the child fiercely. I tossed the other two quarters after the first, and she scrambled to scoop them up. The child started to cry so I hurried on. I'd been raised listening to my father rage about the worthless poor, an easy thing to do given his overflowing bank account.

Seventy-five cents wouldn't save this woman, but the gesture helped steady me. I was a Fairchild in name only and I'd give my money away whenever I felt like it.

I reached into my pocket, hoping there'd be another coin. Empty. No coins meant no streetcar. Still, the woman needed those coins more than I did. I had more money at home. She had neither money nor a home.

The walk cleared my head sufficiently that images from the night began to return. Unfortunate pictures of a nameless man, suffused in magic. Prior to that, there was something about a dog.

"Vincent Fairchild," I murmured. "You're a plain idiot."

My stomach gurgled in agreement. Food might have settled me, although I'd tossed away my means of obtaining anything. I'd have to hope I had a leftover crust in my room to gnaw on.

When I finally did reach my rooms, I discovered I'd have little time for scrounging breakfast, because a letter had been slipped under the door.

Mr. Fairchild,

Please present yourself in the office of Madam Agatha Munro at your earliest convenience.

Thank you.

The florid signature was likely Madam Munro's secretary. The Madam and I had only met once, and she did not strike me as the type who had the patience for curlicues.

Those who possessed power, whether through inheritance or — like me — an accident of birth, were governed by a local witches' council, and those councils rolled up to a governing Congress. Magic was an open secret; most mundanes knew that witches possessed power, but they only admitted it when it served their purposes. The councils and Congress were tasked with keeping practitioners in line so as not to upset our mundane neighbors.

My landlady didn't normally allow strangers to roam her halls, however it was unlikely Madam Munro had delivered the missive by any normal means. Since my room was otherwise undisturbed, I didn't waste time with worry. It was a simple place with a bed, a small wardrobe, and a desk. Simple, yes, but mine. I paid the rent weekly, out of money I earned. Yes, I had access to a trust from my grandmother, but I took pride in supporting myself.

The Lighthouse Keeper

The letter energized me, although coffee would have been as effective and a lot more enjoyable. Still, it gave me something to do besides worry about Rutger. I washed and shaved, put on a clean collar and a more subdued vest, and gave my coat a good brush. My hair needed a trim, but a dab of pomade kept most of it smoothly out of my face. I say *mostly* because a single curl insisted on breaking free and falling over my forehead.

Ignoring it, I replaced my bowler, tucked a clean handkerchief in my pocket, and adjusted my necktie. Vanity insisted that I keep a small mirror on the wall near the door, and I gave myself a final once-over. My gold watch chain hung just so. Dark circles ringed my eyes and my cheeks were sallow, giving me the look of a romantic poet. Practicing the smile that no one could resist — or so I'd been told — I squared my shoulders and departed.

Once I'd been the spoiled youngest son of a Fairchild. Then my gift had emerged, and although my magic was little more than a parlor trick compared with some, I'd been pruned from the family tree, a routine occurrence when a mundane family discovered a child with magic.

Nice people had no time for anything that couldn't be bought and sold.

Fortunately, my parents let me keep my name and the San Francisco Witches' Council appreciated my pedigree, if not my charming ways. In gratitude, I'd sworn to take on whatever challenge Madam Munro chose to throw at me.

This summons had to do with what had happened last night. It had to. My optimistic side hoped I would learn what had happened to Rutger. My less sanguine side couldn't shake a feeling of dread.

The hike to the Council chambers was just long enough for the foggy damp to slide down my neck and numb my fingers. The streets were quiet — nothing had yet opened for business on this Saturday morning — and the air had lost its dead fish smell. The exercise kept me warm enough, and when I reached the building where the Witches' Council kept offices, a glimpse in a dark glass window showed me that my cheeks had turned an attractive pink.

I wasn't vain enough to think that would matter to Madam Munro, but it made me feel slightly better.

The building was on the corner of Market and Hayes Streets, taking up most of the block. A variety of small shops filled the lowest level, and a more formal entrance opened halfway down the block on Hayes Street. The door was unlocked, surprising for a Saturday, and the lobby itself was an echo chamber of marble and polished brass. I rode the elevator to the third floor, breathing deeply to calm myself so Madam Munro wouldn't smell the stink of my fear.

Fear, because my gut told me something had gone very wrong last night. Something had happened to

Rutger, and to me, and I might soon find out what. While it made my jaw tight with fear, I had to be man enough to pay the consequences.

Madam Munro's secretary, a young witch even prettier than I, waved me through to her office. I paused for a heartbeat before opening the door. No amount of preparation was going to help at this point, so I took a deep breath and went in.

The head of the San Francisco Witches' Council sat behind a desk as impressive as her title. Broad, dark mahogany, with muscular carvings on the corners ending in clawed feet. Madam Munro was even more imposing. Her strong nose, high cheekbones, and upright posture brooked no insolence, her hair was a jet black mass of braids and curls, and her bodice of midnight taffeta rose high on her throat. If her hair and dress weren't the latest fashion, no one in their right mind would question her for it, least of all me.

"Come in, Fairchild."

I did as she asked, parsing her tone for meaning. If I'd been in real trouble, she'd have dragged me in front of the whole Council. Seeing her alone and not obviously angry did much to calm my nerves.

"You asked to see me, ma'am?"

She didn't respond right away, instead checking the time on the small clock that hung from an Albertina chain around her neck. "You seem to have had quite a night last night," she said finally, glancing from me to a piece of paper on her desk.

"Apologies, ma'am. Rutger and I went out for a bite after work and…" My voice trailed off. Rutger and I worked together in one of the Council's offices, mostly involved in dealing with the mundane city government when problems arose between witches and mortals. Rutger did the calming, I did the charming, and most of the time we all went home happy.

"Yes, well, the part that comes next is what's concerning me. I cannot seem to locate Mr. Smit, and you" — her gaze pinned me where I stood — "apparently turned a man into a dog."

"I…what?" They say when you're about to die, your life flashes before your eyes. I wasn't dead — yet — but the shock of her words triggered a similar reliving.

"Turned. A man. Into. A. Dog." She spoke slowly, deliberately, as if both giving me time to react and herself time to judge my reaction.

"I can't believe that."

She lifted the page from her desk and read from it. "Council investigators encountered three men and a canine on the edge of the Chinese quarter. Men were distressed, claimed the canine was their friend. J. performed a counterspell and the canine rose up to become a fourth young man. All four were taken by me and J. to the nearest Council office where they described the events and identified a witch who fits the description of one Vincent Fairchild. The men were calmed and their memories altered. Signed, L. M. Peabody, Council Investigator, dated 16 October, 1898." She glanced up at me again. "Is that sufficient?"

Madam Munro hadn't invited me to sit, but my knees were so weak I collapsed in the closest chair. "I suppose."

She folded her hands on her desk. Her smile might have reassured me, if I hadn't been worried that she was preparing to strip me of what little power I possessed. My composure shattered, I had to blink fast not to burst into tears. Using magic on an ordinary person was a witches' equivalent of a mortal sin. She'd be well within her authority to assign any punishment she saw fit.

"The thing is," she said finally, "you're of more use to me as a living witch than as a dead mortal. That Fairchild name..." She let her voice trail off in a way that wasn't altogether reassuring.

I almost protested, telling her that in my case, being a Fairchild meant absolutely nothing. Before I could dig myself in deeper, I asked my most pressing question. "Where is Rutger? He was not there when I woke up."

"We don't know. Smit hasn't been seen since he left the office with you. Something went wrong last night, something bigger than Peabody's report entails. Yes." She drummed her fingers on the desk. "I need you alive and out of the way. I'm afraid the rest of the council will take rash action before we learn what's really going on."

Rash action, like stripping my little parlor tricks from me. All the more reason for me to learn what really happened. "I could start by asking questions at the place we went after work. Someone there must have seen us." And they may be able to shed some light on what had happened next.

"Start where? No, you misunderstand me," she said, reaching into a drawer and pulling out a large envelop. "I recently received notice of a situation. It's not quite your usual sort of assignment, but you're a smart young man. I trust you to use your head."

My throat had gone so dry I needed to cough in order to speak. "But Rutger. I need to find out what happened last night."

"Leave that to me." Her expression stiffened. "A weatherwitch who'd been assigned to a lighthouse near Seattle has died, and we need to send a replacement."

I was too confused to put up much of an argument. "I… can change a thing's appearance, but I'm not much help with the weather."

"You won't have to worry about that. Your task will be something much more delicate. The recently deceased, Martin Gallagher, was rumored to have stolen a very powerful magical object, the Ferox Cor. We don't know whether or not the rumors are true, but he'd never before worked as a weatherwitch. Could he have used the power he gained from the Ferox Cor to influence the weather? Possibly. The larger issue is, what else could he have used it for? He's been up there at the edge of civilization for a number of years."

I sat up straighter. Dear Lord, was this a way out or would it land me in even more trouble? "And you want me to find this Ferox Cor?"

"I do, yes."

"And if I decline?"

She paused for a moment, giving me her full attention. "Then more than likely, the full council will vote to strip you of your power and send you on your way."

To hell. "I find your argument quite persuasive."

"I thought you might. Gallagher lived with his wife Della and a son. Don't know much about the boy, but I knew Della when she was very young. She's a Barron, and that family's not going to tolerate some jumped-up thaumaturge."

"She must be grieving, if her husband just passed."

"Correct, and who knows what you'll learn if you give her a sympathetic shoulder to cry on."

"They'll need another weatherwitch, though."

She smiled, passing me the thick envelope. "Margaret Barnes will be going with you. I've made travel arrangements as far as Portland, but after that you'll need to find your own way. Margaret will help, of course, but I want her to pay more attention to what's going on in the atmosphere."

"Of course, ma'am." From what I knew of her reputation, Margaret Barnes was going to run this whole show. She was a few years older than I and no one's shrinking violet. "I'm sure we'll get on just fine." I knew no such thing, but times like these, it paid to be charming.

"Find the Ferox Cor and bring it to me. Peabody and his boys will find Smit and figure out what caused you to use your power on a mortal, and then you can go back to beguiling our city leaders with your fine manners and wit."

"I hope so." Because the alternative did not bear thinking about. I'd already been cut off from my family. Getting cut off from the magical world would leave me very much alone. That threat, more than anything else, straightened my spine. I had no idea how I'd find this Ferox Cor, but I could not afford to fail.

"Keep in mind, though, that in the wrong hands, the Ferox Cor can bring down nations. Tread carefully and bring it to me — *only* me — so the Council can make arrangements to keep it safe."

I'm sure my eyes were as big as a pair of moons. "I will."

I left soon after, and when I hit the street, the fog had lifted. I walked the first few blocks in the warm

The Lighthouse Keeper

October sun. I'd have called it an omen, but I hadn't gone far when the fog settled in again, weighing my spirits with its gloom.

Chapter Two

I keep an emergency fund in my room, a habit that has stood me in good stead. The bank would not open until Monday, and Madam Munro had promised to send a train ticket as soon as her secretary made the arrangements. Given the uncertainties around this excursion, I handed my landlord enough money for two months' rent and packed such sundries as I would need for an indefinite stay.

Two suits, four shirts and four vests, several clean collars, underthings, handkerchiefs, and two packets of pipe tobacco would see me through, or at least I hoped they would.

The Lighthouse Keeper

As promised, by suppertime an envelope arrived with a train ticket for 3pm on Monday, October 17th. That gave me Sunday to find Rutger, a task I failed to accomplish. He had not been seen at his rooming house since Friday morning, nor had he visited any of our usual haunts. Leaving felt disloyal, selfish, even. While I had no choice but to obey Madam Munro, uneasiness sat heavy on me.

The noisy platform at the Market Street train depot did little to calm my nerves. I recognized Miss Barnes, having seen her once in the Council offices. In addition to being older than me, she stood some three inches taller. Today, she wore a suit of a soft dun color the same shade as her hair. Her face was broad, her smile reserved, and her only bit of brightness came from an emerald grosgrain ribbon around the crown of her straw boater. My sack coat and trousers were a somber black, yet with my paisley waistcoat I felt like a peacock accompanying a hen.

Madam Munro had provided us with seats in a sleeper car, the type that folded out to make a low bunk with an upper bunk that dropped down from the wall. We sat facing each other on cracked leather benches. Miss Barnes eyed every passenger as they passed, as if sizing each one up for possible villainy, while I struggled to come up with something to say.

The car was half empty, so it wasn't long until people stopped moving around. It took a few minutes longer for Miss Barnes to relax.

In a misguided attempt at conversation, I gallantly offered to take the upper bunk.

"Unless we take on quite a few more passengers, we shouldn't be required to share."

I gave her a sparkling smile. "You're probably right."

"And since we aren't wed, I hardly think we should so much as discuss sharing accommodations."

She sounded so prim, I had to fight to keep from laughing. I could have said her virtue was quite safe with me but had just enough sense to see that she might take it as an insult. She *was* quite safe, however. My tastes ran fast in another direction.

Which was ironic, really. I might have been able to keep my inclinations a secret from my family, but if they'd ever found out, they would have cut me off as surely as they had for witchcraft.

I'd apparently been destined to be a Fairchild in name only.

"Are you the oldest child?" I asked. She had the air of authority I associated with my oldest sister.

"Pardon me?"

"The oldest. Are you the oldest child in your family?"

She blinked, clearly weighing her response. "Again, I'm not sure we've reached this level of familiarity, but as we'll be working together, I see no harm in answering."

She paused until I prompted her with an, "And…?"

"Yes." Her head tilted slightly. "And I suppose you are the youngest?"

I laughed at that. "Excellent guess."

"I should have known."

Her tone did not invite further conversation. With little else to distract me, I rifled through the packet of papers Madam Munro had sent with me. "I wonder if some of this is for you," I murmured, trying to make sense of a diagram of… cloud patterns?

"She gave each of us what we need to know," Miss Barnes murmured back without looking up from the book she'd opened, her incurious tone daring me to continue.

C'mon, you went to Harvard. Figure this out.

I examined the diagram more closely. The abstract circles and random dashes and arrows failed to resolve into something that made sense, so after a moment I set it aside. The next page contained a detailed description of the Ferox Cor.

"Gold amulet studded with rubies and emeralds, housed in a small box. Doesn't sound all that threatening." I spoke insistently, perhaps rudely, but we needed to find a way to work together.

She didn't look up, but she paused in the middle of turning a page. "Keep reading. A necromancer created it over five hundred years ago, imbuing it with the ability to grant the holder unlimited power."

19

"Lord."

"They say, though, that the Cor has its own will, and whoever claims it will eventually be turned to evil."

"This seems a lot more complicated than keeping the peace with the city council," I muttered, mostly to myself.

"Yes, it does seem odd that Munro sent someone so obviously ill-equipped to the task."

That brought me up short. Miss Barnes continued to read, ignoring me completely. Almost despite myself, I sent a puff of power in her direction. The book she studied so assiduously turned into a squawking chicken for just long enough to make her jump out of her seat.

She stumbled, but when I reached up to help her, she pushed my hand aside. "If you think you've got any real defense against my magic, you're mistaken."

Water trickled down onto my head. I glanced up at a small, dark cloud that had suddenly formed. Snickering, I took a coin from my pocket and gave it some power. A sturdy black umbrella opened up, protecting me from her magical rain.

She scowled and flicked a finger. A gust of wind hit me, strong enough to blow the umbrella inside out. That was a mistake. It was one thing for us to tease each other with magic, quite another to upset the mortals who rode the train with us.

The couple behind me yelped at the gust of wind.

"What the hell?" The man jumped up, looking wildly around the train. "Where'd the breeze come from?"

"It blew my hat clean off." His companion clutched the feathered monstrosity in her lap.

Another man yelled that the train must be coming apart, while people on the other end of the car were bewildered by all the hubbub. Rising to my feet, I picked up one of the silk flowers that had blown off my neighbor's hat.

"Everything's fine," I said, handing the flower to her. "No one's in danger here."

"I know what I felt, mister, and —"

I cut him off with a raised hand. This is where Rutger proved so valuable. He was a supreme administrator, assuming the mantle of authority with ease. I did not possess his gift, but I pretended I could spread calm. "Everything is fine. Please return to your seats."

They did as I asked, and while the couple closest to us still muttered about poorly maintained rail cars, there was no more distress.

For her part, Miss Barnes gave me a subtle salute, her fingertip touching her brow. "Touché."

I shrugged with pretend annoyance, resisting the urge to laugh.

"And I apologize for calling you ill-equipped."

She sounded sincerely contrite, so I allowed myself a brief smile. "Consider it forgotten. Now, if you don't mind, tell me what this is and what it means."

I held out the chart covered with abstract circles. She took it, and she taught me the basics of weather charts and how to read them.

Our destination, the West Point lighthouse, sat at the north end of Elliot Bay, the body of water along which the city of Seattle had been built. While the bay boasted a deep-water harbor, the sand spit surrounding West Point was too shallow for all but the smallest vessels.

The rotating light helped keep water traffic to the deep shipping lane. It was made up of a dozen panels that flashed every ten seconds, and the mechanism had to be wound every couple of hours.

"From there, a weatherwitch can divert the worst of the storms," Miss Barnes said. "But any small change creates a reciprocal action elsewhere. No one gets to have the sun all the time. Those charts show places of power, nodes and ley lines, that allow us to influence air currents."

That's how magic worked, although I tended to ignore the costs involved. "They must have ended up in my packet by mistake then." I didn't quite smile, but she did, giving me a wry grin.

"Maybe she meant for you to study them."

"Indeed." Miss Barnes was most certainly someone's annoying older sister. She was also right. I did need to learn more about magic. I got by on charm and parlor tricks, but that wouldn't suffice for the present situation. "Why do they need a weatherwitch in the first place?"

"Every lighthouse has one, because it's easier to see weather patterns in such isolated locations."

"You're not telling me witches control the weather."

"We don't control all of it, but we'll give it a nudge every now and again." She folded her hands modestly in her lap but couldn't quite disguise the hint of pride in her voice.

I nodded, hoping my smile wasn't too blank. I'd thought weatherwitches operated on hope more than actual power. Miss Barnes showed me my error. "So, what do you think this Ferox Cor can do?"

With a sigh, she set her book aside. "As it says in the packet"—she glanced pointedly at the papers in my hand—"the Cor is thought to amplify the power of anyone who possesses it. Martin Gallagher had been a fairly ordinary witch, or so I've heard, but he apparently functioned as a weatherwitch for over twenty years."

"I wonder why."

Her eloquent shrug was answer enough. "I suppose that's what we'll need to find out."

"One of the things, anyway. Madam Munro was quite specific that we bring the Ferox Cor to her. Why do you think—"

"You really are just like my brother. I don't know. Whatever it is, we'll find out when we get there." Her smile was full of fake annoyance, but before I could compose an appropriately tart response, the porter called us to dinner.

Dinner was no better than I'd expected it to be, and soon the lights dimmed and everyone readied themselves for sleep. The porter made Miss Barnes and me separate beds, pulling velvet window curtains along tracks to make private compartments. In this semi-privacy, I stripped off my coat and waistcoat and took off my shoes. We took turns in the water closet, and I for one was ready to sleep.

I must have dropped off right away, for soon I was dreaming something awful; me, all alone, lost in a void. No matter how hard I ran, I couldn't find another soul. My breath came short, sweat ran down the sides of my face, and pain stabbed my side.

With a yell, I flung myself off the bunk. My legs tangled in the velvet curtains and I went down hard. Landing on all fours, the carpet burning my palms, I struggled to catch my breath. I didn't put too much stock in dreams, but this one left an aftertaste of fear.

All around me voices cried out, and someone turned on the car's central light. Miss Barnes had positioned herself in front of me, an impressive dagger in her hand. She hid it, most likely before anyone else had noticed. If the man who'd been upset by the wind could have killed me with a frown, I'd have died on the spot. He began to rant about young men who couldn't hold their liquor, which gave me an idea.

Picking myself up, I dropped into an awkward curtsy. "I do apologize for waking you with my nightmare. I'll ask the porter to bring a bottle of brandy and glasses for anyone who needs some liquid restoration."

Most people waved me off, though one man did insist I'd owe him a cup of coffee in the morning. The porter turned the lights back down and the car descended into silence.

Miss Barnes stayed at my side, and when we were the only ones left, she put a hand on my arm.

"I don't know what that was about, but I doubt I'll get any more sleep. Let's dress and ask the porter to put away our bunks."

"Are you certain? I apologize for waking you."

She tightened the belt at her waist, having covered her nightclothes in a corduroy robe. "It's only an hour till dawn, and, after that performance, I couldn't sleep if I wanted to."

"I do apologize."

With a brief squeeze, she released my arm. "One of my cousins was given to having nightmares. At least you were able to charm our fellow travelers."

"I may need to buy that fellow coffee in the morning, but no real harm done." We shared a smile.

I might have dreamed I was all alone, but here and now, I had an ally if not yet a friend.

Once we reached Portland, it was easy enough to find a train to take us the rest of the way to Seattle, a much shorter trip. After only a few hours we were dumped off at a busy station, crowded with men all bent on talking louder than the other fellow.

"Well." I stood with my arms akimbo, surveying the scene. "Madam Munro's instructions regarding how to reach the lighthouse weren't terribly specific."

Miss Barnes frowned at a piece of paper she'd taken from her clutch. "If there are other witches in the city, they haven't drawn attention to themselves."

"Seems odd there wouldn't be any, and we can't simply walk up to a stranger and ask."

Her sidelong grin was much more pleasant than her frown. "You're right about that. Perhaps we can find a policeman?"

"Or we can find a saloon and ask the bartender. They know everything." I had great faith in the power of gossip. A good barkeep would tell us what we wanted to know, either out of kindness or in response to one of the stiff new bills I had in my wallet.

I might be a Fairchild in name only, but I had few qualms about greasing our way with family coin.

We didn't have to go far from the train station to find a likely saloon. In fact, we had our choice of four. I let Miss Barnes decide, concerned I'd pick a place that would offend her sensibilities. I shouldn't have worried. She chose a place called the Merchant's Café, and if she was the only woman present, she remained completely unruffled by that fact.

She did ask to sit at a table rather than the bar itself. The place was longer than it was wide, with the bar along one wall and small tables lined up along the other. She took a seat facing the door and I went to the bar.

"Afternoon," the bartender said. He was a pale man with eyes that bulged. "Still have a pot pie. It's generous-sized, if you two want to share it."

"We would, thank you. We'll take that and a couple of root beers if you have them." We'd earned a treat.

The bartender poured our soft drinks. "I'll be out in a minute with the pot pie."

"Thank you." I put down three dollars, giving him the kind of warm smile that smoothed my way in most every circumstance. "Before you go, I have a question. We need to find our way to the West Point Lighthouse. Do you know how we get there?"

His answer came slowly. "No good reason to go there, so far as I'm concerned."

I put down another dollar. "I know my own business, you see, and I'd appreciate anything you can tell me."

"It's your funeral," he said, and shrugged. "Gotta go by boat, and good luck finding someone who'll take you."

With that, he stomped off. I returned to our table with the root beers, leaving the money on the bar. "Did you hear that?" I asked Miss Barnes.

"Your natural charm certainly worked wonders."

I narrowed my gaze at her in mock offense, amused by the way she'd decided to treat me like a wayward younger brother.

"I do believe they could have heard him out on the street." She took a prim sip of her root beer.

"Excuse me." A gentleman approached our table. His well-made suit had seen some living but his hands and nails were clean. "I couldn't help but overhear —"

We cut him off with a gale of giggles. "I'm sorry," I finally managed to gasp.

Miss Barnes picked up the apology. "We were just saying he could have been overheard on the street."

The stranger gave us a lopsided grin. "Name's Richardson, and my brother-in-law pilots the supply boat that goes out to the lighthouse every Friday and most Mondays. I expect he'll have space for passengers on his next trip. His name's Barnard, and you can find him down at Pier 56. The boat's called *The Lucky*."

"Sounds like a good omen. We'll look for him this afternoon."

Richardson gave us a small salute. "You'll probably want to arrange for a round trip. I've never been there myself, but there's a reason not many want to go."

"Thanks for the warning," I said, my smile never flickering. The barkeep chose that moment to show up with our pot pie. Richardson excused himself and we made short work of our lunch. Later we went to Pier 56 and found *The Lucky*. Her captain, Barnard, looked askance when we asked to go to the lighthouse, but the twenty dollar bill in my hand cheered him up.

We agreed to return at nine o'clock Friday morning, which left us something more than two days to fill. I spent much of the time lurking in the neighborhood taverns, trying to learn anything I could about the lighthouse and about the local witches.

Miss Barnes set herself the same task, although she kept to dress shops and cafés. Altogether, we learned very little. No one wanted to talk about the lighthouse, and if there were other witches in Seattle, they stayed hidden from the general public.

Friday morning dawned cold and rainy. If Barnard was surprised to see us, he kept his opinion to himself. The water was choppy and a steady rain fell, wrapping everything in a layer of mist. Miss Barnes and I huddled together under an umbrella I conjured while our pilot regaled us with adventures at sea.

After the better part of two hours, he pointed to a mass of shadowy darkness. "It's in there. *The Lucky*'ll get hung up on the sand bar if we get any closer, so we'll have to row in."

A fitful light pierced the gloom at regular intervals. The lighthouse? Miss Barnes and I shared a skeptical glance, but nevertheless we clambered into the rowboat. Barnard provided the muscle and the lighthouse flashed overhead, illuminating a stretch of shallow water, maybe thirty feet between our boat and a stony beach. A narrow dock jutted out into the water, our apparent destination.

Closer in, the flashing light revealed a collection of buildings huddled on a patch of grass, like a pile of long-forgotten child's blocks. The buildings were surrounded by the wedge-shaped beach and backed by a steep, tree-covered bluff. Smoke rose from a chimney near the rear, and only one window glowed with light, making the place feel more desolate.

"I suppose it's livelier when the sun is shining," I said.

Miss Barnes' only response was a tight-lipped smile. If I'd been trying to cheer either of us, I'd failed.

Barnard must have overheard, because he chuckled. "Naw, it's gloomy on a good day."

I forced some enthusiasm. "I'm sure it's not as bad as all that."

Miss Barnes gave an unladylike snort, but otherwise didn't comment.

When we reached the dock, I clambered off the boat, hoisting both my satchels and her valise. "Don't be an idiot," she muttered, snatching her bag from my hand.

Barnard followed us out, piling the boxes of supplies on the dock. "If you all have a change of heart, I'll be back on Monday."

We shook hands and I slipped him a few bills, not at all sure I wouldn't take him up on his offer.

The lighthouse flashed again, and this time it illuminated something new. Something, or someone.

A man stood between us and the buildings. Wrapped as he was in darkness and mist, I couldn't make out his features, or truly ascertain his very presence. Miss Barnes halted her progress, evidently brought up short by the same sight.

We stood side by side, the last of the dock's planks between us and the beach.

"Hello," I called. I tried to smile, but it was forced at best.

"What do you want?" His voice was deep, the threat barely hidden. Behind us, a steady splashing told me Barnard and his rowboat were making tracks to return to the city.

"I have a letter of introduction from Madam Agatha Munro, the head of the Witches' Council in San Francisco." I held out my hand, though we were too far apart to shake. "She sent us here when she received word that Martin Gallagher had passed away."

The man hadn't moved, though his silhouette seemed to loom over us. "We don't need help from strangers."

A door opened, a square of light in the darkness. "Let 'em come, Rafe. I wrote her myself, and there'll be more trouble otherwise."

A woman's voice, tired, beaten down by life. "Are you Della Gallagher?" I asked.

"I am. Rafe, let 'em past."

The man stepped aside and I felt a shift, as if something solid had given way.

Or as if a spell had broken.

The darkness lifted, although the rain didn't stop. Miss Barnes and I shared a glance. The crease in her forehead showed her concern, something I seconded.

If Martin Gallagher had been the witch, who had set the spell that wrapped the lighthouse in darkness?

And who the hell was Rafe?

Chapter Three

The man, Rafe, walked toward the house. We were almost there when I noticed his cane. Rather than lean on it for support, he held it in front of him, the tip low to the ground, and swung it gently from side to side. *Odd*.

Della Gallagher looked as weary as her voice. She stepped aside so we could enter her home, her shoulders slumped and her hands clasped tightly in front of her.

I stopped before going more than a handful of steps into the small foyer. I tried a sympathetic smile. "My name is Vincent Fairchild, Mrs. Gallagher, and my associate is Margaret Barnes. We traveled from

San Francisco to offer you any help you should need in this difficult time."

Miss Barnes gave me a sharp look, likely for speaking on her behalf, but she didn't interrupt. Mrs. Gallagher, however, sighed, as if my words had increased her heavy load.

"Say the word, Mother, and I'll see that they're gone."

Mother? I glanced from Rafe to Mrs. Gallagher. "You're the boy?"

For the first time, he turned in my direction. He had several inches on me and in his black cloak he looked twice as broad. His features were strong, his mouth well formed, though a pair of amber spectacles concealed his eyes. "Boy?"

His raw contempt set me a step back. Fortunately, Miss Barnes spoke up. "Madam Munro told us Martin Gallagher lived with his wife and a child, a boy."

Mrs. Gallagher glanced at her son. "The Council doesn't know what's what," she said, then closed her mouth as if to keep in more thoughts.

"I have a letter…" I held it out in Rafe's direction. His expression never changed, nor did he move to take it, so I passed it to his mother. We all waited while she opened the seal and began to read, her mouth moving over the words.

"I shouldn't have written her," she said finally. Rafe made a scoffing sound, but offered no other opinion.

"I did wonder why Seattle's Council didn't make arrangements." Miss Barnes spoke prettily, almost as charming as I could be.

"Because Seattle doesn't have a Witches' Council."

Rafe spoke over top of his mother. "Martin would never allow for such a thing."

Martin? Despite my curiosity, I saved my question for later, reasonably sure the reason Rafe called his father by his Christian name would prove interesting. "Thank you both for accommodating us, then, especially while you're grieving."

Rafe's laugh held more bitterness than humor. "Are you sure, Mother? We have too much to do to parry platitudes with these two."

Stung, I all but gasped, the heat rising in my cheeks. Miss Barnes again proved better at maintaining her composure. "I'm a weatherwitch," she said simply. "It was the Council's intention that I should offer my assistance while they develop a more permanent plan."

"It's too late, son." Della Gallagher's deadened tone made my own heart hurt. She wasn't yet fifty years old, but grey speckled her wild curls, the kind of curls that were never really tamed. "They couldn't leave now anyway. There won't be another supply boat until Monday at the earliest."

"We brought provisions," I said, lifting the heavier of my bags, hoping to prove we'd cause as little trouble as possible. If Rafe and his mother sent us away, we'd have no way to get back to the city.

And no way to find the Ferox Cor.

"Where will they sleep?" Rafe might have aimed the question at his mother, but he seemed to be staring off to her right. *Odd. What were those glasses for?*

Mrs. Gallagher shrugged hopelessly. "There are only the two bedrooms. The girl can bunk with me and you and the other—"

"No." A single word, calling out a line he would not cross.

"If you have a tent..." I said weakly.

"Be reasonable," Mrs. Gallagher said, ignoring my offer.

"I will not."

"Then you'll sleep in the workshop. You do anyway," she snapped, her sudden harshness making me blink.

Without a word, Rafe spun around and stalked out the door. Mrs. Gallagher mustered a tired smile. "Some welcome, I'm sure. Miss..."

"Barnes," she said.

"Miss Barnes, if you go through the parlor, the bedroom door is on the left. And Mr. Fairchild?"

"Yes, ma'am."

"I apologize for my son's rudeness. He's had a difficult time of it."

"Of course, ma'am. I understand." I'd just as soon not share a bed with someone who disliked me, even if he was tall and dark. *And fairly compelling*. I winced, ready to smack myself for such an inappropriate thought.

"The kitchen's in the back, and Rafe's room is the door on the right. Why don't you both unpack some and I'll see what I can make for dinner."

"I'll help, of course," Miss Barnes said. I would have offered, too, except when it came to the kitchen, I was as helpless as a kitten. Instead, I left the bag of provisions and went to the room I'd been assigned.

I hadn't expected a cheery greeting, given that they were in mourning, but Rafe's anger felt excessive. And we'd triggered some kind of spell, probably for protection. I'd felt it break when we came ashore.

Martin Gallagher hadn't been much of a witch, at least until he found the Ferox Cor. Madam Munro's notes had stated frankly that neither his wife nor his child should have possessed the kind of gift it would have taken to set such a spell.

But then, her notes also said Rafe was a child.

Was it possible the Ferox Cor had passed on to Rafe when Martin died? I needed to study Madam Munro's notes, to discover anything she'd written between the lines. Then I'd start my search. I didn't expect to find a box labeled "Ferox Cor" in a corner somewhere, but stranger things have happened.

The room Mrs. Gallagher directed me to was only a bit larger than the single cot pushed up against the far wall. No wonder Rafe objected to sharing. There might be space to make a pallet on the floor, but if so, whoever was in the bed would have to step over it to leave the room.

Such a small space didn't lend itself to decoration, but still I was struck by the bareness. No pictures, no books, nothing that might give me insight into the man. I set my valise by the door.

A wardrobe just fit between the foot of the bed and the opposite wall, close enough that the door couldn't completely open. I'd packed light, well, as light as was possible for me, but the narrow cabinet looked too small for two.

I shouldn't have worried. Rafe owned fewer things than I'd brought with me. The shelf at eye level was nearly empty, and only two of the five pegs along the cabinet's back had clothing hung from them.

Unpacking my valise, though, would be a statement of sorts. My spare suitcoat and trousers, rumpled from my bag, would announce me, would say that I'm here.

That I'm staying.

And in all honesty, I felt unfit for the task at hand. My skills — charm and prettiness chief among them — wouldn't do me much good at all here on this lonesome sandbar. Madam Munro must have truly feared for my life if sending me to this patch of wilderness was her safest recourse.

The Lighthouse Keeper

Despite my doubts, I unbuckled my valise and lifted out the first thing my hand touched. My toiletries. Setting the small leather case on the cot, I reached in for more. Barnard said he'd be returning on Monday. I could last that long, and with any luck, we'd find the magical device before then.

Gripping my determination with both hands, I unpacked my things and, rather than review Madam Munro's notes yet again, I gave in to the urge to move. I found Miss Barnes in the kitchen, pawing through the bag of provisions.

"Where's Mrs. Gallagher?" I asked.

"She said she had to wind the light." She lifted up a bundle, two loaves of bread wrapped in printed cotton. "Apparently there's a mechanism that keeps it flashing at a regular interval. They wind it every couple of hours."

The kitchen wasn't a lot bigger than the bedroom I'd been given. A black stove squatted on one wall, flanked by small cupboards with painted doors. A table took up much of the rest of the floor, which left precious little space for more than one person.

The room had only one window, its glass splattered with raindrops. Beyond loomed a mass of deep green. The forest. "Not much to this place. Seems like finding a bejeweled magical box should be fairly easy."

Her chuckle had a touch of indulgence. "We can hope so."

"I just meant we should be able to find it by Monday," I murmured, struggling to avoid sounding like an annoying little brother.

She tsked, setting a jar of jam on the table. "They need a weatherwitch, so I doubt I'll have the luxury of leaving any time soon."

Her detached attitude gave my concerns little to hang onto. The stove's steady heat had warmed the air enough for me to realize my hands and feet were numb from the damp cold. "Did you feel the spell?"

Her busy hands stilled. "What spell?"

"When we arrived. The spell that had been wrapped around this place."

"You felt it too?" A frown creasing her brow, she went back to disemboweling the bag, lifting out a jar of green beans and another of tomatoes.

I rubbed my hands together, grimacing at the prickles that meant my fingers were warming. Everyone we'd met had discouraged us from coming here. Perhaps that spell was part of the reason. "When our boat first grounded, the house was wrapped in darkness. When Mrs. Gallagher gave us permission to come closer, I felt a pop and the darkness lifted."

Miss Barnes' grim expression likely mirrored my own.

"Some kind of concealment spell. Either that or one for protection."

"There's no one here who could have set such a spell." Mrs. Gallagher came through the door behind me. I spun toward her, unable to disguise my gasp of surprise.

"Don't go looking for trouble, you two," she said, pushing past me. "Now what's all this?" She waved at the food Miss Barnes had unpacked.

"We didn't want to put you out any more than absolutely necessary," I said.

"Good. The stuff Barnard brought won't feed four people for long. You'd best plan on heading back to Seattle on the Monday boat."

Miss Barnes and I shared a glance. I could only hope my expression didn't show how eager I was to do just that.

"I don't expect you'll be able to run the lighthouse for long without a weatherwitch." Miss Barnes spoke with an admirable level of composure.

Somehow Miss Barnes' argument added even more heaviness to Mrs. Gallagher's worn features. "Let me worry about how to run the lighthouse. I've been doing it long enough."

"Our notes say that Mr. Gallagher was the weatherwitch." I spoke without thinking.

"He...was." The pause hinted that she had trouble referring to him in the past.

Miss Barnes' smile was a fine balance between caring and determination. "Then I'd be happy to keep storms at bay until a more permanent arrangement can be made.

Mrs. Gallagher clenched her fists and for a moment her jaw worked. Then, with a sigh, she gave in. "As you like. It won't take you long to regret that offer."

Her words carried an undercurrent of something close to fear, reinforcing that notion. Wondering how long it would take for us to learn what she was afraid of, I retrieved my hat from the bedroom and headed outside.

In all honesty, I wanted to find a trail through the woods. *There must be another way to escape*. The rain had diminished to a faint mist, and I took the time to really get a sense of the place.

The lighthouse had been built on a stony spit, surrounded on three sides by water. Behind the house, the land rose sharply in a forested bluff that permitted little to escape.

Every ten seconds, the tower's light flashed, as if the building itself had a pulse. The tower wasn't particularly tall, rising above the building's roof by only a story. A round, windowed chamber surrounded the lamp, and a narrow porch with a railing encircled that chamber. I didn't see a ladder, so there must be a stairwell inside. Taller than the tower was the flagpole, its empty cables slapping in the wind.

Behind the tower, furthest from the ocean's rage, was the house where the Gallaghers lived and where we'd be staying. The third and smallest section butted up against the rocky shore and would likely catch the worst when a storm hit. Curiosity almost drove me to sneak into that small room, but something held me back. Neither Gallagher had been particularly welcoming, and while I'd need to search everywhere, I didn't want to be told I could swim back to the city tonight.

For a moment I simply watched the light flash on and off. Such a lonely place. So cold. Though when I left this place on Monday, Madam Munro wouldn't welcome me home. Heck, maybe I could join up with some other fellows and try my luck in the Yukon.

A gust of wind reminded me that we'd left San Francisco in mid-October and that the weather was only going to get colder. A trip to the Yukon might be out, but surely there were other places to stay out of sight, even in an infant city like Seattle. Because sure as shootin' I didn't want to stay on this dreary little spit of land any longer than absolutely necessary.

Chapter Four

Rather than return to that barren little house, I decided to explore the forest. I produced a small witchlight, a simple magic that almost all of us can perform, and followed the line of the shore on the south side of the lighthouse.

The beach went on further than I expected, but eventually my progress was blocked by the encroaching forest. The thick pine scent woke something within me, as if the trees themselves could feed my magic.

A tangle of huckleberry and some low-growing shrub with leathery leaves filled the spaces between the trees. Most were evergreens—pines, hemlock, cedar—but the browning leaves of a few maples covered the forest floor. I extended my little light and noted that the undergrowth thinned where the trees grew denser. With that in mind, I made my way along the line, looking for any kind of break.

I found one, a path of sorts. Looked at head on, it wasn't visible. From the side, however, I could see that someone had created a space of some ten or twelve inches between clumps of green. The path had been paved with shreds of bark and pine needles and it wended its way through the trees.

The witchlight brightened with no effort on my part. My heartbeat sped up. *Who's in control here? Me or the forest?*

There were two kinds of witches: those who cultivated their gifts and those who treated them more like a religion. I hadn't had much time for church before my gift appeared, and even less time since. The thought that I could attribute my current circumstance to some all-knowing Mother Goddess didn't sit well with me, so I ignored the idea as much as possible.

The light, though, spreading unbidden between the gnarled old trunks, made me wonder.

Once found, the path led me deeper into the woods. The air was misty and smelled of growing things. The ground began to rise, not steeply, not yet, but it soon would. The quiet allowed me to take a deeper breath, at least until something abruptly drowned out the expected rustling of small creatures.

A man spoke, his voice riven with anger. "Damnation."

I picked up my pace, moved by a mix of curiosity and concern. Walked faster still, broke into a jog, and some two hundred feet up the path, I found my quarry.

Rafe Gallagher knelt on the ground in a clearing, surrounded by a circle of fir trees and vine maples. Holes had been dug at regular intervals and he held one hand extended several inches about the dirt. He muttered something, words that were unfamiliar but recognizably powerful. At some unseen cue, he produced a trowel from his cloak. He dug up dirt and pine needles and threw them aside. When he'd made a pit that was deep enough to hide the trowel, he stopped, again holding out a hand.

While I didn't know what we were waiting for, his tension had me hold my breath.

Whatever he wanted, it was not there. Crawling, he found another spot and began to dig, still muttering. If he noticed me or my light, he gave no sign.

The strangeness of his behavior both intrigued and repelled me. Logic suggested that he too searched for the Ferox Cor, and if he, with all his power, couldn't find it, I didn't stand much chance.

Still, when he threw the trowel to the ground, I cleared my throat. He froze. Something in his stillness frightened me more than his wild digging had done.

"Who's there?" he snarled.

I cleared my throat again. "Vincent. Vincent Fairchild."

"Did Mother send you?"

"No. I'd hoped to find a way to some sort of civilization."

"You won't. Not here." He spoke calmly, as if his hands and nails weren't black with dirt. "The bluff is too steep to climb, and unless you know one of the natives who called this place Per-co-dus-chule, you'd never find your way."

"Per-co-dus-chule?" I mangled the pronunciation, though Rafe didn't seem to notice.

"This place we guard. Did you think our name was the only one?" He swiped a hand across his face, leaving a streak of dirt and blood.

"I guess I never gave it any thought."

His laugh was bitter. "I'm not surprised. Did you know the first man to sail a tall ship into Puget Sound named the bluff behind us Magnolia, because he mistook the madrona trees for the pretty flowers he'd known in his youth?"

A collection of rainwater dripped off my hat as if to punctuate the absurdity of the situation. "I didn't know that either."

"Hmph." He found the trowel and tucked it away. "Find my cane."

"Pardon?"

"My cane. Where is it?"

47

Now I was thoroughly confused. "There, leaning against that tree."

The witchlight wasn't sufficient for me to read his expression, but since he didn't seem to be joking, I retrieved his cane and held it toward him. "Here."

Standing, he reached in my direction, making one unsuccessful swipe before clasping the cane in hand. Without any thanks, he tapped the ground, pausing between taps as if listening for a response. He began to walk in my direction. I was too caught up in his actions to get out of his way. He only stopped when we were chest to chest.

"Move, Fairchild." His tone brooked no argument, yet I held my ground.

Sometimes I have very little common sense.

He might be strange, and rude, and more than a little frightening — hell, he didn't even show me respect by meeting my gaze — but Rafe Gallagher intrigued me.

"Move, now," he repeated. From this close he smelled of smoke and burning herbs, though I saw no evidence of fire.

Gathering my courage, I looked directly into those amber glasses, and though it might have been a trick of the light, it seemed his eyes were wholly black.

I got out of his way, my movement closer to a jump than a dignified step. He brushed past without another word. I stood, my witchlight dwindling, until I could no longer hear his footsteps through the brush.

The Lighthouse Keeper

Rafe Gallagher was not a boy and he possessed more power than the Witches' Council knew. And unless I was very wrong, something almost demonic had stared at me through his eyes.

Could he have the Ferox Cor?

As his footsteps faded, the normal music of the forest resumed, the fluttering and crackle of birds and small creatures creating a reassuring counterpoint to what I had experienced. The rain resumed in earnest, giving me little choice but to return to the house. As much as I dreaded entering the small space, I couldn't stand out here in the woods until Monday.

Once I'd cleared the forest, I let the witchlight go out completely. Either the sun set early here or I'd spent more time outside than I'd realized. An oil lamp shone through the house's windows, a comforting beacon, even as the intermittent light from the tower pierced the gloom.

With luck, I'd be able to talk to Miss Barnes alone. A weatherwitch would likely have a better understanding of earth magic than I did, and while she couldn't tell me what Rafe had been doing out there in the woods, she might have some rational explanation for his eyes.

At the very least, I needed to warn her.

Luck was with me. I hung my wet coat and hat in the bedroom, angling the armoire door so the jacket wouldn't drip on the bedclothes, and found her alone in the kitchen. She had her back to the door and stirred something that smelled like chicken soup.

"Miss Barnes?" I kept my voice pitched low. "I've just had the most disturbing experience. Do you know where Mrs. Gallagher is?"

"Aren't we past the Miss Barnes and Mr. Fairchild stage?" She spoke without turning around. "You're welcome to call me Margaret if I may call you Vincent. After all" — she shot me a smile over her shoulder — "we're stuck here for the time being."

Smiling at her unexpected offer, I came further into the kitchen. My boots squelched on the linoleum floor but at least I didn't leave a trail of mud. "All right, Margaret." Her name felt comfortable on my tongue, as if we'd known each other longer than just these few days. "You're right. High time we became more familiar."

She raised an eyebrow and her tone had some starch in it. "Not *that* familiar, I hope."

"Oh no." I held my hands up, appalled. "I don't mean to be disrespectful."

Margaret's laugh was closer to a snicker. "Hogwash. Now what is it you wanted to tell me?"

I took a seat at the small kitchen table, tracing the outline of a squirrel that had been carved lightly in the wooden surface. "I'd hoped to find a path through the woods, you see," I began, then told her what I'd witnessed. "I've never studied earth magic. There was no need in the city. Have you? And does any of this make sense?"

She stared soberly into the soup, stirring more slowly as if the action allowed her mind to go free. "A weatherwitch must learn earth magic." Her words were thoughtful, carefully chosen as if I'd judge her for them. "But it sounds more like he was looking for something, rather than trying to pull power from the ground."

"That was my impression, yes, but the power seemed to come whether or not someone called it."

"Hmm." She stirred more quickly. "I wonder if he can see. The glasses, the blackened eyes, the way he had you find his cane make me think he might be blind."

"He moves around easily enough, but he does seem to look past the person he's talking to. It makes you wonder."

"Wonder what?" Mrs. Gallagher strode through the kitchen door. Her hair and her shoulders were damp, as if she'd been outside without a coat.

I smiled up at her, thinking quickly. "Whether it ever does stop raining here."

"You should have planned your visit for July," she said, dismissing me with a glance. "I hope that soup didn't burn."

"No, ma'am," Margaret said. "My mama still has a wood-fired stove, so I'm used to the peculiarities."

51

"We'll eat, then." Mrs. Gallagher went to a cupboard and pulled out four generous-sized bowls, the four spoons. She took one of the loaves of bread — a lovely San Francisco sourdough — and put it on a cutting board. "You can serve yourselves and cut your own bread. Rafe and I will eat later."

On the one hand, her plan made sense. There were only two chairs, and all four of us wouldn't have fit around the table even if there were more. How had they managed when Martin was still alive?

Surely the day was dark enough for it to be suppertime, and breakfast was a distant memory. Still, something in her tone made me uncomfortable, as if there was some other reason she wanted to be alone with Rafe.

Maybe he eats small children for his dinner.

The thought had me choking on a laugh, one I declined to share even after Mrs. Gallagher left us. I dared a glance at Margaret, but she was dishing up two bowls of the soup. "This is good," she said. "Nice and thick."

I set myself to slicing bread. "Smells wonderful." *But why are we talking about soup with all that's going on?*

We sat opposite each other, steam rising from our bowls and thick slices of buttered bread at the ready. The first spoonful of soup reminded me of just exactly how hungry I was, and for a while we simply ate without speaking.

The Lighthouse Keeper

Once I slowed down enough to breathe between bites, I looked up to find Margaret watching me. "There's something strange here, isn't there," she said, with none of the lift in her voice that would make it a question.

"What makes you say that?" I agreed with her wholeheartedly but wanted to hear her point of view.

Her nod said she knew what I was up to. "There are too many things that don't match up. I'm beginning to wonder if Martin Gallagher even existed, and if finding the Ferox Cor is some kind of snipe hunt."

I laughed despite a twinge of pain. As a youngster, every time my uncle visited, he'd take all us kids on a snipe hunt. We'd sneak through the neighborhood after dark, trying to catch those elusive beasts. Only later did we learn that there was no such thing as a snipe and the adults found the game just as entertaining as we did, though for different reasons.

"I think he existed," I said, bringing myself back to the problem at hand. "Madam Munro's information might be somewhat inaccurate, but I can't imagine she'd be so completely mistaken."

"You're probably right." Margaret turned her attention to her bowl.

Before I took another bite, however, I shared a thought that made me uncomfortable. "If Rafe has taken possession of the Ferox Cor, he might have acquired the power to set that concealment spell."

Margaret glanced at me, her expression grim. "Let's not borrow trouble."

"Of course." I turned my attention to the stew, reasonably sure trouble would find us whether we borrowed it or not.

Once we'd sopped up every bit of our dinner, Margaret taught me to wash dishes. A hushed conversation told us mother and son were in the tiny sitting room, which I would have to pass in order to reach the bedroom.

Mrs. Gallagher returned my soft "good night," although Rafe stayed silent. He tracked me, though, his dark attention a soft weight until I closed the bedroom door.

Rather than immediately climb into bed, I packed my pipe and lit it. With only the light from the pipe's cherry, I recreated the image of Rafe's stern profile in my mind, noting the play of candlelight and shadow.

Especially those shadows cast by his amber glasses.

Chapter Five

I woke to darkness. It was easier to conjure a witchlight than to light the oil lamp. Climbing out of bed produced a chorus of snaps and groans as the muscles in my back let go of the cot's imprint. I fished my watch from the pocket of yesterday's waistcoat. Seven in the morning. From my window I could see only the shadowed forest behind the house.

Had the sun refused her daily rise? Or had this faraway place been abandoned by the light?

I shivered, shaking my head to rid it of fancies. The subtle hum from the kitchen let me know that others had already risen. I dressed in clean underthings and a fresh collar, hoping yesterday's shirt and suit would suffice.

I needn't have worried. No one but Margaret made note of my arrival in the kitchen, although Rafe did nearly knock into me on his way out.

Margaret had made coffee, for which I was deeply grateful. A slice of buttered sourdough and one of the eggs Margaret scrambled made up my simple breakfast. Mrs. Gallagher helped herself to an egg, too, and after a few bites she murmured thanks.

"You can leave the dishes," she said, but Margaret responded that cleaning up would be no problem. They were still negotiating when I left, though both offered me a cheery goodbye.

Back in the bedroom, I pulled out the packet of papers Madam Munro had given me. It occurred to me that if Margaret made a friend of Mrs. Gallagher, we might find what we were looking for more easily. Immediately I regretted that thought. Mrs. Gallagher seemed to be a lost soul, and it would be cruel to gain her trust, only to abuse it.

Madam Munro's papers contained no surprises. A typewritten sheet with as much detail about Gallagher's life and family as the Council possessed, two pages of information about the Ferox Cor written in a nearly indecipherable hand, and a letter from Madam giving us her official blessing. According to these documents, Rafe was a child, Martin Gallagher was a weatherwitch, and no one knew what Gallagher had done with the Ferox Cor. The facts were laid out plainly.

The Lighthouse Keeper

She'd included a map. The lighthouse sat on the tip of a wedge of land that jutted out into Puget Sound like a bird's beak. South of this location, Eliot Bay provided the deep harbor the city depended on. Areas where the wilderness had been tamed were blocked out in neat little squares. The bird's beak, the area behind the lighthouse, was empty. We were miles from civilization.

After pawing through the papers a second time — or a third or fourth time, all together — I gave up. Donning overcoat and hat, I made ready to go outside.

Margaret met me in the front room. She was also dressed to go out. "Where's Mrs. Gallagher?" I asked.

"Winding the light's mechanism."

"I thought I'd poke around a bit outside, maybe look in that room on the other side of the tower."

"Do you think we'll find the Cor there?"

I almost laughed. "Anything is possible, and the sooner we find the thing, the sooner we can go home."

On that note, we went outside. The sun shone weakly, though the bank of clouds hovered in the west. The wind was brisk, however, raising little whitecaps on the surface of the water. The tide was out further than it had been on our arrival. I strode to the water's edge, stepping over damp rocks and the little pockmarks made by clams under the sand.

"Wonder what that is?" I pointed at the green shadow of land lurking across several miles of open water.

"Della says it's called Bainbridge Island."

I glanced at her over my shoulder. "Della?"

Margaret shrugged. "Just because we won't be here long doesn't mean we can't be friendly."

"Good point. Attract more flies with honey, et cetera, et cetera."

She pulled a face. "Didn't you tell me you're known for your charm? Maybe you should try using it on Rafe."

Before I could conjure an appropriately scathing rejoinder, I saw a boat. It was coming from the south, slicing through the waves with sails caught full in the stiff breeze.

"Hoi!" I jogged forward until the waves lapped against my boots. I waved my arms, though the boat was likely still too far away to see me.

Margaret clattered across the stony beach to stand next to me. "Wonder where they're going."

The boat turned, heading away from us, and my arms dropped. "Now we'll never know."

The words had just left my mouth when the boat turned again, this time heading toward us. When level with the lighthouse, its sails went slack, as if whoever was in the boat meant to stay. Even though the boat was a couple hundred feet from the beach, I hollered a second time. "Hey! We're here."

"Who are you?" The sailor's reply was faint, but his challenge came through.

"Name's Fairchild, and this is Miss Barnes."

The Lighthouse Keeper

"Where's Gallagher?"

I glanced at Margaret. Did no one know the man had died? Yelling about it seemed a poor form of delivering the news. "Rafe went out this morning. Not sure where he is."

"Rafe?" The man was too far away to accurately read his expression. "I meant the old man."

"What?" I needed to buy some time to figure out how to respond. If Della Gallagher had kept her husband's death a secret from the sailor, there must be a reason.

"You are not welcome here." Rafe strode down the beach, cane swinging and black cloak swirling, hand raised as if he meant to push the boat away by willpower alone. *Willpower or magic.*

The man on the boat laughed. "Surely you can say hello to a neighbor."

A frisson of power raised the hairs on my skin. Margaret clasped my arm, drawing closer to me, for which I was grateful. I'd seen witches cast spells before, powerful witches, intent on each other's destruction. Rafe's incantation put them to shame.

The air around us darkened, as if the clouds from the west had rolled across the water, blotting out the distant island, the waves, the man in the boat.

"I'll be back, you devil, and next time Martin won't be here to protect you." His words, a threat and a promise, came from an even greater distance than before.

Rafe did not reply, unless you counted his subterranean murmur, sounds I could not decipher.

We stood frozen until Rafe dropped his hand, releasing the spell. He stood some six feet ahead of us. I increased that distance by several steps. Margaret came with me, both of us backing away until we reached the grass. Still Rafe stood facing the water.

My mind was a jumble of questions and from that jumble, I pulled a single thread. Della Gallagher said she'd written to Madam Munro, but had she told no one else? Hadn't there been a funeral, an announcement in the newspaper?

And where was Martin Gallagher's body?

"What do you suppose that was all about?" Margaret asked.

I gave her a wry smile. "I have no earthly idea, but the best way to find something out is to ask."

She glanced in Rafe's direction. "Would you think less of me if I said I'd talk with Della while you…"

Her voice faded and I had to laugh. "Wish me luck."

With a quick kiss on my cheek, she trotted across the damp grass. I smiled after her. We'd gone from strangers to affection more rapidly than I would have guessed, and I found I didn't mind at all. I needed one bright spot in the midst of all this gloom.

The darkness had faded enough for me to see only empty waves where the sailboat had been. Empty waves and the black silhouette on the beach. There was nothing welcoming in Rafe's rigid posture, so I approached cautiously, as if tiptoeing past a sleeping bear.

"Stop."

His single command came when I was several feet away from him. Still at the edge of the beach, I waited for him to make his next move.

Which was apparently to wait for me to make my next move. After several fraught minutes, I gave in. "Who was that?"

Tension built in the silence. I was very close to trying another question when he answered.

"His name is Oliver Stevenson, and he's a witch."

I'd assumed he'd had power — how else had we heard each other across the waves — and I made a mental note of the man's name.

"If Seattle had a witches' council, he'd run it, but he's more talk than anything else."

"It surprises me that a city as big as Seattle doesn't have its own council."

Another pause, this one filled with something like sadness. "Martin wouldn't allow it." His voice faded and some of the tension left Rafe's posture. "Do you know what day it is?"

We'd arrived on a Friday, so — "It's Saturday."

"The date?"

"Um..." I quickly counted on my fingers. "The twenty-second of October, I think."

"That means we're nine days from Samhain. You know what happens on Samhain?"

"The veil thins?"

"Yes, the veil thins, and the dead can reach through. *Martin* can reach through."

His words held an anguish I couldn't begin to fathom. I looked him over; tall, gaunt, and so very powerful. "Why would he do that?"

"For reasons too dire for you to understand."

Good Lord. I bit down on a knuckle until I could say something diplomatic. "Then we need to make sure he can't."

He spun around to face me, the weak sunlight reflecting off his amber glasses. "There is no *we*. You and your lady love will be on the supply boat when it leaves on Monday. Mother and I are more than enough to fight this on our own."

I stifled a laugh, deciding to defer an explanation of the nature of my relationship with Margaret. "Fight what?" I waited until I was sure he didn't intend to respond, then gave voice to a question that seemed even more important. "Why are you so afraid of help?"

His sneer hurt more than it should have. "Help? And what help would you offer?" He came toward me, taller and broader with every step. "I can sense what is in you. What you call magic barely deserves the name. When Mother sent word to Madam Munro, she had hopes that we would be sent real help, not some carnival barker and his lover."

"Carnival barker?" I crossed the gravely beach faster than I could think. *Enough is enough.* I reached back to take a swing at him. Let my fist fly.

He grabbed my wrist with an iron-hard grip, his smoldering gaze sliding right over the top of my head.

We strained against each other, neither yielding.

"Go to hell." I jerked my hand free, nearly falling on my ass in the process.

"I will."

My wrist felt as if it had been burned. "You know nothing about me." My tone was haughty, as befits a Fairchild. "Despite the fact that Madam Munro sent me, at your mother's request, you dismissed me from the moment our boat made the shore. From where I'm standing, it looks like you've got enough power to go against any number of devils, but you don't have the sense God gave a chipmunk." I exhaled hard. *Chipmunk? Where had that come from?* "You don't need power, but you clearly need help. Perhaps Madam sent me because she knew I could save you from yourself."

Rafe's lips thinned, his hands clenched. Power swirled around him. Still holding my burning wrist, I turned toward the house.

Because turning my back on an angry witch was the height of wisdom.

Fortunately, I nearly ran into Mrs. Gallagher. "You're right," she said. "Listen to him, Rafe. Madam Munro wouldn't have sent him if he didn't have something to offer."

"Certainly, Mother. Let's tell him everything since you think he's so special."

"Rafe." Her voice carried an edge and a breeze tossed her wild curls. Wind, or power. She might not exceed her son, but she held her own.

They stayed locked in conflict for several long heartbeats. Rafe gave in first, striding off in the direction of the trees with a disgusted huff. I watched him go, wondering what had just happened.

Because call me a stubborn fool, but I took his scorn as a challenge. I wouldn't be leaving on the next delivery boat. I'd be staying on this little bird's beak of land until we'd locked Martin Gallagher away for good.

Chapter Six

Mrs. Gallagher peeled my fingers away from my injured wrist. "Not many woulda tried to take him on."

I should have pulled away, but I found myself surprisingly meek under her touch. Rafe's grip had left a red mark on my skin, with small blisters forming along one edge. She brushed the blisters with a fingertip. "Fool."

"Me, or him?"

"Both, I think." She glanced at me and for the first time I noted the clear blue of her eyes, the way they sparkled with humor. She had a heart-shaped face, the kind that showed a streak of kindness no matter what the circumstances. "Come into the kitchen. I've got some salve that'll cool this off."

"I'd appreciate that."

I followed her lead. Margaret stood poised in the doorway, as if she still couldn't decide whether or not to run. Her fists were clenched, and though she yielded a step so we could enter, she didn't relax. She helped me out of my coat and hat. With a little shove, she sent me in the direction of the kitchen.

Mrs. Gallagher rooted through one of the cupboards and came up with a brown glass jar. She opened it and motioned me closer. The salve smelled of herbs, lavender most notably, and she scooped some up with two fingers.

"We'll cover this with a bit of cotton," she said, painting it on my wrist. "Rafe didn't mean to hurt you. He doesn't have the best control."

I couldn't help but laugh, both at Rafe's control and the relief brought by his mother's touch.

"That's like saying a shotgun didn't mean to go off when he pulled the trigger." Margaret's tart comment made me laugh harder.

"Your son is an interesting man," I said.

Mrs. Gallagher gave me a weary smile. "He is, at that. Now wait here while I find something to wrap this with."

As soon as we were alone, Margaret turned on me. "What in the world did you think you were about? You were just supposed to ask him about the man on the boat, not start a war."

The salve seemed to be affecting more than just the burn. A heaviness came over me and I dropped into one of the dining chairs. "He told me the man's name, Oliver Stevenson, and said that if Seattle had a witches' council, Stevenson would be the one to run it."

"That seems harmless enough."

I had to fight to keep my eyes open. "Well, then I asked why Seattle didn't have a council already and things went downhill faster than a cable car on Powell Street."

"I've never been on Powell Street, but still, I thought you were going to come to blows."

Raising my injured wrist as evidence, I said, "Fisticuffs is usually my last resort, but a man who can't see won't be impressed when I change my pocket watch into a cudgel."

"True."

"And he's apparently immune to my most lethal weapon." I gave her the brightest smile I could manage. "My charming personality."

She all but rolled her eyes. "Consider me immune as well."

"Immune to what?" Mrs. Gallagher asked. She came in with a length of plain muslin, her smile cautious as if she didn't want to catch us unawares.

"His lethal smile," Margaret said dryly, earning a laugh from our hostess.

"He is quite pretty."

I scowled at both of them without offering any further comment.

Margaret pulled up the second dining chair and took a seat next to me. Mrs. Gallagher turned her attention to the breakfast dishes, and for a moment we sat in a companionable silence. Or something close to companiable, anyway.

"Before we were so rudely interrupted" — Margaret grinned at me — "I was just going to tell you we saw a man in a sailboat near the lighthouse this morning."

Mrs. Gallagher stilled. After a moment, she reached for a dishtowel and turned to us, drying her hands. "I figured that's what set Rafe off."

"He said the man's name was Oliver Stevenson."

"Stevenson," Mrs. Gallagher finished with me. "Yeah, he and Martin have some history."

I fought off a yawn. "I figured."

"You see, Martin was a practitioner of the old ways. Earth magic. And Ollie, well he's capable enough, but he relies too much on his ability to manipulate water. He's a fisherman, of course, but he only uses his gift to lift himself up."

"What did Martin use his earth magic for?" Sweet as pie, Margaret posed a question that interested me greatly.

Mrs. Gallagher's gaze sharpened. "Same as any weatherwitch. Shift the currents to keep boats off the sandbar and settle storms before they cause too much trouble. He might have also tried to keep the witches in this town out of the clutches of a jumped-up fisherman who wanted to horde everything for himself."

To diffuse the tension, I raised my injured arm. "Is this stuff supposed to put me to sleep, because — " my words were cut off with another jawbreaking yawn.

Both women laughed. "Might be the salve," Mrs. Gallagher said. "Might also be that cramped little cot in Rafe's bedroom."

I had to agree with her. "I've slept in larger beds."

"Such good manners," Mrs. Gallagher said, laughter lifting her sadness for a moment. "If it's any consolation, Rafe's sleeping on the floor in the workshop."

"I expect I got the better part of the deal."

Once she pointed it out, I realized my sluggish humor had more to do with a cramped cot and the let-down after a fight than it did with the salve. I shook myself, and after a glance at Margaret, I tested the waters of our newfound cordiality.

"It did seem odd, though, that Stevenson didn't know Martin had passed away."

Whatever I'd expected, it hadn't been laughter. "Oh that," Mrs. Gallagher said once she'd composed herself. "Martin didn't want to give that man any advantage at all." She sobered. "People fear the unfamiliar, you know, and Seattle is a brand new city. Since there wasn't an established Council to keep everyone in line, Martin always put some distance between us and them. He made us promise to keep his death a secret for as long as possible. He's still protecting us, you see."

Her mix of affection and sadness left me at a loss. I had no idea what to say.

"Rafe told you about Samhain, didn't he?" she asked, filling the silence.

I nodded my agreement, though Margaret made a puzzled sound. I patted her arm, a promise to explain later. I didn't want anything to interrupt Mrs. Gallagher.

"When Martin knew death was near, he vowed to cross through the veil on Samhain. He still wants to take care of us, no matter what the cost to himself."

"And then what would happen?"

She didn't answer, except to look at me, her eyes glassy with tears.

That put me off asking any more questions. "I'm sorry for distressing you, Mrs. Gallagher."

"Della." She gave me a watery smile. "Call me Della."

"Thank you, Della. Please call me Vincent."

"But don't call him late for dinner," Margaret said, making all of us laugh. Mrs. Gallagher — Della

— said she had to draw water to start the supper, and Margaret volunteered to help.

Feeling more awake, I took a moment to think through what we'd learned. Della clearly mourned her husband's death, and she believed Martin had tried to protect his family, even after he passed away. Neither she nor Rafe had mentioned the Ferox Cor, but logic told me Martin's threat to cross the veil must have something to do with that magical object. No matter the reason, what Martin proposed could only end in disaster.

Rafe was a piece that didn't fit in the puzzle. I needed to examine him more closely, though the very idea made me blush.

To distract myself, I decided to look into that room on the ocean end of the building. For all we knew, Martin Gallagher's body was being kept there, which didn't disturb me as much as it should. The burn on my wrist felt quite comfortable, though the bandage snagged on the sleeve of my overcoat. Still, the sun shone weakly, enough to let me know I wouldn't get rained on.

I left my hat in the house and the wind whipped my hair into a disordered mess. Keeping close to the building, I crunched along the gravel path surrounding the house. The bank of dark clouds in the west had moved closer, and I had to give the sun credit for shining despite that ominous bulk.

Before trying to enter the room, I walked around it. There were three windows — one each wall, with a door on the south side. Cupping my hands on either side of my eyes to cut the sun's weak glare, I attempted to look through the south window.

Clutter. Boxes, tools, and some sort of detritus, small objects covering the flat surfaces. No Rafe, which I took as a good sign, and no Martin either. I couldn't make out any further detail, so I moved to the door. Locked, as I assumed it would be. I picked up a stone and stared hard at the lock, as if I could see into its inner workings.

With a small push of power, the rock turned into a key, one that fitted neatly into the lock. I cautiously opened the door, still worried I'd find either Rafe or Martin hiding in the shadows.

The sight before me took my breath away. I'd stumbled upon a workshop, a place where an artist plied his craft. The jumble of small objects I'd seen through the window were, in truth, small carved creatures. Animals, mostly, horses with delicate hooves, sea birds with their wings stretched in flight. Some had been painted, intricate decoration with fine detail. It was as if Noah's Ark or some magical circus had set up shop here at the end of the world.

Once I could breathe again, I entered, moving slowly so as not to disturb anything. The Ferox Cor could well be in here, hiding amongst all the stuff. The artist's tools hung on the wall in neat rows and the floor was clean of shavings and sawdust. A small chair had wheels on its legs so someone could move from one desk to the other. I picked up one of the creatures, a tiny mouse. The surface of the wood was silky and polished to a faint shine. Fine whiskers had been painted on its little face, the tail a fragile curl and each small foot tucked against the body.

I'd never seen anything so breathtakingly fine. I set it down and picked up another, a goat, its expression so lifelike I expected it to bleat. There were barn cats and proud lions and fish of unimaginable colors. Was Della the artist, or had Martin made them before he passed away?

I soon had my answer.

A shadow blocked the thin light from the door. I glanced up, managing to set down the conch shell without breaking it. "Rafe?"

"What are you doing in here?"

If this morning he'd been angry, now his voice had a deadly calm that frightened me even more. "I'm, uh, sorry." There were too many possible weapons hanging on the wall for me to say anything else.

"Please leave. No one is allowed to enter. No one."

His words fell on me like stones. My heart beat fast, then faster, and my breath grew short. "But," I gasped, gesturing at the creatures on the table. "These are so beautiful. I've never seen anything like them. Who made them? They're so very good."

Perhaps my sincerity appealed to him because he let go of a deep sigh. "I made them."

I took a moment to respond. The Rafe I'd seen so far — cold, hard, angry, and threatening — was also capable of creating beauty. "You're… amazing. But how…?"

He stiffened, then sighed again. "I allow the Mother to show me."

Quite obviously the Mother he referred to was someone besides Della. So, like his father, he was a proponent of earth magic. I had no rebuttal for that, sure that my ability to turn a rock into a key didn't come from some mystical Mother Earth. His creations, however, were lovely.

"I'll ask you again. Please leave." His voice held tension, as if he'd have yanked me out more roughly if doing so wouldn't threaten to break things. "You should not have been able to enter in the first place."

"My gift is in transformation. I simply turned a rock into a key that would fit your lock."

"And how did you get through my wards?"

"Not deliberately, I assure you."

"There must have been a flaw in the spell," he murmured, reaching for one of the little carvings. "Leave this place and don't come back."

I did as he asked, though I had to carefully edge around him to reach the door. I confess his scent, smokey and herbal, drew me in a way I couldn't explain. I glanced up, intending to apologize, only to find him leaning toward me. His gaze seemed to glide past me, those pitch-black eyes burning through the amber glass. *What could he see?* I froze, locked in the moment for a heartbeat too long.

Instead of something demonic, I surely saw desire.

"We're not lovers," I whispered, voice raw as if I'd been screaming. "Margaret and I. Only friends."

He swallowed, the movement in his throat as enticing as the curve of his lip. His gaze grew even more intent, and for a heartbeat I thought he might kiss me. He even leaned closer, just a hairbreadth. My body stilled. If he tried, I knew in my bones I'd kiss him back.

He shuddered, then straightened and looked away. I lurched out of his range, stopping in the doorway, breathing hard. "I'm sorry," I gasped. "I did not mean to intrude."

His only response was to fix his attention on the little carving he'd picked up. It was a hummingbird, its wide-spread wings so thin the light shone through them. He drew a finger down its long, impossibly narrow beak, and all I could think about was how his fingers would feel on my body. A blind man's touch would be unlike anything I'd experienced. But was he truly blind?

Before I could do anything utterly irrational, I left him alone.

Chapter Seven

Rafe absented himself for the rest of the day. He could have been in his carving room, although the windows were dark. He might not need a light, after all.

Margaret helped Della with the cooking and the washing up, while I tried to find something useful to do. The only place I hadn't explored was the lighthouse tower. There didn't seem to be a passage to the tower from inside the house, so after lunch, I donned my overcoat a third time and set out.

The clouds from the west had moved in, blotting out the last remnants of sunshine. A brisk wind blew off the water and cut right through the wool of my coat. White foam from the rising tide sprayed across the grass when each wave hit.

The door at the base of the tower was blessedly unlocked. Neither Rafe nor I would fare well if he caught me breaking into another place. As it was, I entered a small room with a wood floor and not much else. The bottom steps of a wide spiral staircase took up most of the space, with a column at the center that traveled from one floor to the other. A pair of oil lamps sat in sconces on opposite walls, giving me enough light to navigate the first few stairs.

The briny smell of salt and fish seemed more concentrated here than it had out of doors. *Odd.* I climbed the staircase and it spit me out onto the second floor.

This was the true heart of the lighthouse. The lamp itself sat in the middle of the space, surrounded by a cage of glass. Near the top of the stairs, a handle had been mounted on a wooden box on the wall. From the base of the box, a pair of cables snaked down the wall and into the column at the center of the stairwell. This must be the mechanism that kept the light running.

Across from the stairs, a door led to a narrow widow's walk, a porch and railing that surrounded the lamp. I stepped outside, blinking into the wind. Madam Munro's notes had said that this body of water was called a *sound* because it was hemmed in by islands. To me it looked the same as the great Pacific

Ocean, though wilder than those stretches of beach near San Francisco.

If forced to make a list of the benefits of being cut off from the rest of my family, I confess it wouldn't take me long. I'd put the ocean near the top. Its endless expanse and its absolute disregard for human wants and desires were intoxicating to me. I envied the fishermen who threw their lot in with her every day, and for the most part lived to do it again.

If I had a mental image of the Mother Goddess, she resembled the ocean: cold, endless, and uncaring. I didn't believe she granted me power, such as it was. Power was in the air, the ether, in unlimited supply. As far as I knew, power was meant to be taken and manipulated by those who had the gift.

I stood on that little platform, the lighthouse's lamp blasting me from behind every few seconds, until my fingers were stiff and numb. Only then did I climb down, keeping myself open to any sign of magic, whether good or evil.

There were none, nor did I stumble over the body of Martin Gallagher. It unsettled me to think that he must be around here somewhere, but if people in Seattle didn't know he'd passed away, there can't have been much of a funeral procession. I hadn't asked if Rafe and his mother had a boat of their own, though it seemed obvious that they must. They couldn't depend entirely on the delivery boats. Could they?

At the bottom of the stairs, I found Margaret.

"There you are. I'd run out of other places to look." Her smile took the sting out of her words, and I hung my head, abashed.

"I do apologize. I climbed up to the lamp to see if there was anything magical lying about."

"Magical?"

"You know, the Ferox Cor or maybe the body of Martin Gallagher."

She took hold of my arm, drawing me closer. "Martin Gallagher…" She shook her head, as if the dead man was a subject she would avoid if she could.

"Any idea how to keep him from crossing the veil?"

"No," she said shortly. "But we must somehow prevent it."

"My thought exactly. Which is why I've decided not to get on that supply boat the next time it arrives."

She nodded, her expression grim. "I'll need to stay longer still. Della is many things, but she's not a weatherwitch, from what I can tell. I'd thought to climb to the tower now to see whether I can coax this storm to take its ire out on someplace less populated."

"Surely Madam Munro will send a permanent keeper soon."

She laughed wryly. "I'd like to be that permanent keeper. I'm well past my apprenticeship and have had more than one temporary assignment. It's my turn."

Her clear-eyed determination impressed me. "Then I'll do whatever I can to help you."

"Finding the Ferox Cor will help a great deal, as will keeping Martin Gallagher on the other side of the veil."

"You're very persuasive." We shared a smile. "As Rafe said, we have nine days. Let's see what we see."

Margaret went her way and I went mine. Despite my best efforts, however, I had little luck. I didn't find any stray sources of magical power, nor did I find a dead man's body. Rafe appeared after dinner, looking both unwell and unwashed, his hair a tangle, his nails half-moons of black. Clutching his cane, he barely acknowledged his mother and Margaret, instead directing his full attention at me.

"You'll be on that supply boat when it leaves tomorrow."

He had me at a disadvantage, as I'd been tucking into another of Della's savory stews. He was markedly taller than me when I was on foot. In this rickety dining chair, he towered over me.

"Not until after Samhain," I said, keeping my voice firm.

"No. You will leave tomorrow."

I glanced at Margaret. Her eyes were so wide I couldn't tell if she meant to laugh or cry.

From the stove, Della's voice came as calming as one of her salves. "Vincent, why don't you give Rafe your seat."

I rose. He did look like he was about to topple over. "Please." I gestured to the seat, realizing he was unlikely to see me.

He found his way, however, collapsing into the chair as if his limbs simply could not hold him any longer. Della brought him a bowl of chowder, though she grimaced when she saw his hands. "Let me get a towel."

With a damp, soapy towel, Della knelt at Rafe's side and took hold of his hands. "You shouldn't push yourself so hard, son. I've taken their measure. Both of them. They're willing to help us."

"They don't know what we need of them, and if they did, they'd run." Even beaten down, anger twisted his tone of voice. That same anger — *or was it fear?* — reminded me that Rafe Gallagher wasn't some tortured hero. Hell, he might even be possessed by a demon. That glimpse of his woodshop had shown me a softer side of the man, but his was still a dark and dangerous soul.

Girding myself for battle, I stepped into the fray. "Tell us. If you tell us what you're afraid of, we can understand how best to help you."

Rafe's cane toppled to the floor. Both of his hands were fisted in his lap and the veins stood out in his neck. "I'm not afraid for myself." The words came from between clenched teeth. "I am ready, but I can't be distracted by a dilettante and his —"

"Rafe." Della spoke sharply.

"Mother," he snapped back.

Margaret eased herself from the other dining chair and came to stand next to me. "We've decided," she said. "We're not leaving till after Samhain."

Della looked up from Rafe's hands. "Thank you," she said.

He did not respond to her, nor did he look up from the floor when Margaret and I left.

We hovered in the front room. Though we'd become friends, we weren't close enough to take refuge together in a bedroom. Della's voice rose, and I made a deliberate effort to ignore her words. If Rafe responded, he spoke too quietly to overhear.

"You are something of a dilettante." Margaret's sly smile took the sting away. If she meant to make me laugh, she succeeded.

"Yesterday he called me a carnival barker."

"I don't know whether I should laugh or feel jealous that he hasn't called me anything at all."

I returned her smile, though my effort felt stretched. The entirety of the room's furniture included a padded bench near the window and two straight chairs with pillowed seats. A diminutive table sat between the chairs, the oil lamp taking up most of its top. The floral fabric covering the bench and seat cushions added warmth to an otherwise spare space. There should have been a picture on the wall, or maybe a bookcase.

Or maybe even a shelf filled with Rafe's handiwork.

Feeling as if I'd stumbled onto an unfinished stage set, I settled on the bench. "He might be right."

Margaret took one of the chairs, anchoring both of us in place. The lamp threw her profile into relief. While she wasn't conventionally pretty, her strong features and ready smile made her a striking woman. "Who might be right?"

Rafe, obviously. "Forget I said anything." I pulled out my pocket watch, unwilling to whine about something so petty. "What time does the sun set in this town? It's only five-thirty yet it's already getting dark."

Margaret's smile was way too perceptive. "We're far enough north that the nights get long at this time of year."

"Of course." I reached for another topic, one that would divert her focus from me. "You must have had luck with the storm." It hadn't started raining yet, at least.

That gave us something to talk about, and Margaret went into some arcane detail explaining how she'd controlled the air currents, balancing them in order to diffuse the force of the storm. "It's tricky work, though. When I move something close at hand, things may shift on the other side of the world."

"Astonishing."

"Not really."

"My tricks aren't nearly as impressive," I said, "but I've never worried that drawing the power needed to change a coin into a baseball would influence anything else."

"It's all one world, Vincent."

"It is, and when a leaf falls here, they'll hear the echo in China," Della said. She came into the room, her face pale and her expression grim. Rafe must have stayed in the kitchen, unless he'd snuck out through a wall or window. Della took the chair across from Margaret, and it struck me how appropriate the two of them looked sitting together like that.

Blinking, I let the image clear. Margaret and I had made the first overtures of friendship, but I knew Della much less well. I needed to find the right entry, the combination of words that would encourage her to tell us what Rafe so feared.

"I hope Rafe feels better after he eats something." It wasn't a lie. I did hope he felt better, but I also wanted her to open up.

Her gaze sharpened, as if she recognized my ploy. "He will."

Shut down in two words. I needed to do better. "I saw his workshop. His creations are extraordinary."

Both women pinned me with their gazes. "What creations?" Margaret asked.

"How did you get in?" Della's question overrode Margaret's and I raised my hands helplessly.

"I was poking around outside. Neither of you have said anything about the smaller shed on the other side of the tower, so I looked through the window."

"Neither of us have said anything because it's none of your business." Della's blatant annoyance flared into anger. "Besides, neither of you have asked. If you had, I'd have told you to stay the hell away from it. Now, how did you get in?"

I cleared my throat, surprised by the cold, distant person she'd become. Rafe came by his moods honestly. "My gift is transformation. I turned a rock into a key that would fit the lock, and I went in."

"What did you see?" Margaret asked.

"Never mind." Della rose. "Least said, soonest mended. Just promise me you'll stay out of there."

She rose, heading for the door to the kitchen. When she reached the threshold, she turned to me. "Promise."

"Of course. My apologies for causing you distress," I said, fingers crossed behind my back. Her response had moved the workshop to the top of my list of places to search for the Ferox Cor.

Chapter Eight

The early sunset chased me into bed sooner than I might otherwise have gone. The little light cast by the oil lamp made it difficult to do anything but think about the Ferox Cor and rub my hands together to keep warm.

Not that it was going to be any warmer in bed, but if I slept, I might find a clue in my dreams.

The next morning was noteworthy because Della brought Margaret into the tower to show her how to wind the mechanism that worked the light. And because Barnard arrived with his delivery when the tide was the furthest in.

Rafe wasn't around, so I volunteered to help with the delivery. Barnard had again dropped anchor some distance from the dock and then loaded a rowboat with our supplies. This time there was a crate with eggs and two bottles of milk, along with some late apples and other items wrapped in paper. Everything in the second crate was wrapped, and the rowboat held three more bundles wrapped in white cloth. I helped unload the supplies and carried them up from the dock.

"How do I get the crates back to him?" From what I could tell, *The Lucky* was already underway.

"We burn 'em for firewood," Della said.

With a shrug, I carried the bundles toward the house. Della brought one of the crates and Margaret the other, but when I dropped my load and would have headed out to get the rest, Della stopped me.

"Wait. There's a letter in this one."

Margaret moved to her side, resting a hand on the other woman's shoulder. "What is it?"

"We do solemnly declare that the Seattle Witches' Council does exist and is made up of the undersigned. The president of said Council, Oliver Stevenson, instructs you to attend our meeting on Tuesday, Oct 25th. A boat will arrive to transport you, and if you choose not to comply, there will be consequences."

Her stilted delivery made a mockery of the letter's solemn tone.

"Can they do that?" I asked.

Della shrugged, her shoulders slumping. "Whether or not they can, they have. They must have guessed that Martin is gone."

Her dejection tugged at my heart. "They can't have been anointed by the Congress." The Congress had authority over all witches' councils, and like every form of authority, they worked slowly. "Are you going to go?"

She roused herself with a shake. "I should probably talk to Rafe first."

I agreed with her, but my mind was already jumping ahead. Della probably shouldn't go alone, and it would be a sincere surprise if Rafe didn't insist on accompanying her. That left me and Margaret running the light, which could work to our advantage.

If they were both gone, we'd have more time to search for the Ferox Cor. And finding the Cor would allow us to leave this barren place. We'd only been here two days, but already I missed the energy of the city. The place was too danged quiet.

On the other hand, when I tried to imagine Rafe's response to a roomful of witches claiming they had jurisdiction over him, it almost made me laugh.

No, Rafe couldn't go on this little jaunt.

If Margaret and I went, we could speak as representatives of the San Francisco Council, which would buy Rafe and his mother some time before they had to admit Martin was dead. But then we wouldn't be able to search for the Cor, which was our main task.

Although… perhaps without Rafe and Della present, Oliver Stephenson might give up a clue.

I had no idea which would be the best avenue, a situation I still hadn't resolved by the time Della called us all to meet with her in the front room. She and Margaret again took the chairs, I sat on the bench, and Rafe lurked in the doorway, as silent and disheveled as ever.

Though my heart beat just a little faster whenever he turned my way. If it seemed he turned my way with increasing frequency, I chalked it up to the tense situation rather than any interest on his part.

Because surely he wasn't interested in me, except as an irritant.

"And what do you think those consequences could possibly be, Mother, the ones they mention in the letter?" Rafe's tone gave away how little he thought of those who had summoned them.

"Don't, Rafe." Della sat with her arms crossed, as if she knew there'd be a fight no matter what she said. "They've summoned me, so I shall go."

"*We* shall go."

I glanced from Rafe to his mother. "I mean no disrespect to either of you, but as a representative of the San Francisco Witches' Council, I could speak for you and for the Congress."

"And how will that help?" Rafe sneered.

Why did he have to be so attractive and so unpleasant at the same time? "For one thing, I can tell them they're full of beans, unless they have an order from the Congress."

"If Vincent and I went," Margaret said, "we could assess their authority and get word to Madam Munro in San Francisco."

Rafe's glower deepened while he and his mother had a wordless conversation.

"We can't all go," Della murmured.

"Then you stay here, and I will represent us," Rafe said.

"Not alone." Della conceded the point, giving the words a finality that didn't brook argument. "If I stay behind, perhaps you should stay as well, Margaret. A storm could blow in…"

"I'd be happy to."

I had to stifle a smile because Margaret's tight lips and the crease between her brows made a lie of her words. "So Rafe and I will go," I said, "and Della and Margaret will hold the fort."

"I don't need help." Rafe tapped his cane on the floor as if he could shake free an argument. The way he fidgeted, though, made me wonder if he believed his own lie.

Since my winning smile would be wasted on him, I settled for a shrug. "Before coming here, I worked in the liaison office, keeping the peace between the city's mundane government and the Council. You may not need my help, but I'm here and I believe my skills might come in useful. Might as well put me to work."

The amber glasses shielded me from the full effect of Rafe's glare, that and the way he stared past me.

"That sounds quite reasonable, Mr. Fairchild," Della said.

"Vincent," I corrected.

"Of course. Vincent. We appreciate your offer." Della tucked the envelope in her pocket. "It's decided. Rafe will respond to the summons, and Vincent will accompany him."

Where I would do my best to both keep him out of trouble and learn more about the Ferox Cor. And where I wouldn't moon over him like a lovesick calf.

With that decided, we dispersed to get ready for the following day. The rain returned, hammering the roof and sending rivulets of water down the windows. During dinner, I had the opportunity to question Della further.

"I know so little about this area."

Della set a plate in front of me. "Chipped beef," she said, and I thanked her.

"Do you have much contact with the other witches, the ones who made the new council?" Margaret asked, nodding her thanks as Della set a plate in front of her.

Della straightened, hands on her hips. "Martin was a singular person. He didn't tolerate others getting in his way."

"Amazing that he possessed the kind of power it took to prevent the formation of a council." I kept my tone light, flirting with the real reason for our presence. *Where did his power come from if not the Ferox Cor?*

I got a sad glance for my trouble.

"My husband was a good man. He did his best to protect us from outsiders, and he took care of this town for many years. He secured the territory and kept the people who lived here safe from more than just the weather." Her voice rose as she warmed to her subject. "It was my honor to help him, and I won't brook anyone speaking ill of him in my presence."

"Pardon me, Della. That wasn't my intention."

She pressed her lips together, as if fighting the urge to say more. I waited for her next move, tension tightening my jaw. Margaret's little cough broke through to both of us.

"This beef is delicious, Della. You must share your recipe."

Della chuckled, her posture relaxing. "I surely will, Margaret, just as soon as I put your young man's mind to rest. Martin Gallagher was far from perfect, but he did what he could. There was no one in the area who could match him, and every one of them was jealous."

"It must have been lonely for you and Rafe."

"You get used to it, being out here. It comes with being a weatherwitch."

Margaret put a hand on Della's arm. "She's right. I expect I'll end up someplace just as remote."

"It was good of Madam Munro to send you." Della gave each of us a tentative smile.

I felt lifted up in her estimation; not high enough to ask about the Ferox Cor, but close. "Madam Munro knows what she's about. Now, tell me about this Oliver Stevenson so I don't say the wrong thing tomorrow."

"He's a fisherman and he's got power over water. He's not strong enough to call himself a weatherwitch, so I guess this council thing is his way of grabbing power."

The longer she spoke, the warmer she sounded, so I kept her talking. I learned that there were likely six witches on the new Seattle council — if it could really be called a council — each in possession of some manner of talent. There was one who could take animal forms, one who had the power of invisibility, and two sisters who were accomplished herbalists.

The sixth was some kind of psychic, which caught my attention. "Tell me more. Can he read anyone's mind?"

Della picked up Margaret's empty plate and brought it to the sink. "She's a woman, Mrs. Morrison, and she's an odd one. She's only been here a year or so and she's not married, but she keeps rooms in town and a house on the banks of the Duwamish River. They say she's a skilled clairvoyant, but I've never met her, so I don't know."

"She must make her money somehow."

"That's what people say. Of course, they also say she'll make you a love potion for a dollar, so who knows what is true. Just be careful when you're around her. Rumor has it that if she steals a thought our two, she'll use them to hurt you."

Margaret and I exchanged a glance. "Thank you, Della. I'll do my best to put your information to good use."

And in the meantime, I'd best find a way to protect myself against a psychic. The last thing I needed was for her to announce what she saw in my head, whether those thoughts had to do with the Ferox Cor or with Rafe himself.

After Margaret and I finished our dinner, we browbeat Della into sitting at the table. Rafe was nowhere to be found, but Margaret served her some of the chipped beef and I made a mess of the dishes. Once Della was settled, Margaret elbowed me out of the way and took over the clean-up.

I was left to my own devices.

The rain had stopped, the clouds rolling back far enough to let some moonlight through. I put on my coat and hat and wandered down to the beach. I should be looking for the Ferox Cor, but it seemed we'd exhausted our possibilities. For now.

The tide was out, the moonlight casting a gloss over the rocky sand. There was a dim light in Rafe's workroom, and though I tried to ignore it, inevitably my steps headed in that direction.

I cupped my hands on either side of my eyes, cutting the moon's glare. The figure within was indistinct, a silhouette in motion. He made quick, repetitive movements, polishing or sanding an object in his hands.

After several minutes the motion jerked to a halt. A muttered curse, barely heard, brought my hand to the door. I turned the handle. Locked. Acknowledging that this was likely a mistake, I knocked.

The cursing grew louder and more plain. "What the devil do you want?"

Rafe jerked the door open, causing me to stumble. *What did I want? More than Rafe could likely give.* "I asked your mother about the people we'd be meeting tomorrow, and she mentioned a Mrs. Morrison."

"So?"

"Your mother says the woman is a psychic."

"I'm aware of her skill."

"So unless you want your secrets spread across the town before nightfall, you should be prepared to deal with her. I, for one, don't want my thoughts snatched by a stranger."

He exhaled, an exercise in frustration, and for a moment I thought he would slam the door in my face.

He didn't.

"Come in," he said, holding the door so I could pass.

The Lighthouse Keeper

I confess I hesitated, uncertain I wanted to be in such a small space with a volatile man. I'd been there once.

As if irritated by my hesitation, he stormed out of the workroom, damn near knocking me over. He slammed the door. I spun around to face him. "Do you know anything about her?"

He was halfway to the corner when he paused. "Yes. I know she can read minds, and I know that I can put up shields to prevent her from reading mine. I also know" — he hesitated, as if he already regretted what he was about to say — "that if you stand close enough, I can shield you, too."

With that, he disappeared around the corner of the workshop. I stayed put, wondering whether he'd given me a glimpse of his softer side.

Or whether I'd imagined it.

"Hey," I said, jogging to catch up with him. "Thanks. What happened to the thing you were working on?"

He kept his back to me. "It broke."

The defeat in his voice landed like a blow. I wanted to ask him why or how, but he went into the tower and shut the door. Since I'd already intruded on him once, I didn't want to push my luck.

Instead, I reminded myself that he was grieving and went back to the beach. The steady pulse of the waves calmed me. My mind settled, and I gave the situation some thought. From what Della had said,

Oliver Stevenson's main power was his ego. I should be able to cajole him with flattery and a few well-placed mentions of the Congress and Madam Munro.

The others, except for Mrs. Morrison, should be manageable as well. As far as the psychic was concerned, I'd stay close to Rafe, and hope that his shields worked.

And that his proximity didn't produce any of the kind of thoughts that could get me in trouble.

Chapter Nine

In the morning, Margaret met me in the kitchen with a gloriously warm mug of coffee.

"Thank you."

"Are you ready for today?"

For a moment I ignored her question, letting the fragrant steam settle the chills running through my body. "Of course," I said finally, striving for more confidence than I honestly felt. "This council doesn't worry me."

"They don't worry me, either. Rafe, though, could give you a harder time."

I agreed with Margaret, although saying the words out loud made them more real, so I held my tongue.

Liv Rancourt

"At any rate," she said briskly, "while you're gone, I'll do some exploring. Della's beginning to trust me, I think, and if—"

Della's arrival cut her off. "I think I see sails to the south. Whoever they've sent should be able to drop anchor in another twenty minutes or so."

"I'm at your disposal." I raised my mug in toast, giving Margaret a grateful nod, filling in the rest of her thought in my own mind. If Della trusted Margaret, she might give her some clue as to the location of the Ferox Cor. My own errand was likely to be less directly helpful, though I'd keep my eyes and ears open.

An undercurrent of sadness weighed down Della's smile. "Rafe should be along any time. I swear, if you do nothing else, keep him from angering them. You don't want them to refuse you a return trip."

My smile never faltered, though her warning heightened my nerves. "They've only offered us a one-way ticket?"

"I'm sure they mean to bring you back." She clasped her hands in front of her belly, a protective gesture that gave more of a warning than her words. "Unless they won't."

"Then I will do my best to charm them like they've never been charmed before." I gave her a little bow, and her answering laugh had more life to it.

"If anyone can do it, it'd be you. Rafe has many gifts, but sweetness isn't one of them."

The Lighthouse Keeper

I murmured something noncommittal. It'd never do to agree with too much enthusiasm. Finishing my coffee, I bundled up and went out to the beach.

Either the sun rose later than normal, or the thick clouds prevented the passage of light. Rafe waited on the small lawn, his attention somewhere over the horizon. Certainly, he didn't notice me.

He was clean-shaven, his hair neat under a sporting bowler hat. Rather than his leaf-and-twig bedecked cloak, he wore a handsome overcoat. His boots were glossy black and he'd even traded his normal cane for one of ebony. I approached him slowly, giving myself a few moments to enjoy the view.

As soon as he opened his mouth, I had no doubt he'd be back to his old acerbic self.

"He's out there."

Surprised by his acknowledgement, I stopped at his side. The boat — ship? — was some two hundred yards offshore. It had two masts and was larger than most fishing vessels. Across the sound, mist softened Bainbridge Island's deep green profile. "Looks like he's lowering a rowboat from over the side."

"The sandbar makes the water too shallow for any vessel with a keel."

"Therefore, the lighthouse." Stupid of me not to recognize that before now. "I blame my Midwest upbringing." He greeted my confession with silence. *Lord, he is a stiff one.* Rather than give up, I tried a different approach. "I confess there are excursions I've been more excited about."

"Stay here, then."

If I'd hoped to put him at ease by sharing my own uncertainty, the attempt failed. Whatever measure of cordiality we'd reached last evening had not carried over.

I dared a glance in his direction. His stern profile gave little away. "Generally, when approaching a meeting like this, I find it's helpful to anticipate as many possible outcomes as I can conjure up."

I took his silence to mean I should keep babbling. "It's possible they will invite you to join them." No response. "Or perhaps they'll ask you to leave the city, to tell you they've assigned the lighthouse to someone else." They had nowhere near the authority to do that, but they could try.

"No."

"They won't ask you to leave, or they won't assign someone else to the lighthouse?"

He stood so still I wondered if he was even breathing. The man in the rowboat made steady progress in our direction.

"Neither." He spoke quietly, but with utter conviction.

"How do you figure?"

"They'd have to kill me first."

Interesting. "All that would take is a well-placed bullet."

The Lighthouse Keeper

He laughed, though it wasn't a happy sound. I let the silence settle around us, imagining what his real laugh would sound like. Rusty, creaky, as unused as the pump for a forgotten well.

A wave pushed the rowboat those last feet to the dock. We strode out to it. The young man nodded at Rafe alone.

"Where's your mum?" he asked. Rafe, unsurprisingly, ignored the question, climbing over the gunwale and settling himself on a bench close to the stern.

"Mrs. Gallagher is staying here to run the lighthouse. Rafe will speak for her, and I will speak for the San Francisco Witches' Council."

The young man blinked in surprise. Still, he stepped aside so I could climb aboard. Once I was seated, he used his paddle to shove off. I had to shift my feet to keep them out of the puddle at the bottom of the boat, and for the first time I wondered if perhaps I should have let Rafe go it alone.

Yes, I could speak for the Council and by extension, the Congress of Witches, but what good would that do here, in a place where they'd let one man rule them for some twenty years? Martin Gallagher had apparently held them in thrall, and Rafe seemed intent on furthering his father's rule. *Especially if he now possessed the Ferox Cor.*

That thought gave me something new to worry about. I'd volunteered for this job so I could soften his sharp edges, but what if they truly angered him? Whether he relied on the Ferox Cor or not, he still possessed a world more power than I did. He could flatten everyone in the room before I could do more than wring my hands.

The closer we got to the fishing boat, the lower the clouds drifted, until it seemed we were paddling through their thick, misty depths. The only sound was the flap and splash of the waves and the paddle. Any seabirds around had had the good sense to hide in their nests, out of the dreary cold. Before we reached our destination, I had to clench my teeth to keep them from chattering.

An older man, clearly the one in charge, awaited us on the ship. If he had questions about the missing Mrs. Gallagher, he kept them to himself and invited us aboard. I let Rafe go first. He passed his cane over, then gripped the side with both hands. This ship rode a good two feet higher in the water than the rowboat, but Rafe managed to climb over with a fair amount of grace.

I was not so fortunate, but at least I didn't go swimming.

We were ushered into the cabin where — thank the Lord — a small iron stove burned merrily in the corner. My hands were nearly as numb as my feet. Before, Rafe's silence had invited chatter, but now he squashed it. I still didn't have all the pieces of the puzzle, and I could only hope the missing bits wouldn't cause us too much trouble.

It took less time to reach the city dock than I'd expected. A good thing, too, as the wind picked up, rocking the boat and adding nausea to my list of complaints. The captain and his crew of one tied us up to the dock. Rafe climbed onto it, testing the surface with his cane.

It was the first time I'd seen him move with anything less than complete assurance.

He took several steps and stopped, his posture so stiff I thought he might snap. I scrambled after him. Once I reached his side, I waited a moment to see if he'd lead the way. When he didn't, I guessed that he might need some assistance.

And that he'd cut out his own tongue before asking for it.

I laid a light hand on his arm and spoke quietly. "It's this way."

He shook me off with something like a growl and took an uncertain step. Though his difficulty was plain, we'd never discussed anything unusual about his vision, and this was not the time nor the place.

"Would it help to put your hand on my shoulder?" Again, I spoke low, my tone soothing, inoffensive.

"No." Tapping with his cane, he made his hesitant way down the dock. I stayed close to his side, all the while wondering why I bothered. He'd more than likely meet my concern with rudeness. It seemed to be his way, and I had no idea how to earn his trust, a situation that fell outside my previous experience.

If there was one thing I was good at, it was making people like me.

Still, as we neared the end of the dock, I said, "It's down a step to the road, and then some six feet away a cab appears to be waiting for us."

"Thanks."

"You're welcome." I said nothing more but made sure to stay close to his side.

A gust of wind caught us as we approached the cab. Inside, we found blankets folded on the seats and a pair of heated bricks on the floor. I debated offering to help Rafe get settled, then decided I'd done enough. He sat as still as a statue, lips compressed in a small frown. I gave up trying to plan for eventualities and simply enjoyed the warmth.

We'd deal with the newly born Council when we were faced with them.

The driver took us up a hill steep enough to make me worry for the horse's health. In the gaps between houses, we caught a view of distant water, though the rippling surface suggested a lake rather than the ocean.

We reached a neighborhood where small lawns and young trees filled in the blank slate left by new construction. The cab came to a stop and the driver pointed us to a stately Georgian, with balanced rows of windows on either side of the deep red front door. If I stayed close to Rafe's elbow, he moved with greater confidence, so together we went up the center walkway.

We were greeted by an older woman, her dark gown and upswept hair from an earlier era. She directed us to a comfortable dining room, where half a dozen men and women were seated around a large mahogany table.

Rafe took the seat closest to the door, opposite the man I guessed was Oliver Stevenson. I sat at Rafe's right hand, putting my back to the windows, so I wouldn't be distracted by the view. In this house, in this room, Rafe appeared reduced, shrunken somehow. His normal pallor took on a sallow hue, his cheeks sunken, his eyes distant behind his amber glasses.

In the interest of keeping us both safe, I made an effort to meet each person's gaze with a smile. If they wondered about my presence, no one spoke their concerns out loud.

"Thank you for joining us, Mr. Gallagher." The man at the head of the table spoke serenely, giving himself airs that I wasn't sure he deserved. "Perhaps you could introduce me to your companion."

Rafe went from stiff to rigid, his gaze directed at the tabletop. "This is Mr. Fairchild. He's a representative of the San Francisco Witches' Council."

If that news surprised Mr. Stevenson, he didn't let it show. "Welcome, Mr. Fairchild. I hope your stay here has been fruitful."

I gave him a smile intended to dazzle, and his short intake of breath proved my success. "It's very nice to meet you, Mr...." I allowed my voice to trail off, inviting someone — anyone — to fill in the missing information.

"I'm Oliver Stevenson," he said, and going around the table, he introduced his companions, Mr. Ford, Mr. Trilby, and the sisters Misses Franklin, distinguishable only because one wore a dress of shocking purple, while the other's gown was an appalling orange.

When he reached Mrs. Morrison, I noticed a subtle hum, right at the edge of my awareness. The psychic. With luck, that hum was Rafe, blocking her power.

Otherwise we might have a problem.

If there was a Mr. Morrison, no one mentioned him. The Mrs. was the youngest one present, her silvery silk dress the very height of fashion, and on her introduction, she gave me a smile that rivaled one of my own.

"So very nice to meet you, Mr. Fairchild." Her voice had a musical trill, a note of falseness, that immediately raised my hackles. If she noted my suspicion, however, her expression didn't change.

But then I expect someone who could read minds must be better than most at schooling their expression.

Our sparring smiles were interrupted by Stevenson, who rapped on the table. Everyone turned to him. "Thank you all for coming," he began, his chest puffed up as if he truly were the most powerful one in the room. "I must ask, however, why your father didn't make the journey. I hope he's well."

"My father is too busy for such fool—"

I cut him off. "I believe the senior Mr. Gallagher is otherwise occupied by an impending storm. He did send his regrets."

"Is that so?" Stevenson smirked in a most annoying way. "I thought perhaps he had left this mortal plane."

I turned toward Rafe, my expression falsely puzzled. He ignored me, but at least he wasn't raising a burning ball of power to throw at Stevenson.

"He was hale and hearty when we left him this morning," I lied.

Mrs. Morrison laughed. "Oh, you are telling a tale. Martin Gallagher died two weeks ago. I saw it in the stars."

In the stars. My Lord. "I hesitate to cast aspersions on your—"

"Martin Gallagher lives, and he sent me to tell you to leave off this foolishness. Seattle will not have a Witches' Council," Rafe said.

"Why not?" Stevenson's question seemed to have escaped his mouth against his will. He rubbed his chin, collecting himself, then continued. "The city is growing, and the mundanes need a formal way of interacting with us. Where is the harm in it?"

Rafe fisted both hands. "Because you're only in it for your own profit. Elect someone else to lead — "

"How dare you?" Stevenson rose to his feet, palms flat on the table. "I've been here, doing the work without the title, while all you've done is hide in your godforsaken tower. I'll have you know we don't need your permission to form this Council, and you will join with us or deal with the results. This is the last time I will ask."

"No."

Under different circumstances, the flatness of his tone might have made me laugh. As it was, the tension in the room made my ears ring and I dared to let my hand rest on his forearm. "You must understand Mr. Gallagher's point of view. He and his parents have been on their own for so long, I can see where he doesn't understand the benefits of joining with you."

A surprising flash of heat had me remove my hand from him and again I had to stifle a laugh. *Dear Lord, could these fools not see the power radiating from him?* Even in a diminished state, he dominated the room. Stevenson and his friends were playing with something stronger than fire, and I didn't know if I should warn them or let them learn the hard way.

"Of course," Mrs. Morrison said. "Perhaps you could enlighten him, Ollie dear."

Ollie dear? How very forward. The other men must have become used to her, for neither reacted. One Miss Franklin, the one in purple, pursed her lips in a moue of distaste, but her orange-garbed sister maintained a benign smile.

Appropriate or not, Mrs. Morrison's request calmed the waters. Stevenson made an obvious effort to control himself and resumed his seat. "Yes, well it saddens me that you don't see an immediate benefit to joining with us."

"No," Rafe repeated, and I had to cross my legs to keep from kicking him in the shin.

"Generally," I spoke loudly enough to draw everyone's attention, "when a new council is formed, there's some written…"

Stevenson interrupted me. "And I'm sure you'll be happy to provide said affidavit for us."

"Of course. Just as soon as I notify Madam Munro by telegraph."

My smile did not falter but Stevenson's did. "We don't need to bother her with something so insignificant."

I leaned forward, forearms resting on the tabletop to emphasize my sincerity. "But it's not insignificant at all. The foundation of a new Council is an event to be celebrated. Why, when Portland established their Council, I hear the party lasted for days."

Oliver Stevenson frowned as if I'd somehow insulted him. "We have better things to do with our time."

"Regardless, you'll need the National Congress to approve your organization."

"Like hell. We've made our own arrangements. No need to trouble anyone further up for any reason whatsoever." His snarl surprised me, but Rafe's response surprised me more.

"You will be civil, Stevenson, or I'll give you a lesson in manners." His calm, measured words were so far from the Rafe Gallagher I knew that I glanced quickly to make sure he hadn't been replaced by a counterfeit.

"You always have been an expert on manners," Stevenson murmured. Rafe inhaled, as if he meant to respond, but I bumped him with my elbow.

"Perhaps," I said, grateful Rafe took my cue, "you could provide us with more details regarding your plans for your new Council."

Mrs. Morrison tilted her head, fixing me with a smile. "You would know better than all of us." Her gaze flicked from me to Rafe. "You persuade him."

Despite myself, I felt the color rise in my cheeks. *Had Rafe's shields failed?* "The Council in San Francisco does a great deal. My own function is to help keep the peace between the magical and the mundane."

"Obviously, we'll assign someone to do the same here."

Stevenson's lofty superiority made my jaw clench. Given that Margaret and I had spent days in this town without coming across other witches, they had much work to do.

"Our work will be much more effective if the Gallaghers join with us," Mrs. Morrison said. "They do possess such amazing… talents."

This woman was dancing on the blade of a knife, and her tiny smile said she knew it. One of the sisters blurted, "And they've kept it all to themselves. It's time for them to share."

I blinked in surprise at how quickly the mood had changed. Tension rang through the room, and everyone sat forward, expressions ranging from excited interest to fear.

Stevenson, however, looked more amused than anything else. "The way I see it, the Gallaghers have little choice but to join with us."

"How so?" Rafe's tone was deadly.

"Well, it's a matter of consequences, you see." Stevenson spoke with too much bravado for a marginally talented waterwitch. "Join with us or I can guarantee you won't like what happens next."

For a moment it felt like everyone in the room held their breath. Even Mrs. Morrison's sly gaze was fixed on Rafe, as if she couldn't help but wait to see how he'd respond.

In fact, he met their challenge with… nothing.

"If that is all, Fairchild and I will be going." Rafe stood and, as if willed by his motion, I did, too.

"We're not done yet," Mrs. Morrison trilled. "Tell them, Ollie."

"Sit," Stevenson commanded, sending a flash of power our way. It broke over us like waves on a rock, fading into nothing.

Neither of us obeyed him.

"We'll see ourselves out," Rafe said. He turned, and I did, too. He stood between me and the door, so with a surreptitious hand on his elbow, I guided him out.

"We'll have it, you know. We know Martin's secret, and when we come looking, you and your mother and your pretty new friend will not be able to stand against us."

Rafe jerked to a stop so sharp, I came close to bouncing off his back. He turned more slowly, taking off his glasses so that he faced Stevenson with eyes as black as bottomless pits of tar. Power came off him in waves, and from the dumbstruck faces around the table, I wasn't the only one who felt it.

Only Mrs. Morrison seemed immune, her hands crossed calmly on the table, her head tilted as if she heard things the rest of us did not.

"If you disturb us, you will come to regret it." Rafe maintained his measured tone, but his power swelled further, raking across my skin. The Misses Franklins huddled together, Ford and Trilby grimaced, and even Stevenson frowned, as if he hadn't expected this kind of display.

"Don't threaten me," he snarled, but at Rafe's sharp intake of breath, I placed a quelling hand on his arm.

"I don't believe I heard a threat, actually," I said. "More of a promise, I suppose. If you leave the Gallaghers alone, they'll leave you to your" — I glanced around the table — "silly little games."

I gave Rafe a slight shove, and he started to move. Together we reached the street and stood on the front walkway, both of us breathing hard.

"I don't suppose they're going to offer us a return trip," I said, my hands on my hips.

Rafe simply grunted. "Come on. There should be a streetcar in a few blocks."

"I did notice one on Madison Street."

Rafe nodded, although he didn't make a move. With another quick brush of my hand on his arm, I indicated the direction we should take. He stayed at my side, and I kept to a pace he could follow. When we reached the first intersection, he glanced down at me. "Silly little games? I thought you were supposed to be the amiable one."

I couldn't suppress my laugh, and for the first time, I saw Rafe Gallagher's real smile. It warmed me as if the sun had burned the clouds away. Though amber glass hid his gaze, the creases at the corners of his eyes moved me. "Couldn't help myself, I guess. They were like children playing dress-up."

He sobered. "Yes, but those children can still make trouble."

Despite his dour reminder, my heart remained buoyant, a floating bobble in my chest. All because of a single smile, a gift that fueled my foolish hopes.

After all, he'd never smiled at Margaret.

It occurred to me that this might be an opportune time to ask what Stevenson meant about Martin's secret. Reluctant to shatter this tentative truce, I let the moment go.

We'd be back at the lighthouse soon, and I could tolerate a few more days of confinement. I'd have other chances to learn the truth. I'd *make* other chances. Meanwhile, I'd learned that the Seattle Witches' Council knew Martin was dead and they knew about — or guessed at — the existence of the Ferox Cor. They were also a great deal cockier than their relative power indicated.

Which had me wondering who else might be involved.

Chapter Ten

I managed to find Barnard and his boat *The Lucky*. He looked askance at Rafe and charged me a good deal more for the trip, but we were home in plenty of time for dinner.

He refused our offer to stay the night, saying he'd rather take his chances sailing by moonlight.

"Why?" I asked. We didn't have the space to accommodate him, but I was curious why everyone in town acted like this place was a corner of Hell.

Barnard simply tipped his hat, his eyes on Rafe, who strode down the dock. "Some folk say there's evil here. I don't know about that, and Mrs. Gallagher's nice enough, but my wife'd have my hide if I stayed."

I had no good response to that, so I simply gave him an extra five dollars and sent him on his way. Was there evil here? There was power, and those who didn't understand might call it evil. If Martin Gallagher met his goal on Samhain, though, that would truly be evil.

For once, the clouds had dispersed and the sun wouldn't set for another half hour or so. Taking that moment of weak sunlight as a more positive omen than perhaps I should have, I followed Rafe up the dock.

Della met us on the beach. "What happened?" she asked as soon as we were within earshot. "Why did Barnard bring you back?"

I settled my hat more firmly on my head. Rafe should be the one to answer, but when he stayed silent, I spoke up. "Stevenson and his gang invited you and Rafe to join the Seattle coven, and he wasn't inclined to accept a polite refusal."

She crossed her arms, gaze narrowing. "And who issued that refusal, you or him?" She tipped her head in Rafe's direction.

"I did, Mother." Rafe kept walking up the beach, though I couldn't tell whether his intent was to avoid questions or change out of his fancy duds as quickly as possible.

"Then I can only imagine how *polite* you must have been." Her emphasis made her sarcasm clear.

Rafe stopped, his back to us. "I left the flowery speeches to him. That's why you insisted he come along, isn't it?"

Apparently I didn't even merit a name. "Is he always this difficult, or am I just lucky?" I addressed the question to Della, but it was Rafe who gave a snort of disgust. He strode up the beach and disappeared into the shadows surrounding the tower.

"He's had to deal with more than you can guess," Della said quietly. There was no judgement in her voice, yet I felt chastened.

"He maintained his composure better than I'd anticipated. Stevenson and his lady friend Mrs. Morrison were just..." I searched for an appropriate word. "Inexperienced, you might say. They didn't recognize real power when it sat across the table from them. You poke a bear enough times, you're going to see his claws."

She gave me a faint smile. "That's what I was afraid of."

"They did say one odd thing. They said they knew Martin's secret, and they implied they'd come for it."

Her smile faded and her gaze frosted over. "Martin's only secret was that he practiced earth magic, and if they come to take that, well, I wish them luck."

She spoke firmly, leaving me alone on the beach. I needed time to think, to create order out of all the day's experiences. Judging that I had a few minutes

119

before Della called us to dinner, I headed for the tower.

I wanted to stand out on the widow's walk that encircled the light, to watch the waves and hear the sea birds shriek and squabble. Never been much for introspection, but it felt like time to start a new habit.

Opening the door, I stood for a moment, listening to the silence. Wherever Rafe had gone, I didn't hear him here, so I entered and climbed the stairs. On the way by, I checked the light's mechanism. The cables at the bottom of the box moved slowly down, as if something pulled them from the lower floor.

I came out on the top level. The light flashed, temporarily blinding me. When I could see again, I noted someone out on the widow's walk.

Damn. I should go back downstairs. The profile was masculine, which eliminated Margaret from the list of possibilities. So, Rafe then. I debated whether to turn around, but my need for companionship won out. I circled the light, squinting when it flashed in my direction, and stepped through the door onto the widow's walk.

Though I'd lost Rafe in the glare of the light, I spoke up. "Apologies for following you. That wasn't my intent."

He did not respond.

The glare faded so that I could distinguish light from shadow. Rafe was several feet away from me, looking out over the ocean. I looked more closely. There was something off about his posture. "Rafe?"

Still no answer, though this time the figure turned in my direction. The light flashed and for a moment I could see nothing. Still, I eased back a step, acting on instinct more than anything else. When the glare faded, the figure was much closer. Close enough to touch.

It was not Rafe.

He was shorter, this silent man, and dressed in a fine black suit. A strip of linen had been tied around his head to keep his jaw closed, and instead of eyes, he had two copper coins.

Fear made my muscles tense as every impulse told me to run. I could not run. I could not move. The figure drifted toward me and raised his arm. Instead of a hand, he had a blackened claw.

My breath coming in ragged gasps, I forced myself to take another step back. This time I reached the door frame. The figure stopped moving. Slowly, he came apart, strands of his image peeling off. Those strands coiled on the wooden deck, writhing like a clutch of baby snakes under a rock.

Then those snakes stilled, as if they'd heard a wordless call. Fear blotted out conscious thought when those snakes turned as one in my direction. They began to glide toward me. From some base, animal part of me came one command.

Run.

My body finally responded. I dashed through the door, around the light, and down the stairs. Heedless of anything but escape, I failed to notice Rafe until I plowed into him.

He caught my arms, keeping me upright. "What?" His glasses had been knocked askew by the impact and for a moment I was trapped in his black, black stare.

"There was" — I coughed into my fist, dragging more air into my lungs — "something. Someone. He turned into snakes."

Rafe turned his head toward the stairs. "Someone?"

"There... he... there were coins where his eyes should be."

Apparently satisfied that I would remain upright, he gave my arms a squeeze and released me. "Go back to the house. Mother has some brandy." He settled his glasses in place, but not before I caught a flash of concern. "She'll take care of you, and I'll have a look around."

"What? Who?" I still couldn't make any sense of what had just happened, though my body made note of his concern and the warmth of his hands on my arms.

"Go. I need to reinforce the spell."

Whether justified or not, his confidence reassured me. The feel of his touch lingered all the way to the house.

Margaret met me before I reached the door. "What is it? You look distressed."

"Distressed?" I managed to laugh. "I'm not sure where to start."

She put an arm around me, steering me toward the beach. Heavy clouds hung over the horizon, though the setting sun had managed to sneak a few rays from under them. In that fading glow, she brought us to a halt.

"I learned something today," she said, keeping her voice low, her solid presence alone enough to calm me.

"As did I."

Her arm still around my waist, she laughed softly. "I imagine you did. Let me get this off my chest and then you can tell me about the meeting."

Meeting? I almost laughed again. The snakes had driven the Seattle Council and their machinations clean out of my mind. Still, it was easier to let Margaret talk than to describe my recent experiences.

"Della is a Baron." She seemed to think I'd grasp the significance, though I stared at her in confusion.

"Madam Munro mentioned that. She said that family wouldn't tolerate... um... a jumped-up thaumaturge, I believe is what she said." I slung my arm around Margaret's shoulder, comforted by her warmth. We'd never be lovers — I knew myself too well for that — but I was increasingly grateful that she treated me as her little brother.

"That's right. The Barons are one of the oldest families of witches, and no, they'd have little use for one of their members dealing in dark magic."

A lot like the way the Fairchilds wouldn't tolerate a witch in the midst of their distinguished lineage. I nodded, grateful to her for taking my mind off the scene in the tower.

"It makes sense, you know?"

I must have been more disturbed than I'd realized. "I'm not sure what you mean."

"We came here to find the Ferox Cor with only Madam Munro's say-so to go on. So far, we haven't found anything close to an object of power, and neither Della nor Rafe have given anything away."

"Madam Munro was wrong about more than one thing, though it seems unlikely she'd make such a grand mistake."

Margaret shook her head. "Yes, and if Della *Baron* Gallagher wed someone powerful enough to steal the Ferox Cor, she'd have the strength to convince him to hide it away."

"I see your point," I said, the connection lighting up inside me. "The Seattle witches surely think Martin Gallagher had something powerful hidden here. They all but came out and said so."

"Good. We aren't just wasting our time, then." Margaret tipped her head, resting against my shoulder. "Now we just have to figure out where it is. I wish we could just ask Martin himself."

Her comment reminded me of the vision. "I should have, when I saw him in the tower."

"What?" She lurched around so she could glare at me. "You saw Martin Gallagher and you let me carry on like some kind of idiot?"

I didn't want to talk about it here in the darkness. "Let's go find Della. She'll want to hear about it too."

Over her budding protest, I led the way across the small lawn to the house. There, Della lifted something savory off the stove. Reaching for a large spoon, she greeted us with a mournful smile.

"Sit, you two. I want to hear about your day, Vincent."

Margaret and I took seats at the small table, and Della served us bowls of meat pie and slices of fresh bread. At her prompting, I described the meeting with the Seattle Council, happy to have another excuse to avoid talking about my vision.

"I'm glad Rafe stood up to them," Della said when I finished. She stood with her fists on her hips, her blue eyes sparking. "As if Ollie Stevenson could do anything to us."

"None of them felt particularly powerful," I said, reviewing my memories of each Council member. "Aside from Mrs. Morrison and Stevenson himself, the rest are marginally talented at best."

"They'll never reach us." Della tilted her head, as if listening to something only she could hear.

After a moment, the door opened. Rafe stood breathing heavily, his hair wild and studded with bits of leaf and branch.

"What is it?" Della reached for him, but he flinched, stopping her hand in mid-air.

"His body is there. In the cave." Rafe's voice was a bare rasp.

"Who? Martin? Where else would he be?" Della's voice rose to a shriek.

"He" — Rafe nodded in my direction — "saw him in the tower."

Rafe's gaze was fixed on me with a rare intensity. "He's right. I went to the top of the tower and saw…" Fear choked off my words. Fear and the sense that when Rafe looked *at* me, I was somehow stripped bare.

"He saw Martin." Rafe entered the kitchen, his face the very definition of grim. He stopped next to me, as if to protect me from some unseen danger. "Martin can break free of the grave, and we have less than a week to stop him or the whole world will know of our failure."

Margaret gasped and Della hugged herself, grimacing. "The world?" I managed.

Rafe gave his mother a look of raw grief. "Martin has vowed to overcome death itself. He may be successful, but it's possible his power will prove insufficient. If so, he'll destroy anyone with enough power to stop him and will subjugate the rest."

The Lighthouse Keeper

"We won't allow that to happen," Della said, her words a balm against the stark image Rafe had cast. "We will not. We cannot."

I could only hope she was right.

Chapter Eleven

Y ou should wash up, Rafe." Della spoke calmly, as if she could will away our distress. "You need to eat something. There's warm water in the bowl."

"I'll go out to the pump." With his cane tapping across the floor, Rafe left us. Although I no longer felt hungry, I swallowed the last bit of meat pie and wiped my bowl clean with the crust. Margaret and I needed to know more about Martin and to do that, I needed to find the right approach.

"Rafe accused Stevenson of establishing the Witches' Council for his own gain." I kept my tone casual, hoping to stir the pot without ruffling feathers.

"That was Martin's argument." Della carried my empty dinner bowl to the counter.

I folded my hands, wondering if I should offer to help wash dishes. "We did our best to keep Martin's death a secret, but Mrs. Morrison said she'd seen it in the stars."

With her back to me, Della responded slowly. "Well, it was going to come out sooner or later."

"They must be very confident of that clairvoyant's skills." Margaret brought her bowl to the counter. "Not sure that's a gamble I'd take."

Margaret's common-sense observance made me appreciate her all the more. "You make a good point. What would Martin do about this, I wonder, if he was alive?"

The thump of Rafe's cane announced his return. "He'd have retaliated."

"How?"

I rose, giving up my seat for him. Rafe settled into it, his hands and face still damp from the pump, his gaze directed at the floor. "Stevenson takes his fishing boat out most mornings, early. Martin would have found out when he was sailing, and what direction he'd headed, and then sent a storm."

Margaret set a bowl down hard on the counter. "That's completely against the rules."

Rafe snorted, and even I had to laugh. "I don't get the impression that Martin Gallagher had too much patience for rules."

Della took the other seat, her expression warming to something like a smile. "You're quite right. Martin made a good life for us out here. He got to be his own boss, and it gave him a chance to right some of the bad decisions he'd made in his youth."

Bad decisions like stealing the Ferox Cor? The words were on the tip of my tongue, but I could not force them out. Della became slightly more forthcoming, as if she'd finally decided to trust us — though not enough to talk about the Ferox Cor.

She told us how she and Martin had come to this isolated spit of land. "They wanted a weatherwitch up here," she said. "So Martin took the job."

"How old were you, Rafe?" I still wanted to know why Madam Munro's information listed Rafe as a child. If I was fishing for other reasons, like making sure he and I were the same age, I couldn't be faulted.

There was an agelessness about him; while I could tell he wasn't a child, I wouldn't have been surprised if he was either eighteen or thirty-eight, or anywhere in between. As to why I hoped we were near each other in age, the reason would make me blush. I'd become much too interested in Rafe Gallagher.

Much, much too interested. It wasn't just his power and his dark good looks that attracted me. The glimpses he'd given me of the real Rafe Gallagher, the artist, the one whose smile I'd seen only once, intrigued me beyond measure.

The Lighthouse Keeper

In a sense, I was like a hermit crab. I could survive on my own, but I was stronger if I scuttled into someone else's shell. I'd relied on my family and the Witches' Council. And now, apparently, I wanted something similar from Rafe.

The object of my affection didn't deign to answer me, but his mother tilted her head, her smile bemused. "Oh, Rafe was just a baby. We've been here twenty-two, maybe twenty-three years."

Good. He wasn't much younger than me. Still, twenty-odd years at the edge of the sea... "What a lonely place to grow up."

The words were out before I could catch them. Margaret laughed, covering my gaffe. "We can't all be Fairchilds," she chided.

"True." I gave Della a contrite nod. "I'm sure Rafe's upbringing was just fine."

"We did send him off to school when he was a boy. But you're right. After a point he wouldn't leave us, despite being so far away from town."

"I preferred it here," Rafe said. "Still do."

Which would account for his roughness. He'd had little chance to acquire any polish. "The three of you must have got on pretty well, then."

Rafe made a sound that in another man I would have called a chuckle. "Martin and I didn't get on at all."

"I'm shocked," I said dryly, and the women laughed. Rafe didn't, but one side of his mouth curled, as if he was making a conscious effort not to smile.

Reminiscing about Martin had certainly taken the edge off our fear. I stood in the doorway while Margaret served Rafe and Della their supper, debating if I should bring up anything difficult.

"Della, I think it's time to wind the light's mechanism, isn't it?" Margaret gave me a pointed look, as if she could read my mind. "I'll be right back." *And don't upset anyone.* I couldn't hear her, but I knew what that look meant.

"Keep to the path closest to the house," Rafe said. "The fog's come in."

As if to emphasize her words, a horn sounded from somewhere outside, loud and low-pitched. "Foghorn?" I asked.

"It'll keep the ships away." Della's eyes were weary, as if we'd used up all her good humor. "I lit the coal to run it earlier this evening."

Left with nothing to do, however, the situation overwhelmed me; the Seattle Council, the ghostly visitor, the whereabouts of the Ferox Cor. This was as close as Rafe and Della had come to admitting Martin possessed the missing magical object, but, "Too many pieces of this puzzle," I murmured.

"What?" Della's question made me realize I'd spoken aloud.

"I wish my friend Rutger were here. He's better than I am at making people do what he wants."

Rafe ignored my comment but Della paused between bites. "And here Margaret's been telling me you're the charming one."

"Oh, I am." I aimed a smile at both of them. "Rutger's a whole lot bossier." Bossy, and good at organizing things. He'd have us giving the Seattle Council the heave-ho before they knew what hit them and ferret out Martin's secret at the same time.

Still, I was here, and I'd survived an encounter with the restless spirit of Martin Gallagher. There was something to be said for that.

Rather than supervise their dinner, I took a seat on the bench in the front room. Margaret should soon return from winding the light's mechanism. I wanted to discuss the meeting with her, sure that her sharp mind would notice things I hadn't.

The stove had kept the kitchen warm, but little heat reached the front room. The chill air and my own nerves soon numbed my fingertips, and still Margaret didn't return. Della and Rafe murmured together in the kitchen, apparently unconcerned by how long Margaret had been gone.

I pulled out my pocket watch. Six-o-five. I hadn't checked the time when she left, but night had truly fallen.

I stood and peered through the window. Fog encased the house, thick enough that I couldn't see the beach. Something must have happened to delay Margaret.

Grabbing my overcoat, I returned to the kitchen. "Margaret's not back yet. I'm going to go look for her."

Buttoning my coat, I stepped outside. I created a small witchlight, just bright enough to guide me along the path to the tower. The oil lamp near the tower door hadn't been lit, and while I could hear the steady beat of the waves, fog obscured the beach.

The ground level room of the tower was also dark. The mechanism was at the top of the stairs, and halfway up, I noticed the lighthouse's flashing eye had stopped.

My first clue was the silence. While the light's mechanism wasn't loud, it did create a steady whirr. All I could hear now was the pulse of waves on the beach. That, and Margaret's absence, had me on guard. Still, I wasn't prepared for what I found.

Margaret, at the top of the stairs, slumped against the wall, hands covering her head.

"Hey," I whispered, touching her shoulder. She flinched but didn't otherwise respond. "Margaret, what happened? What's wrong?"

Her fingers flexed, clawing at the neatly coiled braid in her hair. I dared touch her again, hoping to bring her away from the dark place she was visiting.

"Margaret?" When she didn't flinch, I shook her. "Margaret!"

She gasped, grabbing ahold of my arm. "Don't. They'll hear us."

"What?" I squatted to bring myself eye level with her. "No one is here. Just you and me."

"Oh." She blinked, her gaze meeting mine with some level of understanding. "Of course. I must have been dreaming."

I stood and offered her my hand. "You decided to stop for a nap before winding the light's mechanism?"

We managed to get her standing upright. "I... didn't? I don't know." Brows drawn, she frowned at the floor. "I remember... leaving the kitchen. Stopping for my coat." She patted the woolen lapel. "The tower... the stairs." Her frown turned to a grimace of anguish. "I don't know."

I put my hands on her shoulders. "You're all right now. Let's just wind the thing and go back to the house."

Tears welled in her eyes. "You mustn't touch it. They'll know if you do."

Giving her a gentle shake, I let go and turned toward the mechanism. "I don't know who you mean, but the light's gone out. Between that and the fog, there are boats out there who could be in real trouble."

"You're right. I must have been dreaming." Her drawn brows gave her an uncharacteristically puzzled look.

I reached for the handle. Her plea must have had some effect, because I moved slowly enough to feel the frisson of power before grasping the metal arm. "What's this?" I whispered.

"Do you feel them?"

"Not sure who you mean but let me try one thing. Do you have a coin? A hairpin? Something small."

Margaret pulled a hairpin from her braid, allowing it to spill down her back. "Here."

Running the bit of wire between my fingers, I pushed the little power I possessed into it. Instead of a hairpin, I held a pair of pincers about eight inches long.

"Let's see if this'll work," I murmured, reaching for the mechanism's handle. I grabbed it between the pincers' teeth, fighting the repellent feel, as if I forced magnets together by their opposite poles. Just keeping hold of it had sweat breaking out on my brow.

"Pull on my arm." I managed to grind the words out, my teeth clenched with effort.

Margaret understood, and with the addition of her effort, I managed to drag the handle down, restoring the mechanism to action. The sudden flash of light near blinded me, and when the glare faded, I held a misshapen hair pin. I couldn't help laughing, and Margaret joined me.

"What the hell is going on up here?" Rafe appeared at the top of the stairs, his cane crowding Margaret closer to me.

The fierceness of his scowl sobered me. "Someone put a spell on the handle."

"What are you talking about?" Rafe mounted the final stair, attention fully on the winding mechanism.

He reached for the handle without acknowledging my muttered, "Careful."

As I had done, though, he stopped just short of grabbing hold. He brought his hands together, palm to palm, and for a moment he stood very still. When he again reached for the handle, there was no hesitation. He grabbed it firmly and after a moment I felt a sharp pop.

"There," he said. "That's taken care of." He rubbed his palms together, expression unreadable. "I'll leave you to it then."

Somehow Margaret beat him to the stairs. "Someone needs to figure out what that was. I can't help you, so if you don't mind, I'll go back to the house."

She clattered down the stairs, leaving Rafe and me alone. Unfortunately, the first words out of my mouth were fairly thoughtless. "Your father's been busy today. I found Margaret trapped in some kind of terror triggered by the spell on the handle."

"Wasn't Martin." He stood awkwardly, half turned toward the stairs.

I blinked. "I saw him here not that long ago."

"If Martin had set the spell, she'd be dead."

Martin Gallagher must have been thoroughly horrible. "Maybe someone from the Seattle Council?"

"I'm not sure." Rafe wrapped his cloak more closely around his body. "None of them have enough power."

"Could they have purchased the?"

"From whom? I could have made it, but I assure you that was not my work."

"Someone just traveling through?" My voice faded as I became aware of his proximity.

He must have made the same realization. Only a few inches separated us, not as far as a foot apart. Once again, he looked at me, his cold, dark gaze penetrating the amber lenses. For several heart beats, neither of us spoke.

I licked my bottom lip and he tilted his head, as if curious about something. I thought about asking if he'd ever kissed someone or if he'd mind if I kissed him. One of us should say something. Anything.

"You are unusual, Vincent Fairchild. I didn't intend to like you, yet I find I do."

Though the nightmare spell still echoed around us, I smiled. "You're not an easy man to like, yet I find I like you, too."

His gaze was no longer cold. In fact, it was hot enough to make me sweat. I could not have looked away for any reason. I reached for his hand. His fingers were warm and strong, and I gathered my bravery, ready to ask for that kiss.

The light flashed again, catching me dead in the eye. I flinched, dropping his hand, and the tension between us fell away. I blinked hard, trying to force my eyes to adjust to the darkness. When my sight returned, Rafe was smiling. I laughed, and so did he.

Good Lord, but he was handsome when he smiled.

His gaze drifted away from me and he clutched his cane, his knuckles turning white.

I exhaled slowly, wondering how far I dared go. "Thank you for breaking the spell on the handle." Those weren't the words I wanted to say, but they'd do for now.

"You're welcome." His faded smile hadn't entirely disappeared. "Now, if you'll excuse me, I need to reset the protection wards."

A-ha. "It *was* you. I noticed a spell when we first arrived."

He turned toward the window, shutting me out. "Yes."

"I'll leave you to it, then, though… I hope we can talk, soon."

He nodded, his attention already on his next task. "Tomorrow."

"Of course." I clattered down the stairs, certain I'd hold him to that promise. By the time I left the tower, however, that certainty had turned to frustration. I should have asked him how he went about setting a protection spell and whether or not he possessed the Ferox Cor. I should have asked him if he'd ever kissed a man, or if he'd ever wanted to.

I should have asked him many things, but Rafe Gallagher, with all his rough edges and fearsome power, could damage me in more ways than one.

I'd save my questions for another day.

Chapter Twelve

I warmed my palms with a morning cup of coffee. "How do you think someone set a nightmare curse on the winding mechanism despite Rafe's protection spell?"

Margaret and I were alone in the kitchen. She'd poured my coffee after I'd filled her in on the conversation I'd had with Rafe. Most of it, anyway. I left out our mutual confession, although knowing that Rafe Gallagher found me appealing made me slightly giddy.

"I think…" She set the coffee pot back on the stove. "There aren't too many possibilities. Either one of us set it, or there's someone out there with more power than Rafe."

I raised my mug in toast. "Which is saying something."

"True. He might be the most powerful witch I've ever met."

A wind gust sent a splatter of rain against the kitchen window. "My Lord, does the sun ever shine? Can't you conjure something?"

Margaret's laugh was amused without offering any promise that she'd make good on my request. She tightened the woolen shawl around her shoulders. If I wouldn't look ridiculous in a shawl, I'd have begged her to lend me the thing. The cold had settled so deep in my bones I wasn't sure I'd ever warm back up.

"Have we established what Della's gift is?" I asked, mainly as a distraction from my self-pity.

Margaret grimaced, rinsing soapy dishes in a pot of clear water. "She's pretty cagey. All I know for sure is that she's not a weatherwitch. She's a Baron, so whatever her gift, she's powerful."

"Could she have set the nightmare curse?"

Thrusting a towel and a clean dish at me, she asked for help without words. I rose and took them, drying the clean dishes as she washed and putting them in a neat stack.

"But why would she?"

"I don't know." Frustrated, I picked at something even further from our control. "When we find the thing, how will we get it back to Madam Munro?"

142

"How will *you* get it back, you mean." Margaret grimaced at the bucket of soapy water. "Let's cross that bridge when we have the Ferox Cor in hand."

"Good advice." I bumped my shoulder against hers, grateful for her solid presence. One way or the other, I'd accomplish the task Madam Munro had set for me. Somehow…

Someone cleared their throat behind us, and I whirled around.

Rafe stood in the doorway, arms crossed, his frown so deep I could get lost in it. "I don't suppose there's any breakfast left."

Margaret gestured to the stovetop. "I've kept some oatmeal warm for you."

He stalked through the doorway, sending sparks swirling in my belly. Without his ever-present cloak, his body was slimmer than I'd expected. Wiry even. And so very strong. I looked away, hoping no one had caught the gleam of lust in my expression.

Rafe took a seat at the table and wordlessly Margaret served him. She'd found a small dish of raisins and a pot of cream, and when my stomach rumbled, she set down a second bowl for me. Rafe clearly hadn't shaved since our excursion, and the stubble on his jaw gave him an even more dangerous air.

Because he could be *dangerous, you ninny. He could have the Ferox Cor.* With that necessary reminder, I reeled in my wayward heart.

"Where's Mother?" Rafe asked.

"I'm not sure." I dared a glance at him, but his attention was focused on his oatmeal. *That settles things.* Until we found the Ferox Cor, I'd keep myself in check, and I'd ask some of those questions I'd so far avoided.

To derail my foolish disappointment, I went to work. "Do you know of any other witches besides those we saw at the Council meeting?"

He glared at his oatmeal. "If you mean to suggest that there's someone who could have set that nightmare curse, I assure you there is not."

I leaned back against the chair, feigning relaxation. "Last night you claimed that none of the Seattle Council could have set the spell, and you dismissed the idea that Stevenson could have bought it from someone traveling through. That leaves you or your mother as possibilities."

"You're accusing both of us? Fine manners on the part of a house guest."

His tone held a hint of a threat, one I chose to ignore. "Ah, but we're not ordinary house guests. We were sent here to offer you our help, and in order to do that, we need to know what's really going on."

Rafe rose to his feet, moving slowly, hands still on the tabletop. This allowed him to loom over me, and a smarter man might have felt a quiver of fear. Instead, I smiled. He couldn't see me, but the act lifted my spirits. "I don't really suspect you or your mother.

You'd have no reason to set such a spell. You said the nightmare curse wasn't your father's work, either. That seems to have eliminated all the possibilities."

With that, I stood, too, moving even more slowly than he had. When we were eye-to-eye, something sparked between us. Despite his amber lenses, I could see that he was inches away from taking action.

Though I couldn't guess whether he meant to fuck me over the kitchen table or strike me dead.

"So." I calmly picked up my napkin and dabbed my lips. Neither of us had mentioned the Ferox Cor. That omission tempted me to dig a little deeper. "No outside witch cast the spell. Nor did an inside witch, nor a recently deceased witch. Are there any other sources of power that I'm missing?"

"No." Rafe spat the word, but even so I heard the lie.

"Perhaps, then, you could do me the favor of showing me around the perimeter, the area your protection spell covers."

"Why? It will mean nothing to such as you."

Such a charmer. "I'm just trying to help."

Margaret approached the table, smiling serenely, as if Rafe and I weren't here growling at each other. "He's right, Rafe Gallagher. You can't simply sit there and do nothing until the next spell is cast. I'd think you'd be a little curious about how someone had got through your protection wards."

He smacked the table with an open palm. "Oh, I am more than curious. I just don't want help from some... popinjay and his tart."

That pulled Margaret up short. "Now you listen up, Rafe Gallagher. I am a weatherwitch, and as such I was asked to help keep things running smoothly, but I do not have to put up with being insulted." She yanked the bowl out from in front of him. "I made your breakfast out of kindness, but you can cook your own darn food if you're going to be that way."

She set his bowl on the wooden counter with a dull thump. "Vincent, I'll speak with you later, and you, Rafe Gallagher, will apologize to me before the day is through."

On her way out of the kitchen, Margaret muttered about men who'd been alone too long and how they couldn't make friends. For my part, I directed my attention to my oatmeal.

I resumed my seat and picked up my spoon. Last night seemed a very distant dream. Rafe remained standing, looking over his shoulder in the direction Margaret had gone.

"She's not...?" he said finally. "You're not...?

Part of me wanted to torture him further, but in the interest of preserving the peace, I stayed quiet. "If you're asking whether Margaret and I are involved in some kind of illicit love affair, or hell, a licit one, for that matter, I've already told you we are not."

"But you're always together."

I pinched my lips together to stifle a laugh. "There are only four of us on a patch of land smaller than a city block. You seem to spend most of your time in the forest, but I'm naturally gregarious, you might say, and it would look quite odd for me to spend extended periods of time with your mother."

I took his grunt as a sign of agreement. "I don't like to be alone," I added. And if I stared up at him through my lashes in a most flirtatious way, at least I didn't flutter them.

Not that he could see me if I had, but somehow he seemed to take my message.

"Now," I said, keeping my tone light. "Have you had enough to eat?"

The mention of food broke the tension between us. Rafe didn't relax, exactly, but he resumed his seat. I brought him his oatmeal and after a moment, he began picking at it. I sat, too, and began to chatter about nothing at all. I asked him if he knew his grandparents, the Barons. *No.* I asked if he'd ever traveled as far as Portland, Oregon. *No.* I asked his favorite book, his favorite music, and whether he liked to dance.

"Dance?" His snort came gratifyingly close to a laugh. "I do not dance."

"We should correct that as soon as possible."

He set his spoon down carefully. "What sort of man are you, Vincent Fairchild?"

"A man like any other." *Almost*. "I like good food, the occasional pipe, and a glass of beer every now and again."

"I'm not so sure." He fell silent and to cover my awkwardness, I cleared the table. I felt as if I'd been given a test and come up with the wrong answer.

Whether due to my charm or a latent sense of guilt for having insulted Margaret by calling her a tart, Rafe announced that he would take me to the place his father was buried. "That's where my wards are strongest," he said. "Even you should be able to sense them."

Ignoring the dig, I greeted his declaration with enthusiasm. "I'll meet you in the front room in five minutes."

"If you say so."

"I do."

With that, I left him. I confess that before I put on my hat, I made sure my hair was properly groomed, and I knotted a plaid scarf around my neck. All that, to spend a morning with a blind man. A very handsome blind man, who — I made a point of reminding myself — was entirely capable of setting that nightmare curse that had so distressed Margaret.

And if he was capable of that, what else was he capable of?

I made a promise to myself that I'd find out.

For our excursion, Rafe wore his tattered cloak. His boots already had mud on them and his hair was better combed than it had been at breakfast. That little vanity had me stifling a grin.

He wasted no time, however, in setting off toward the forest. If Rafe was following a path, it wasn't one I could easily see. He moved quickly between the trees, his cane making small arcs in front of his feet. The confidence with which he moved through this uneven landscape was markedly different than when we'd been in town. He managed to avoid the clumps of shrubs that claimed land wherever the tree canopy thinned, though we trod right over patches of leathery-leaved groundcover. Living for so many years on this isolated bit of land must have allowed him to commit the landscape to memory.

Our route took us gradually, and sometimes not-so-gradually, uphill in a series of sharp turns. Before long I promised myself I wouldn't say anything to make Rafe angry, because if he lost me out here in the wilderness, I might never find civilization again.

My upbringing had many benefits, but bushwhacking wasn't one of them.

We'd walked nearly an hour when he came to a dead stop. "What is it?" I asked, only to have him shush me with a sharp wave of his hand.

I kept quiet, except for the sound of my heavy breathing, which I could not muffle. If Rafe was taxed by our hike, he gave no sign. As my breathing slowed, I picked up other sounds — the soft rattle of small creatures in the leaf mould and the murmur of a stream channeling the steady rainfall.

There was little color. Browns and greens from the various trees surrounding us, shades of grey from the rocks underfoot. Ahead a maple had held onto a few of its golden leaves and they shone all the brighter for our drab surroundings.

"Do you see?" he asked, pointing off to our right. There, some ten feet away, was the stream, tumbling its way down the side of the bluff. Beside it, across the water, was the mouth of a cave, a dark maw, a patch of blackness amongst the brown and the green.

Our destination, though it might take us directly to hell.

Cave might not be the correct word. This was more like something miners might have made, stacked rocks framing the opening and a small, cleared area in front of it. Reaching it would require a scramble, but no worse than what we'd already covered.

First, though, we had to ford the stream. "Where do we cross?" I kept my voice low, the hush of the place dampening my eagerness. Something about that dark opening chilled me even worse than the persistent drizzle.

"Come." Rafe swung his cane and set off, aiming our route downhill. We reached a coppice of large shrubs, their leaves a dark glossy green. With one hand, Rafe traced the perimeter of the cluster, and I followed him. We came to a place where the stream narrowed, gurgling happily through a large rock and a giant, jagged stump. Without a pause, Rafe leapt from one side to the other, and with a lot less confidence, I did the same.

My boots squished in the muck on the other side and for a moment I thought I might fall back. Pride kept me upright. We reached the cavern and, following Rafe's lead, I stopped at the edge of the clearing.

The darkness at the mouth of the cave seemed to bow out, a convex shadow, as if it would suddenly erupt and cover the land. I glanced around for something large I could hide behind if that ever happened.

"Put him in here two weeks ago," Rafe murmured. "Do you feel it?"

I did, an undercurrent of tension that spoke to powerful magic.

"We can go in."

The soft dirt in front of the cave was undisturbed, giving no indication hat something had been moved. There were no footprints, not even the ones Rafe had presumably left when he checked yesterday. "You rake that smooth every day?"

"What do you mean?"

"There are no footprints leading into or out of the cave. None at all."

"So?"

I tightened my plaid scarf. "You said you went in there yesterday to check on your father's body. Unless you flew in, you should have left prints."

His body radiated tension, though he didn't speak for a long moment. "Let's go inside. Maybe you'll see something I missed."

Interesting turn of phrase. I stifled a rude chuckle. Rafe crossed the dirt, leaving five clear prints. I waited to see if the ground would magically smooth itself before following him. It didn't. I looked for other signs, broken branches, anything out of place, and though I was far from an expert on forest life, all seemed as it should be.

Gathering my courage, I crossed the little patch of dirt and stepped into the darkness.

And it was very, very dark. "Rafe?" My voice came out close to a squeak. "Where'd you go?"

"Here." His voice was soft and perversely comforting.

I set off a witchlight. The darkness pressed against the light until it illuminated a circumference of just a few inches. "Rafe?" I whispered.

"Here," he said again, this time so close it made me jump.

I reached out blindly and took hold of his arm. "What is this place?"

"I made it when he died. We needed a place for him, you see, and the Mother said she would watch him here."

The Lighthouse Keeper

The Mother? "You used earth magic to make this?" No wonder it squashed my witchlight.

"There is only one magic, though there are different ways of understanding it."

This was neither the time nor the place to dissect magical definitions. "Where is Martin?"

He moved further into the cave, with me hanging off his arm like a limpet. We'd gone several feet when he stopped again. "Here."

This deep my witchlight had no more radiance than a distant star. I couldn't tell where he'd pointed or what we might be looking at.

"And is he there? All I see is darkness," I said, figuring Rafe might have methods of observation that I could not access.

"That's the spell. He's there, though in all honesty, he shouldn't have been able to leave here, even if only in spirit."

"Some part of him left. I saw him." I tried to dampen my surprise.

"I believe you, Now go back to the entrance. I'll follow in a moment."

Going back to the entrance meant letting go of him, and since I had lost all sense of direction in the darkness, I stayed put.

"Fairchild." Rafe's voice was a soft plea. "I'll reset the binding spell, but I don't want to chance catching you in it."

153

Oh. Well. "I'm afraid I won't be able to find my way." If his voice was a plea, mine was a frightened whimper.

"There is no other way but out. Turn and walk in a straight line. If you get off, you'll either hit the wall on the left or on the right, and in either case, just follow it. This place is an oval with one end cut off for the entrance. There are no tricks or turns."

Taking that first step was the hardest part, because his magic made the space between my shoulder blades twitch. Since I had no interest in being bound to this place, I did as he requested, one painful step at a time.

Chapter Thirteen

Stepping out of the cave felt like an escape. I was greeted by the cry of a hawk, a rude shriek that made me jump. The thing perched on the top branch of a young cedar tree, some twenty or thirty feet overhead. The hawk's feathers matched the mottled mix of browns and greys that surrounded us, but its eyes…

Its eyes watched me, and even from twenty feet away I knew this was no ordinary bird.

We stared at each other. If I meant to take the bird's measure, I was unsuccessful. Aside from its extraordinary malevolence, I had no idea who or what this was.

I had a lot less success hiding myself from it.

A harsh sound broke my fixation on the hawk. Rafe erupted from the cave behind me, waving his cane wildly. "Go, demon. Go away from here."

The hawk flapped its wings, lifting off the branch. It flew up and then, when directly overhead, it dove.

I would have scrambled out of the way, but there was no place to go. Rafe held his ground, swinging his cane and hollering "Get away!" until I was sure he would swat the bird like a baseball. As much as I wanted to hide, I pulled a coin from my pocket and gave it a burst of power.

The coin changed into a broadsword, heavy enough to take both hands to hold it upright. My heart hammered. My muscles tensed. I could barely draw a breath.

The hawk screamed, so close and so loud that I echoed it, readying myself for its impact, hoping it would impale itself on my sword before I got clawed. It screamed, and I screamed again.

Then, silence.

Rafe stood at my side, one hand held palm-up, the other arm around my shoulders. The hawk flapped its wings some three or four feet overhead. It rose high, then came at us again, this time with its claws outstretched. Again it stopped overhead, as if we were covered by an invisible dome.

Lowering the sword, I leaned into Rafe, grateful for his protection. He was muttering something unintelligible through jaws so tightly clenched the muscles bulged under his skin.

The hawk came at us once more and was similarly rebuffed. After that it gave up, flapping away until the trees overhead concealed it.

"What, or rather who, was that?" I asked, my voice hoarse from screaming. With a blink, the sword assumed its normal shape.

Rafe stood still for a moment, then shook out his palm and took a step away from me. The spell he'd cast gave way with a subtle pop. He swept the area in front of us with his cane. "Let's go. We need to get back to the lighthouse."

"Certainly." I followed him, but I was done with staying quiet. "We were nearly skewered by a wild hawk and you can't give me even the slightest hint as to what the hell is going on?"

He strode forward. It wasn't until he reached the jagged stump that he paused. "You were brave. Back there. Foolhardy, but brave."

His words were kind, with an unexpected hint of sweetness. Shrugging off the glow rising in my cheeks as a result of his compliment, I made another attempt at finding the truth. "I'm no braver than the next man, and my gift cannot compare with yours." I stopped, my throat closing up. The aftermath of the hawk's attack made my joints feel loose, as if I would topple over in the softest breeze. "But I'll fight more effectively if I know where the battle is coming from."

With one long, leaping step, Rafe crossed the stream. He waited on the other side, his hand extended in my direction. A mad mix of fear, anger, frustration, and yes, lust, nearly had me ignore his gesture. Acting as if I were a puppet of myself, I reached out and grabbed ahold.

The distance across the brook wasn't far; I'd crossed easily on our way to the cavern. The feel of our fingers intertwined, the dry press of his skin against mine, drove every other sensation away. I readied myself and took a long, leaping step, just as Rafe had done.

This time, though, he waited and pulled me close, an arm around my waist. All the air left my lungs and all thought was chased away by the feel of his body against mine. I caught hold of the edges of his cape. His gaze was aimed over my head, but those amber glasses hid so much. He might look in my direction, but what did he really see?

"Is this what you want?" he whispered, the words fluttering against my skin like a hummingbird's wing.

"Yes," I said, though I wasn't sure what I'd agreed to. In the aftermath of our fight with the hawk, Rafe's closeness made me feel safe. Despite, or maybe because of that, I finally found the nerve to ask, "How do you do it?"

"Do what?"

"The glasses... the cane. You move through the forest almost too fast for me to follow, yet I'm not honestly sure what you can see."

He stayed silent for so long I thought he might not answer, yet he did not loosen his hold. Perhaps I shouldn't have asked him something so personal, or I should have waited until some other time, when things were less fraught.

The irony was not lost on me, that I, Vincent Fairchild, who relied so much on his appearance, should be bewitched by a blind man.

"We really shouldn't stay here, in case the demon returns." His voice was rusty, as if, in these last moments, he'd become unused to speaking.

I didn't move a muscle. "Looked like a hawk to me."

"Not a hawk."

"It might not have been an actual bird, but those claws and that beak looked very real."

He released his hold and took a step away from me. "Let's go to the tower. We can talk there."

I shivered, bereft of his warmth. "You lead the way."

He headed down the path and, after taking a deep breath to clear my head, I followed.

The walk to the lighthouse was faster and more direct than the trip to the cave. Rafe crashed through knee-high ferns, using his cane as a scythe. Despite our speed, my mind had time to stray.

For the most part, I feared I'd come to regret having asked him about his sight. He hadn't seemed angry. If anything, he'd held me closer, more tenderly. That wasn't the action of an angry man.

Yet there were so many things I did not know. Those questions plagued me, so that by the time we reached the edge of the forest, I'd decided that if I had my druthers, I'd find my friend Rutger and drink a pint somewhere. Rutger was easy. He'd never tied me in knots like this.

Rutger. What had happened that last night in San Francisco? Something profound enough for Madam Munro to exile me here. With luck, my friend had ended up someplace safer.

Safe or not, I followed that dark, caped figure across the grass, one eye on the sky in case the hawk made another appearance. Why did he need privacy for this conversation? Or did he just want to bring me someplace nobody would see? If Rafe intended to reveal himself as the holder of the Ferox Cor, I would have little defense against him no matter where we were. *Lord.* I swallowed down my fear and kept on.

Rafe reached the door of the tower, opened it, and stood aside so I could enter. The door closed behind us, and for a moment, we both hesitated.

"Should we go up?" I asked.

He stood with his arms crossed, a picture of indecision. This lower floor had no windows, but a thin, grey light came down through the stairwell from the upper floor.

"Maybe I should apologize. I didn't mean to distress you so," I said.

Shaking his head, Rafe took a deep inhale, and there, in the cold, damp tower, he removed his amber glasses.

His eyes were as black and glossy as coal. The focus of his gaze was off to one side of me, and his lips quivered, as if he didn't know whether to laugh or to cry.

"What happened?" I asked, an almost involuntary question. "No, you don't have to answer. I didn't mean…"

What didn't I mean? I had no idea. This close to him, in a place of privacy, my thoughts were as ragged as the wind-tossed surf.

"It's all right." He slipped his glasses back on. "You'll have to forgive me. It's been so long since I had anyone but Mother to talk to." He raked a hand through his hair, an uncharacteristically awkward gesture. "Um… when I was twelve or so, I tried a spell, one well beyond my skill."

"That must have been a difficult spell indeed."

That comment brought the shadow of a smile. "Yes and no. In a way, it was a gift, because by trying and failing, I opened channels to power that I might not have otherwise found. It did, however, permanently damage my vision. I can see only the spirit realm, no more and no less."

With those words spoken, we moved closer together. He wasn't going to destroy me with the Ferox Cor. He might still possess it — Lord, for all I knew, it was behind every spell he'd cast — but this was simply a conversation.

"That's why," he continued, "I can move quickly here. The distances are small, and there's only me, Mother, and Martin to disrupt the ether."

"In the city?"

"It's more difficult, because there are so many people, so many things. It's hard to sort through them all."

"That makes sense. I must admit, the few times I've felt you really look at me, it's as if you can see through to my soul."

He snorted, his frown returning. "People are the hardest. Their spirits are so bright…"

His voice trailed away and for a moment, we both paused, as if neither was sure what would happen next.

We were interrupted by Margaret. She slung the door open and pulled up short when she saw us.

"Is everything all right?" she asked.

"What's wrong?" My question overrode hers, and then we both laughed.

Rafe, however, took her arrival as an escape. Tossing a weak wave over his shoulder, he ducked through the door.

Caught in Margaret's thoughtful gaze, I found myself blushing. "I, well, it's been a morning."

She resumed her route to the stairs. "We can talk about it later. I've got to wind the light."

"Good. Yes. Later," I babbled. Rather than embarrass myself any further, I made for the door.

"Wait," she said. "I'll only be a moment."

I paused with my hand on the doorknob. "Of course."

While she was gone, I attempted to sort through all the things I'd learned compared with all the things I still didn't know.

The second list, unfortunately, was the longer one. Margaret clattered down the stairs before I'd completed my list. I wasn't sure where to start, but she pounced on the question of Rafe's sight. "Only sees the spirit world." She nodded, as if a piece of the puzzle had fallen into place. "That does make sense."

We reached the house, and though Della's presence might put a damper on our conversation, I desperately wanted the warmth of the stove. "I can tell you the rest of it later."

We found Della still sitting at the table, clutching the edge with both hands. Her face was caught in a terrifying rictus grin.

"No." Della ground out the word, although her teeth were clenched. "Mine now. Mine."

Gagging on the stink of magic gone awry, I approached her slowly. "Della?"

"Not yours. Mine."

Margaret, too. approached. "Della?" She spoke softly, hands outstretched, but before either of us could touch her, Della screamed.

I made a rapid retreat, my heart nearly pounding out of my chest. Margaret knelt beside Della's chair, her face gone grey with fear. "I'll find Rafe," I said, and took off at a run.

A gust of wind caught me as soon as I came through the front door, keeping me close to the house. I had no idea where Rafe might be. A huge wave crashed and the breeze carried the spray, making me taste salt. I decided to start with Rafe's workshop, if only because the forest loomed dark and threatening. Fortunately, luck was with me, and Rafe answered my knock on his door.

"Your mother." I managed to get that much out. "In the kitchen."

He brushed past me, his cane smacking my shin. I didn't know how to truly describe what I'd seen, so I simply followed.

Rafe threw open the front door with me at his heels. Margaret still knelt by Della's chair. She glanced at us with a hand over her mouth, tears in her eyes.

"Mine." Della spoke in a guttural groan and then she screamed again.

Rafe would have put a hand on her shoulder, but she jerked out of his reach. "No," she wailed. "No. No. No."

Silence fell. The heavy atmosphere of dread thickened further. My breath came in short gasps, and Margaret was crying openly. Della shuddered, her shoulders twisting.

And then she threw herself backwards, upending the chair.

A hawk's scream broke the silence. Rafe caught Della before she hit the ground. He eased her to the floor, his dark hair hiding his face, making it hard to see his expression. Della did not appear to be breathing. Rafe murmured to her. "Mother? Mother, are you all right?"

"You must not touch me," she whispered finally. Her lips were cracked and dry, as if she'd spent day in the desert. "It tried to bend me to its will, and if it does it again, you must not intervene."

"Nonsense."

She opened her eyes, looking right at her son. "It will try to get to you through me, Rafe. Promise me. I'm strong enough to fight it off alone."

Rafe did not respond. The two of them made a single being, so wrapped up in each other that Margaret and I might not have existed. I extended my hand, helping Margaret to stand. Without words, we retreated, stopping when we reached the door.

Whatever conversation Rafe and his mother were having must have ended, because Rafe stood and pulled Della to her feet.

Only when Rafe sighed, his face as pale as Margaret's, did I dare to say anything. "What just happened?"

My question was simple enough, but neither Gallagher gave me an answer. "Come now," I struggled to keep my tone measured. "Something just happened to you, Della, a fit of some kind. Margaret and I cannot help you if we don't know what's going on."

"Wasn't a fit." Della's voice was hoarse, her eyes shadowed, and sweat beaded along her brow. "What do you think, Rafe?"

Rafe stood with his head bowed. He held his cane in front of him, both hands on it as if it were some kind of magical staff. "I will explain, but first, let me check the wards one more time."

"They're fine." Della wavered, barely able to keep her feet. "They protect us from what's outside, but this, the Ferox Cor, is already here."

"Mother." Rafe's word held a world of warning. Still, I thrilled at finally hearing those words from one of them.

Della shook her head, ignoring her son's admonition. "We cannot fight something that's already behind our defenses, and the Ferox Cor is Martin's legacy. It will be with us as long as he is."

Her knees folded and again, Rafe caught her. "I'll help her to bed, and then I must see to the wards. We can talk tomorrow."

The gravity of his tone weighed on me. We were going to hear something that filled Rafe Gallagher with dread.

Filled me with dread, too.

Chapter Fourteen

Della slept, Rafe absented himself, and Margaret and I stayed in the kitchen where it was warm. Taking advantage of our time together, I described our excursion to see Martin's cave and our battle with the hawk. The end of our discussion could be distilled in two words:

Be careful.

Margaret made a light supper of an omelet with hashbrowns, leaving some on a platter for the Gallaghers. When we'd exhausted our conversation, we both retired. I slept, but it was an uneasy sleep, filled with visions of errant magic and growling dogs.

The next morning, Della invited us to the front room as soon as we finished breakfast. She and Rafe took the two chairs, leaving the bench for Margaret and me. Rafe gazed at the floor, while I leaned forward, my elbows on my knees.

If we were going to get answers, I had to make sure the correct questions were posed.

"First," Rafe began, "I'd like to apologize to Miss Barnes. I should not have insulted you yesterday."

"Oh." Margaret blinked at him. "Thank you."

An awkward silence descended, broken by Della's sharp inhale. "So. Have you ever heard of the Ferox Cor?"

Margaret and I answered in unison.

"Yes."

"No."

We shared a glance. I'd been the one to answer yes. Her jaw clenched and I shrugged. "Fine," she whispered, although I had the feeling that later I'd hear more about this little disagreement.

A gust of wind hit the house hard enough to make the windows rattle. Perhaps the Ferox Cor was stirring things up as a way of delaying our conversation. "Before we left San Francisco, we were warned about rumors linking Martin to a magical object called the Ferox Cor."

A partial truth, but enough for now.

Rafe's grimace made me glad I hadn't revealed our true mission. Della, however, simply looked sad.

"Those rumors were true," she said, pausing when another gust shook the windows, followed by a crashing sheet of rain.

"What the hell?" Margaret spoke softly, but with enough concern that I grew tense. Something was wrong.

Della plowed ahead, oblivious to the storm. "He stole the amulet, unaware of its true properties."

An amulet in a jeweled box. My memory provided the details. "So, why did he want it? What can the Ferox Cor do?"

"It can do whatever the amulet's holder wants it to," Rafe said tersely. "He wanted it so he could play god."

I glanced at Margaret, profoundly disturbed by Rafe's claim, but her attention was fully on the window.

"This storm is not... right." She rose, headed for the front door. "I need to get to the tower."

Without stopping for anything as common sense as a coat, she ran out into the storm.

And I followed. I might have been the little brother, but I'd always tried to protect my older sisters. Even though none of my real sisters had reached out to me after Father sent me away. I hadn't expected them to, not really. They couldn't, not if they wanted to find good husbands, and I would never have soiled them with my stigma. But Margaret gave me another chance at being a good brother, and I intended to watch out for her if I could.

Waves crashed on the beach, tendrils of water swirling around stones and broken mussel shells. A sudden gust of wind caught me off guard. It came from the north, carrying an arctic chill. Salt spray splashed against my face and soon I was drenched to the skin. The wind died away, only to be followed by another gust, this one even stronger.

All around us, evergreen branches thrashed and crackled, and I raced up the stairs after Margaret, frightened by what had been unleashed.

She stood with her back to me, facing out over the ocean. The wind buffeted her, dragging strands of hair loose from her twist at the nape of her neck and sending them flying. She gripped the railing, and though she was standing still, her shoulders rocked as if she was breathing hard.

"What's going on?" I asked.

Margaret waved a hand to shush me. "I'm trying to sort that out. Someone sent this." She sketched a sigil in the air. "Careless. Dangerous." She flicked her fingers. The wind died down, only to start up again even stronger.

Rafe pounded up the stairs, brushing past me on his way to Margaret's side. "Can you stop it or not? If you don't stop it—"

She cut him off. "If I can't stop this, all the world will be affected."

Her tone was grim, and the next sigil she sketched was almost bright enough to see. It blew apart, streaks of scarlet carried on the wind. She tried again, breathing hard. This symbol persisted, black marks that were impervious to the storm.

The wind faded. Della's arrival startled me since I hadn't heard her come up with steps. Margaret trembled, evidence of how much effort this cost her. Her next sigil was more like handwriting in the air. She stroked the air, massaged it, teasing the invisible currents into place.

I'd never seen a weatherwitch work, but from our conversation on the train, I recognized the way she prodded and cajoled, alternating magical signs and simple persuasion, to bring the weather in line with her wishes.

"There," she said finally. Her shoulders sagged, and, elbowing my way past Rafe, I got an arm around her waist.

We shared a glance. Margaret's eyes were heavy, her cheeks sunken, and her face a pale grey. "Back to the house," I announced, daring the others to argue with me.

"Do you need help?" Rafe asked, sounding uncertain.

"We're fine."

He and his mother went down the stairs. Margaret and I followed more slowly. She required enough support that I should probably have allowed

Rafe to help. The tired smile she gave me when we reached the bottom, though, made me glad I had not.

I trusted Della, for the most part, and Rafe some of the time. Margaret, though, was a friend, and I didn't have many of those.

We settled in the kitchen, near the warmth of the fire, Margaret and Della at the table, while Rafe and I propped ourselves against the wall.

"That wind wasn't real," Margaret said. "Or it wasn't natural, anyway."

"What does that mean?" I asked.

"It means another weatherwitch caused it," Rafe said, his frown deepening.

"A sudden change in the weather like that can mean that somewhere, a weatherwitch is being careless," Margaret said. "Someone in Canada, perhaps, or Germany. Their attempt to calm their local weather causes disturbances in other parts of the world."

"This felt more deliberate." Della tapped the tabletop, her hair all the more wild because of the storm.

"Yes, I agree." Margaret reached out and covered Della's hand with her own. "In addition to carelessness, there's another reason for an abrupt change in the weather. Someone can direct foul weather, aim it at another with the intention of doing harm."

"You think someone meant to ruin our morning?" I tried to inject some humor into my voice, but no one seemed to find my comment funny.

"I do, yes." Margaret's expression turned somber. "Though I think this was more of a test than a real attack. I was able to dispel it fairly easily." She shrugged. "I also worked out some of the sender's, well, peculiarities, for lack of a better word. If he disrupts our weather again, I'll be better prepared for him."

"Him? You know it's not another woman?"

That made Margaret smile. "A foul wind is a distinctly masculine weather pattern. A woman would have done something both subtler and more vicious."

I found I didn't want to imagine that set of circumstances. "Assuming you're right, have any of us made sworn enemies of a weatherwitch? Could Martin be practicing from... wherever he is right now?"

Rafe glanced at me for the barest second. "Not Martin, no. More likely Oliver Stevenson is behind this."

"That does seem more likely." I frowned at nothing in particular. "So unless one of us has secretly made an enemy, the instigator behind the weatherwitch's attack was the Seattle Witches' Council."

Della stood up from the table. "That's about right."

Margaret refused to go to rest, instead insisting that she wanted to sit at the kitchen table near the fire. Della brewed another pot of coffee, while Rafe fretted about his wards.

"I'll need to make a new spell, one with stronger wards."

Della gave him a sympathetic smile. "I'd help if I could."

His scowl softened. "I know."

"How?" I planted myself between him and the door.

He faced me, a scowling dark shadow. "Get out of my way."

I yielded, but only so I could follow him. Rafe went outside with me on his heels. The storm had faded to a light sprinkling of rain, though the waves still crashed on the beach, sending up sprays of foam. Broken clouds in the west allowed shafts of sunlight through, enough to prove that it would be sunset soon.

Rafe walked along the beach, heading for the tree line. Glad I'd stopped to grab my overcoat, I followed. He reached the gap in the trees and stopped.

"Go back to the house."

"No." I stood an arm's length behind him, determined to be a witness to whatever he was about to do. "Should your spell have resisted the storm?"

He tipped his head back, as if pleading with the Mother for patience. I didn't really care that I was annoying him. We'd been here long enough that it was time for some answers, and I had every intention of posing the questions.

Without another word, he disappeared between the trees. I took that as an invitation to follow. He sped up the path, his steps sure, his cane carried parallel to the ground. The trail rose and we began climbing the side of the bluff.

After several minutes of rapid travel, he left the path, striking out through the trees. I did my best to keep up, tracking him by sound rather than sight.

Things grew suddenly quiet. *Now what?* I kept moving until I found Rafe standing in the center of a clearing. The space was large enough for a scattering of grass to grow, and I stopped at the edge, content to watch.

"There's a difference between a spell that makes a ward that will discourage people from visiting and one that makes a barrier to keep people out. This new spell will be stronger than the one before."

Though he spoke with his back to me, I took his comment as an olive branch.

Rafe raised his arms and began speaking in a language I did not understand. *"Gofynnaf yn ostyngedig i'r Fam sicrhau'r wlad hon a'n cadw'n ddiogel rhag y rhai a fyddai'n gwneud niwed i ni."*

Lord, was he strengthening the shielding spell or was he calling down the Ferox Cor? Tension clawed at my throat as I waited to see what he intended.

Streams of white light flowed from his palms, rising as high as the treetops. The streams twisted around each other and kept moving, one heading toward the water, the other toward the top of the bluff.

The light streams broke free of Rafe's hands, though their ends seemed to have knotted together, creating an arch overhead. This must be the protection spell, not the Cor. I took a deep breath and allowed myself to relax.

Rafe repeated his invocation, creating two more streams of light. Those rose to the same height as the first, twisted together, then flowed in the opposite direction. The streams broke free of Rafe's palms, and when the leading ends reached the horizon, I felt a shock. Fear tensed all my muscles. *Had he called down the Cor after all?*

The streams of light spread out, creating a shimmering bowl.

No. The feeling of safety created by that dome convinced me the Cor had nothing to do with it. Rafe repeated the words one more time, adding, *"Diolchwn i ti, Mam, am dy ofal hael."*

The glowing dome faded from sight, and only then did I notice how hard Rafe was breathing. I dared take a few steps toward him until he held up a hand.

"Give me time."

His voice was a bare rasp. I did as he asked, waiting until he turned toward me. The amber lenses covering his eyes shone as if they were made of polished brass. Something, some leftover magic, arced between us, washing me in a shower of sparks. I couldn't have moved if I'd wanted to. Rafe, however, either did not notice or did not mind. He came to me, stopping just outside of my reach.

"No one has ever watched before."

I didn't know what to say. Had he truly shown me something he'd allowed no one else to see? His rare moments of vulnerability undid me. My lips parted, though instead of words, I meant to invite a kiss.

Rafe paused, and while his gaze was directed into the trees, he tipped his head as if considering my offer. Considered, and declined. With a slight shake of his head, he started off into the woods. Feeling as if I'd had a bucket of cold water poured over my head, I followed.

The route to the lighthouse was easier as it was all downhill. There was just enough light to keep from tripping over tree roots. I kept distance between me and Rafe, though as we drew closer to the edge of the trees, my attention was drawn to a new noise, a soft hum. My shoulders knotted with tension, as if the sound was raking over my skin. I wanted nothing more than to get out from under those trees and into the open sky.

The Lighthouse Keeper

Rafe seemed to share my discomfort. Both of us moved toward that break in the trees. Things grew darker, branches thickening overhead. The hum grew louder, a buzzing I couldn't escape. "What is it?" I asked, gasping for breath.

"Come." Rafe took my hand, moving fast, almost dragging me with him. He used his cane as a cudgel, clearing our way through the underbrush, and soon we broke free of the trees.

He'd brought us a different way, much closer to the beach. The lighthouse buildings were ahead and to our right, and, just visible through the near-darkness, the hawk sat on top of the tower.

"It's there," I said, forgetting myself long enough to point. The hawk gave a fierce cry. Still holding my arm, Rafe began to run, his cane held straight out in front of us.

Right before we reached the house, I barked that we were close. Rafe lowered his cane and dragged me under the eaves. There we stood, both of us breathing hard.

The forest noise had faded, drowned out by the steady pulse of waves on the beach. Rafe edged closer to the kitchen window, his back against the wall. He rapped on it, then said, "Mother?"

At first there was no answer. He rapped again. This time the window opened a crack. "What is it?" Della sounded as if she was torn between fear and irritation.

"It's on the roof. The Cor." Urgency penetrated Rafe's voice. "Get the door."

Without letting go of my hand, he began to work his way around the house, keeping under the eave. The hawk shrieked. Rafe held up his cane like a shield. Though it likely wouldn't do much, I found a coin in my pocket and turned it into an actual iron shield, something that would have done an Elizabethan knight proud.

If Rafe noticed my shield, he gave me no indication of it. Instead, we crept around the corner of the house. The hawk screamed at us but made no attempt to attack. I held my breath until spots drifted down in front of my eyes. Stopping, I made myself breathe, then continued my slow progress toward the door.

The front door swung open right before we hit it and both of us ducked inside. Della and Margaret waited in the front room, their arms around each other.

"What is it?" Margaret asked. "What's out there?"

"It's the Cor," Rafe said, bent forward, his hands on his waist. "The Ferox Cor."

My heart tripped over a beat. *Now what would we learn?*

"You're tired." Della reached for him, her frown fierce.

Rafe took a step away from her. "I'm fine."

"Where is it?" I asked. "Where is the Ferox Cor?"

He turned in my direction. "Not where, but who."

"*Who* is the Ferox Cor?" I rephrased my question to make sure I understood him right.

"Who." Ignoring his mother's sputter of protest, Rafe continued. "The Ferox Cor is a powerful earth spirit, a demon, really. Years ago, someone bound demon and amulet together. With no one holding the amulet, Martin's death has set the demon free."

I asked the obvious question. "Why is no one holding the amulet? Where is it?"

Rafe and his mother shared a long look, one that spoke of a lifetime spent as allies against some great evil.

"We don't know," Rafe said finally. "Martin hid it before he died."

Chapter Fifteen

So we had at least one answer. Rafe's power was his own, not fueled by evil magic. After the others had retired, I stayed at the kitchen table. I brought out my pipe and filled the bowl with tobacco. Despite my efforts at rationing, the packet was on the light side; I'd need to buy more soon. Della had left lit candles in every corner of the room, promising they'd hold back the Cor, and I used one to light the pipe.

I had doubts about many things. The three of them, Della, Rafe, and Martin, had lived on this tiny bit of land that jutted out into the ocean — the distinction between Sound and Ocean was lost on me — for over twenty years. That didn't seem possible. Rafe had said he only attended school for a few years, yet he spoke like a man with an education. I went to Harvard, so I knew what that meant.

How had he learned? There weren't piles of books around the house, and Rafe likely couldn't have read them if there were. It didn't make sense.

Madam Munro's notes made it seem as if Martin Gallagher had stolen the Ferox Cor for personal gain, but I failed to see the gain in a tiny house some two or three hours by boat from civilization. There was no electricity here, no gaslights, no plumbing. They lit the rooms with oil lamps and witchlights, pumped water from a well, and cooked over wood or coal. If Martin had wanted riches and power, he'd missed the mark.

Della's claim that whoever held the amulet controlled the Cor made sense. If Martin had intended to keep people safe from the Cor's evil, an isolated bit of land would be better than a house in town. I'd come here believing Martin was the villain in this story. Maybe I was wrong.

Either way, I was inordinately relieved that Rafe didn't hold the amulet and therefore control the Cor.

When the clock approached midnight, I was still awake. I tucked my pocket watch away, debating whether to sacrifice more tobacco to my peace of mind. In the end, I gave in to my sense of restlessness and went in search of Rafe.

He wasn't in his workroom, nor was he in the tower. That had me curious and a little concerned.

Unsure where he might have gone, I debated my next move.

I had no intention of wandering through the forest at night. Just being outside was idiotic enough. I'd never seen the hawk at night, but then I'd never looked for it. If Rafe had gone into the forest, however, I might hear him. With that in mind, I stifled my common sense and headed for the place where forest and ocean met. The air felt heavy, as if someone lurked in the darkness, watching.

The steady pulse of light from the tower should have reassured me. The waves kept up their own rhythm, drawing away from the shore only to surge ahead. There was no fog, so the horn was silent, though clouds obscured the moon.

At the edge of the forest, I turned north to follow the bluff. My nerves were taught, every bit of my attention listening for Rafe, or worse, a hawk's flapping wings. The trees were little more than a black shadow, so dark I couldn't imagine that anyone would willingly walk into it.

Anyone except a man with otherworldly vision.

Something rustled through the underbrush, some small animal making its escape from the heavy-footed human. *I hope.* Tension wrapped around my chest like a steel band, and though I kept going, it grew harder and harder to breathe.

The Lighthouse Keeper

Another rustle, this one closer. "Is someone there?" My voice quavered and I cleared my throat. "Rafe?"

Nothing. No one. Not silence, exactly. A soft rustle. A snap, as if something or someone had stepped on a twig.

I walked faster. I should go back to the house. Rafe was probably there waiting for me. An owl's throaty hoot made me jump. *What am I doing?* This was pointless. A rush of feathers, swooping so close the draft ruffled my hair.

"Rafe?" I called out one last time before my courage failed. I'd reached the entrance to the one trail I knew. If Rafe wasn't here, then he was on his own.

He did not respond, and though it might brand me a coward, I turned to go.

A man stood between me and the building. Little moonlight penetrated the clouds. I could make out his silhouette, enough to see it wasn't Rafe. The figure was shorter and broader, poorly defined, a creature of shadow.

Fear traced lightning streaks down my spine. I wanted to run, but he stood between me and safety. The only way forward was through him, so rather than run and hide, I raised a hand. "Hey, you. What are you doing here?"

He did not respond, except to come closer. Dread must have twisted my mind, because he moved without taking steps, in a way no human could. I strode forward, aiming to make a loop around him. He moved again, so quickly I cried out.

We were face to face, me and this shadow figure. He was close enough I could have reached out and touched him. I did not. Instead, I ran the other way, toward the beach, pulling up short when he appeared ahead of me.

The lighthouse flashed, and a sharp pain stabbed my side. The shadow figure vanished in the glare, though when I turned toward the house, he was there. So close. I dodged, but so did he. The faster I ran, the faster he moved. I turned. There he was. I jerked to the side.

And ran right into him.

Dark poured over me, into me, drowning me, leaving me gasping for breath. Every inhalation, though, brought more darkness in. I thrashed, standing on tiptoe, pushing back against this… this… this force.

"No." My attempt at refusal ended in a gag, as if I could vomit up this invading thing.

Darkness, malevolence, evil filled me, stretching out as if to follow my muscles and sinews and veins, to occupy every part. I fought, fists clenched, muscles tense, resisting its progress. The little magic I possessed would do me no good here, as I could no more reach inside myself and change into something else than I could fly to the moon.

The Lighthouse Keeper

I wouldn't give up, though my fight did little good. The voice I thought of as me, myself, my constant inner companion, felt crowded, stifled. A lonely sound in the face of the rushing, howling malice that filled my thoughts. So little space. So little air. I fell to my knees. I would not give in. I would not...

"No, you will not take him."

The words came from a great distance. Rough hands grabbed my shoulders and shook me. My head snapped, rocked, came to rest against a firm thigh. I stayed there, grateful to be able to draw in a breath.

"Leave him." A new power bathed me. This one was warm instead of cold, light instead of darkness. The shadow being thrashed strongly enough to make my arms move, but the steady voice from above kept up a stream of refusal. "You will not have this one. Go back to hell where you belong."

Now when I fought, I was able to gain leverage. My muscles tensed and twisted, and with a cry that started somewhere deep in my gut, I forced the thing away.

And with it gone, I fell to the ground. My world went dark.

"Vincent." Someone shook my shoulder. "Vincent. Are you there?"

"Where else would I be?"

The shaking gentled and strong hands lifted me till I was sitting up, though propped against a warm body. Rafe. I recognized his scent, smokey and herbal, even though I could not coax my eyes to open.

He had an arm around my shoulders, and both of us seemed content to simply rest against each other. Only when he exhaled in something like a sigh did I speak. "I suppose that was our friendly Ferox Cor."

"It was." His voice rumbled against my chest.

"Thank you for freeing me. I couldn't have done it on my own."

"Martin Gallagher overestimated his own strength." He paused, pulling me tighter against his body. "Arrogant fool."

There was a note of finality in his voice, as if he'd said all he wanted to about his father and the Ferox Cor. To be honest, I was fairly sick of both subjects myself. "I was looking for you because I couldn't sleep."

He stilled, a marked enough change that I pried my eyes open. We sat on the edge of the lawn, the gravely beach at our feet. The clouds had thinned enough to let the moon send a shaft of light across the water. I glanced at Rafe and found him looking at me with an intensity that made my heartbeat rise again.

But for an entirely different reason.

"We'll be safe enough now. The thing will need to regain its strength," he said.

My breath caught in my throat. I had no idea whether he was telling me the truth, although I said, "In this situation, I'll bow to your greater experience."

The Lighthouse Keeper

I loaded my smile with all the invitation possible. To be this close to a man who may never have truly seen me added a element of excitement to the experience. Other men had wanted me because I was handsome, but I had no idea why Rafe did.

Those thoughts ran through my head between one heartbeat and the next, and then I reached for Rafe, laying my palm on his cheek. "Do you want me to kiss you?"

Some tension in him melted away. "Yes, and in this circumstance I'll bow to your greater experience."

I straightened, at the same time pulling him in. We paused with our faces so close his breath brushed against my lips. My gut swirling with a mix of desire, excitement, and something like fear, I closed the gap.

He froze, his lips stiff against mine. His body went rigid, and I rubbed my thumb along his cheekbone, the way a rider comforts a startled horse. I didn't push, though my every instinct was to claim his mouth for mine, to taste him in a way no one had before.

Slowly, he relaxed. First, an exhale. Then, his shoulders softened. Finally, he moved his lips, giving me permission to move mine. I eased away, then came at him again, this time flicking my tongue along his lower lip.

He whimpered, an incongruous sound in a man so strong, and with a gentle shove, I lowered us to the ground. The grass was cold and damp and I didn't care one whit. I wanted this man, this dark, strange, vulnerable man.

Given the bulge pressed against my thigh, he wanted me, too.

We kissed, then, stretched out on the lawn. His lips were soft and gaining confidence, which drove me even higher. I lay half on top of Rafe, one leg between his so I could rut against him. He soon returned the favor, and desire threatened to outpace my common sense.

His hands grew rough, raking through my hair, gripping my arms. He startled me by rolling us over, bracketing me with his arms. "You." He ground out the word between clenched teeth. "This cannot be right, but—"

He broke off. Slowly, I reached for his glasses, sliding them off and setting them carefully on the grass. The damp seeped in at my collar and below my coat, easy enough to ignore. I should still be caught up in my panic, but Rafe's presence made me feel safe. Teasing a fingertip along one brow, I murmured, "I do not believe anything so good could truly be wrong."

He sighed. "Mother hopes my feelings for your friend Margaret will grow into something, but since the moment you arrived, I could think of no one else. You're as brave and clever as you are—"

I hushed him with another kiss, catching his head in both hands and holding him where I could go deeper. His gasp gave me an entrance and soon I knew the sweet feel of his tongue against mine. His prick was an iron bar against my thigh. I kept him there until we were both breathless.

"Vincent," Rafe gasped between kisses. "We should… the Cor…"

I closed my eyes and swallowed my disappointment. "You're right." *Though I might always associate kissing Rafe with danger.* "We should go inside." *Where I will sleep on that god-forsaken cot.* "Inside."

"And…" His knees slotted between mine and he sat back on his heels. "I should… we should not…"

I laid my palm against his cheek. "I'll go to my room and you go to yours."

He nodded, gazing around the area, as remote as he'd been when we first met. I pushed up to my elbows and he climbed to his feet. I wanted something, some acknowledgement of what had just happened. Rafe turned, as if to start patrolling the tree line.

My instinct for self-preservation warred with my heart.

Self-preservation won. Rafe stalked off into the night. With soggy trousers and a flagging prick, I headed for the small room with its smaller cot. I hadn't gone far, however, when Rafe called my name.

"Thank you, Vincent Fairchild. You are…" He muttered a curse and I bit my lip to keep from laughing. Uncertainty looked good on him.

"Good night, Rafe. We'll talk more tomorrow." Though I could only guess what he thought of me, I could no more have kept the smile from my face than I could have flown to the moon.

The house was barely warmer than the air outside, and I felt the cold more keenly for Rafe's absence. Before lying down, I stood outside the room where the women were sleeping. One snored softly. Since I didn't hear the ravings of a madman, I judged them both to be safe.

Or as safe as any of us could be, which doesn't seem to be very safe at all. Danger came from behind the wards.

Chapter Sixteen

The next morning, I woke with a gasp, sitting straight up in bed. Gulping air, I fought off memories of the dream.

I lost.

Rutger stared at me from some kind of container. It was tall and wide and made of glass, and it was filled with water. My friend beckoned me closer, his light hair floating around his head, his mouth moving as if he thought to warn me of something. He made no sound, only let out a stream of bubbles with each attempt.

I had to rescue him. That was plain. I spied a ladder leaning against the container and darted up it. But the higher I climbed, the taller the container became. At last I gave up, my heart full of despair. I found myself back on the ground and instead of Rutger, Rafe stood in the water. Tall and angular, he did not attempt to speak, and no bubbles came from either his mouth or nose. His eyes, though, were pools of shadow.

Dreaming about Rutger after kissing Rafe. I poked at my conscience but found no trace of guilt. Rutger and I were friends, companions. Rafe and I hadn't declared even that much.

My friend and companion would not begrudge me last night's kiss, though if he did, well, the problem would be his.

"Rafe!"

Della's cry brought me out of bed. The cold floor burned against my bare feet, and though I wasn't dressed, I opened the bedroom door. Sticking only my head through, I called to her. "What's the matter? Do you need help?"

"It's Rafe." She stood near the front door, arms wrapped around her body as if protecting herself from something painful. "He's not in the workshop and the tower light's gone out."

Margaret stumbled out of the room she shared with Della. Her hair hung over one shoulder in a long braid, and she knotted the tie of her corduroy dressing gown around her waist. "Where else might he be?" she asked.

The Lighthouse Keeper

Della glanced from me to Margaret and back again. "Martin must have him."

Martin is dead, I wanted to shout. Controlling myself, I smiled in a way that I hoped would be comforting. "I'll get dressed and help Margaret wind the light's mechanism. After that, I'll try to find the cavern Rafe made for Martin's body."

Della's eyes widened. "You know where that is?"

"I do." Although without Rafe to lead me, I stood a much better chance of getting lost in the woods than finding it again.

"Della and I can wind the light," Margaret said. "You just look for Rafe."

I agreed with her plan and closed my bedroom door. The memory of the Ferox Cor fighting its way into my body knocked the breath from me. Stifling the urge to scream, I put on the same undershirt and trousers I'd taken off yesterday, figuring they were already soiled. My boots still had smudges of mud on the toes, but I slid them on without bothering to clean them.

And if my shirt still carried Rafe's smoke and sage scent, I did not mind at all.

Once dressed, I donned my overcoat and hat and stepped outside. I didn't see either Margaret or Della. They must still be winding the light. My watch said it was a little after nine a.m., and for once the clouds had scattered and a weak sunshine blessed us.

Rather than heading directly to the cavern, I stopped at the tower door. I caught the murmur of women's voices, confirming their location. If Rafe was in the tower, there was no way they'd miss him.

From there I went to the door to Rafe's workshop. Trying the handle, I found it unlocked. The snap of a spell hit me as soon as I stepped over the threshold and I backed out as fast as possible.

Nothing happened.

I ran a hand over my chest and shoulder, catching the faint vibration of magic. I felt fine, however. No pain, no sudden urge to collapse and die. Perhaps the spell was simply an alarm. If so, I wondered who now knew I'd been in the workshop.

"Might as well go ahead and take a look," I said to myself and crossed the threshold again. This time nothing happened, so I kept going.

Shelves lined the wall directly across from the door, each shelf covered with Rafe's tiny creations. The wall closest to the water had a small grate and the damped coals still gave off a little warmth. A mat lay in front of the fire, a thick blanket folded neatly on one end. A small pillow lay on top of the blanket, and briefly I allowed myself to enjoy the intimacy of the sight.

A pair of tables took up most of the floor space. One was covered with tools, laid out neatly. Rafe must need to know where he'd put something down to make it easy to pick up again.

The other table, though, required a closer inspection. One of the toys — or what was left of it — covered the tabletop. The splintered pieces looked as if someone had smashed the thing with a hammer, and at the center of the table was a pool of red paint. I looked closer.

Blood.

I glanced over my shoulder at the trays filled with tools and found a small pair of pliers. Picked up the largest piece, the one in the pool of blood, and recognized the beak and head of a bird. A hawk, maybe? I set it back down.

Yes, there were two wings and over there was a bird's foot with long claws. The obvious answer was that Rafe had destroyed the hawk in effigy in order to keep us safe. The blood must have been necessary to power the spell.

Unless this was evidence of a fight of some kind.

I put the pliers back in their assigned spot, wracking my brain for the name of someone who could have overcome Rafe. Fists on my hips, I scanned the room again. This time I caught a shadow in one corner. The shadow thickened, took shape.

Martin Gallagher took form, his jaw still held closed with a strip of linen and coins where his eyes should be.

Dread rooted me to the floor.

With no way of knowing what the specter was capable of, I reached for the closest thing to hand. The pliers. Centering myself with a breath, I turned them into a clear glass shield. With luck the shield would be impervious to magic, though fear had my heart beating so erratically that I might drop dead without the help of Martin's ghost.

"Do you know where Rafe is?" I whispered. In response, the thing's mouth opened wide despite the linen and a low, mournful sound filled the small room.

Slowly it raised one arm, the clawed hand even blacker than before. A tight sound escaped me; I was sure I was about to take some kind of magical blast. Instead, Martin's ghost pointed at the door.

"Oh." My feet finally gave up their lock on the floor and I took a step. "You want me to find him?"

Another groan, more pitiful than the first one. Then, before I could draw air into my lungs, the figure disappeared, a shredded shadow that simply drifted away. I snapped the shield out of existence and pocketed the pliers. Good that he didn't turn into snakes this time. Small blessings.

Leaving the room with the shattered hawk behind, I walked along the beach, as far as possible until I reached the place where the forest met the ocean. From there, I followed the tree line behind the house to the trail leading into the forest.

The canopy overhead blocked out most of the sunlight and the air felt heavy, oppressive. Someone watched me; some unseen presence raised the hairs on the back of my neck. I stood a much better chance of getting hopelessly lost than I did of finding that cavern again. "Rafe?" I called out, hoping he hadn't gone far.

To my surprise, he answered me.

"Here."

A weak sound, but recognizable, coming from a cluster of three trees growing closely together. They were young, their trunks slender enough my hands would have spanned each of them. Past them was an old mother, grizzled and bent, her trunk wider than I could reach.

That's where I found Rafe, wrists bound and suspended from a branch overhead. Blood trickled down from the bindings on his wrists. A smear of blood marked his cheek and his lower lip bore a ragged cut.

His glasses were missing and one eye was swollen shut, but the unmarred eye trapped me in its depths. Neither of us said anything. There was no point in asking him what had happened. His injuries were self-evident. Besides, giving voice to my dismay at seeing him so defenseless would have embarrassed us both.

"I'm fine," he murmured, as if he could read my mind.

"Of course." I pulled the pliers from my pocket, closed my eyes, and in a breath I held a pair of long-handled clippers. Stretching on tip-toe, I could just reach the rope above his wrists. It wasn't a clean cut, but I managed to free his hands. He stumbled into me, groaning. His arms flopped forward, his wrists still tied together, but in a moment I had his hands free.

Once he regained his balance, I released him and stepped away, though I would have much rather wrapped him in my arms.

"Do you see my glasses anywhere?"

I wasn't sure he could wear them with the way his eye had swelled, but I looked for them anyway. On the other side of the mother tree, the forest floor had been kicked up and some branches were broken, evidence that Rafe had put up a fight.

But Lord, who could have done this? We weren't all that far from where Rafe had created the dome of a protection ward. The idea that someone had broken through his magic made my chest so tight I could barely draw a breath.

Knowing someone had hurt him turned that fear to anger.

A few paces past the mother tree, I found the glasses hanging on the branch of a young maple that had dropped most of its leaves. I glanced back; Rafe was leaning against the wide trunk, rubbing his hands together. He moved restlessly, turning his head from side to side, as if he expected someone or something to come flying out from between the trees.

Wordlessly, I returned to him. "Here." I kept my voice low because otherwise I would scream. There was every possibility that Rafe's captors were still nearby. Rafe hooked the arms of his spectacles over his ears. The right side did press against the swelling, but if it bothered him, he ignored the discomfort, as if it was enough that those amber lenses gave him something to hide behind.

"Let's go."

"My cane."

Lord. Quickly, I scanned the area. At first I didn't see it, but then, "There. It's... broken."

The cane Rafe used to make his way through the world lay in two pieces, partly covered by dirt and moldering leaves. I scooped them up, more than ready to leave this place.

Rafe took them from me, weighing each with a frown. "They will pay for this."

"Who?"

He didn't respond. After a moment, I took hold of his elbow. "We should go before whoever it is comes back."

Still no answer, but he did respond to my touch. If I'd hoped he would lean on me, I was mistaken. Without his cane, Rafe moved with hesitation, but we might have been strangers, as if we'd never touched each other with any kind of caring.

Fortunately, we didn't have far to go. Rafe's weakness was painful to witness, and I swear I didn't draw a deep breath until we were safely inside the house.

201

"Does the door lock?" I asked.

Rafe pointed at the doorknob and muttered something unintelligible. "No one will be able to open it until I release the spell."

Nodding, I gestured for him to precede me into the kitchen, then realized he wouldn't be able to see me. "Go on," I said, and he did. I came last, the pliers hanging heavy in my pocket.

At least the kitchen was warm, and Lord bless her, Margaret met me with a mug of coffee. That simple gesture helped me calm down, to let go of some of my fear and my anger.

Rafe flopped into one of the chairs, while Della leaned against the counter, her arms crossed. Margaret brought a warm rag and took charge, wiping away blood and dirt from Rafe's wrists and dabbing at the cut on his lip.

"Where's your salve?" she asked Della, who pointed at a shelf over the table.

I stood alone, with little to do besides watch. Rafe barely noticed Margaret, let alone his mother. Or me. I tried to tell myself he was rightfully distressed by the attack, that he needed time to recover.

We barely knew each other, and we were all in danger. Rafe and I would find our way under more secure circumstances. Or so I hoped.

Once the wounds were clean, Margaret took down the jar of salve and smeared some on Rafe's wrists. "I don't dare put it on your lip," she murmured.

"It'll be fine," he said. The memory of those lips against mine made me flinch, a physical urge that burst from deep in my belly. I made fists with both hands, fighting off the feeling I could do nothing about.

At my nod, Margaret took the other seat, and then we all waited to see what Rafe would say next. The silence lengthened, making it clear that he was going to need a prompt. "Who attacked you, Rafe?" I spoke gently, hoping I wouldn't distress him.

Or get my head bit off.

"Two men tied their skiff up to the dock sometime after midnight last night." His voice was heavy, with no inflection to give his words color. "I was in my workshop, so heard them despite their stealth. I meant to chase them off, but one of them possessed an inordinate level of power. I managed a spell that kept them away from the house, though that brief distraction allowed them to restrain me."

"Who were they?" Della asked.

"Not sure. Likely Ollie Stevenson sent them."

Della's glare grew hot. "That man."

"Could the demon spirit have helped them?" I guessed the answer would be no, but wanted certainty. My own experience with the spirit of the Ferox Cor left me sure it would be a contrary partner.

Rafe raked his hand through his hair, a gesture I was coming to associate with uncertainty. "I'm... not sure. Either they managed to use the Ferox Cor or they had another source of power."

"Would they have been able to use the Ferox Cor without the amulet?" Margaret asked.

I took a sip of coffee to calm myself, grateful for her common sense. "From all that you've told us, they shouldn't have been able to. I have the impression that the Cor doesn't obey anyone willingly."

Della stared at Rafe, as if she wanted him to argue the point.

"You're right," Rafe said, without acknowledging his mother. "The Cor will possess creatures, but not on command."

I glanced from Della to Rafe and back, a sense of dread hardening under my breastbone. I had perhaps more experience with the thing than anyone except Della, yet I said nothing. Rafe knew, as he had helped me fight it off. Hell, he'd saved me.

Instead of making a confession, I said something even more terrifying. "So we have two enemies: the Ferox Cor, and someone or something strong enough to break through your wards."

Rafe spoke without looking up from the floor. "Yes."

"That would seem to make finding the amulet even more important."

Margaret's jaw tightened, as if she shared my desperation. "We have a few days till Samhain," she said. "Surely we can find the amulet by then."

"We will. Find it and destroy it, before it causes any more trouble." Rafe's certainty should have settled my nerves.

It did not.

Chapter Seventeen

If I thought Rafe and I had reached a new level of accord, I was mistaken. Rather than stay and help us plan, he absented himself, leaving me in the front room, fighting off the sense that I'd made an awful mistake.

I could not discern whether my kiss was based on true desire or because he'd saved me. Did I want him as one man wants another, or was he another shell my hermit-crab-self wanted to crawl into? Rafe was strange, and he could be hard. Underneath that, however, hid the soul of an artist, a sweetness I'd only seen in glimpses. His infrequent smiles, the time he'd called me brave, and his rare moments of vulnerability all hinted that there was more to him than his cold exterior. There was more to him than his power. I knew that in my bones.

Still, worrying about matters of the heart was easier than anticipating our next challenge. I was still wrestling with the memory of that thing, the spirit that had tried to possess me.

That sense that I'd been drowning in darkness.

Darkness I could still feel, like a pebble in my shoe. Was it the same darkness, or something that had always been there, some part of me I'd never recognized? I couldn't be sure. I sat near the front room's window, gritting my teeth to keep from shivering. Little of the kitchen's heat reached this far, and the slate grey sky did less to warm me.

I rarely regretted my liaisons with men, but the longer Rafe stayed away, the worse I felt.

Maybe he's staying away because he sees the evil in you.

That thought, so unexpected, caused me to jerk upright. That voice was not my own, so where did it come from?

My breath came short, though not from effort. From fear. How did a voice that was not my voice sound in my own mind?

If you're not careful, the same thing that happened to Rutger will happen to Gallagher.

I rubbed my eyes with trembling hands. I had no idea what happened to Rutger and understood the source of these thoughts even less. Swallowing down

207

my rising panic, I got up from the bench. I should find Margaret. Even if I couldn't tell her everything, her solid common sense would be a comfort.

I went to the kitchen, where Della was peeling potatoes. "Do you know where Margaret went?"

"She's winding the mechanism." I would have asked after Rafe, but movement outside caught my eye. Black cloak swirling behind him, he strode up the lawn, headed for the trees.

"What the hell is he doing out there?" I murmured. I hadn't realized I spoke aloud until Della answered me.

"I expect he's going to reset his wards."

"The wards," I murmured. "Of course."

She went back to her potatoes, leaving me alone with my thoughts. "I'm going to find Margaret."

I put on my overcoat and bowler hat and headed out into the rain. Drops of water splashed off the brim, making me grateful they weren't landing in my eyes.

But Margaret wasn't in the tower. I went back to the house, where Della had moved on to mixing something in a larger crockery bowl. "Did Margaret come back in?"

"I haven't seen her."

"Odd."

I would have seen her if she'd been on the beach, and I would have seen her if she'd followed Rafe. That sense of dread weighing me down grew heavier still.

Rather than trouble Della unnecessarily, I went back outside, making a more thorough survey of the beach. There were really no places to hide. I peered through the window into Rafe's workshop. No one there, either.

That left the forest.

But Margaret would have no reason to go there That thought stopped me in my tracks. I needed help. I needed to alert Della. I needed to find Rafe.

If finding Rafe meant going into the forest, I would do it.

"Rafe?" I stopped at the opening to the path and called his name. The relative quiet made the distinctive snap of foot on branch ring all the more loudly. I waited, glancing around both for the cause and a place to hide. "Rafe?" Another rustle, one that could be footsteps. I fingered the coin I always kept in my overcoat pocket, ready to turn it into some kind of weapon if necessary.

"Who's there?" I did my best to stamp out the quaver in my voice. "Rafe?"

He loomed up from behind a large evergreen. "What the hell are you doing?"

"Looking for you."

"You were just going to wander around until you found me? You're crazy. You have no idea what's out here." He carried his ebony cane, the one he'd used in Seattle.

I found it somehow more threatening. "I can't find Margaret."

Raindrops spattered his amber spectacles. "What do you mean?"

Cold. Rude. Could this possibly be the same man who'd kissed me breathless just last night? The same one I'd found beaten near senseless?

I relaxed, letting my hands hang at my sides, as nonthreatening as possible. "Margaret is missing."

Raindrops glistened in his soggy curls. He never wore a hat, something I hadn't paid attention to until now. His rough edges only added to his appeal.

You'd destroy him, you know, and it would be fun to watch.

"Stop it," I bleated. That hated voice.

"What?"

I was tempted to say something, to tell him about the voice, but fear kept me quiet. I didn't want him to think I was demented. "Nothing." My voice stayed remarkably calm. "I didn't mean to upset you. We need to find Margaret."

"I truly don't think—"

"Lord, Rafe, there are only so many places someone can be on this godforsaken rock, and she isn't in any of them."

He grew still, expression even more remote. "All right," he said finally. "Let's go back to the house."

With that, he started off through the trees. I followed as best I could. Rafe had grown up on this isolated bit of ground, and if I squinted, I could see a younger version of him, using cane and memory to move around.

At some point, we'd need to decide whether this flirtation was real, although I knew with some certainty that I'd be the one to start that conversation. *I will do it, too, even if the answer is* nothing.

We found Della in the kitchen. She tossed another hopper of coal on the fire, forehead creased with concern. "I haven't seen her at all."

That gave me a very bad feeling. "All right, I'll check the tower again, Rafe, if you could look for her in your workshop—"

"And I'll look in our room," Della said.

There was really no other place she could be.

Moving quickly, I went to the tower, pounding up the stairs. I let myself out on the widow's walk and made a circuit. No Margaret. Nowhere. Rafe left the workshop, walking across the grass to the house. "Not there?" I called to him.

He shook his head.

Jogging down the stairs, I tried to come up with our next steps. I could not believe that Margaret would desert us. I knew in my bones that she had not left willingly. What, then, had happened?

Perhaps the men who'd attacked Rafe had stayed here, hidden, in order to capture her for their own ends. The obvious response, that we must go after her, was tempered by the fact that we had no idea where she'd gone.

The alternative — that the Ferox Cor had possessed her — was awful enough to make me hope she'd been taken.

On my return to the kitchen, I said as much. "And if so, we must go after her, though I do not know where to look."

Della's grave expression added to my fear. "Here," she said, offering a plain piece of paper covered in a scrawling script. "I found this in our room."

We have your weatherwitch. Agree to join, or we'll send a storm, the likes of which you've never seen.
Oliver Stevenson

I read it out loud, for Rafe's benefit. He simply said, "Mother?"

"Of course," Della said, as if answering his unspoken question. "Give me time to set it up."

"What?" I asked, glancing from one of them to the other.

"She's a searcher," Rafe said. "She can divine a person's location, though she can't find objects."

That left me with more questions than we had time for. I didn't ask any. Instead, I gave voice to my deepest fear. "She has always been kind to me. I have no particular skills to offer this assignment but Margaret didn't fuss when she saw she'd been paired with someone like me."

Rafe stayed quiet for a moment. "I think your Madam Munro doesn't make mistakes. Mother and I didn't need another powerful witch, so much as we needed" — he turned toward me, his expression hard to read — "you."

The weight in his voice told me he spoke the truth, the hidden sweetness piercing my heart. Having a powerful witch hold me in regard was a new experience. People liked my looks, and they liked my family name, but neither of those things mattered a whit to Rafe Gallagher. He might be unsure about kissing me, but we shared a connection, of that I had no doubt.

I hung up my coat and hat, wondering if they'd dry before they froze stiff. Della busied herself setting four candles on the kitchen table. She'd already laid a thin circle of salt, with a small brass dish in the center.

Selfishly, I planted myself close to the little stove, my fingers and toes too stiff with cold to move. Rafe took the chair opposite his mother, his attention fully on the spell she was working.

Della brought out a small velvet bag. She poured the contents — dried herbs of some kind — into the brass bowl. She hummed softly and then struck a match, tossing it on top of the herbs.

As the herbs began to burn, the scent that rose reminded me of Rafe: smoke and sage, though lighter, with notes of honey. From another bag, Della poured a bit of white powder, then smeared it around on the

213

tabletop. Last, she put the note on the powder by her right hand.

Her humming tune drew power into the room, creating a tension that set my teeth on edge. The powder began to shift and blur, making shapes that I could not interpret.

They meant something to Della, though.

"She's not far, but she's moving," Della murmured. She drew a fingertip though the powder and the powder shifted the way iron filaments are drawn to a magnet. "South and east of us."

A current of air brushed past me, tinged with the scent of the burning herbs. Della murmured something, words too soft for me to understand, and began to hum again.

This time her tune was more demanding and the powder responded in kind. The paper vibrated as if tiny hands were shaking it. I'd never seen this sort of magic and was tempted to move closer. My fingers had thawed out enough for me to bend them and I could almost feel my toes.

"Where?" Rafe said quietly.

Della glanced up at him. "She's in a tunnel, somewhere underground. Or that's where she's headed, anyway."

"Could it be the cave with Martin's body?" I asked.

Della didn't respond right away, her attention wholly on the tabletop.

"Should we check the cave or not?" I prompted.

"She's not in the cave." Della traced another line through the powder. "She's further away than that, probably all the way to Seattle, or she soon will be."

"Then we should go after her. Leave now." My desperation made me rather fierce.

"We can't," Rafe said, with a note of finality I could barely stand.

"We must."

Della broke in. "We can't very well leave her, Rafe. Who knows what they'll do to her."

"She could be..." I couldn't bring myself to say the word dead.

"I know," he said, "but there's also the amulet to consider."

"Oh, for pity's sake." I spun around, raking a hand through my hair, and looked desperately from mother to son. "We must go after her. You need a weatherwitch, if for no other reason. I'll go by myself if necessary."

Della exhaled slowly, and Rafe's jaw tightened. She held up a hand, forestalling any protest before he could mount it. "He's right, Rafe, and you know it."

The relief made me sag, though my relief was short-lived as the impossibility of the situation hit me. "Unless one of us can conjure a boat, we won't be going anywhere."

Rafe waved me off. "We have one."

"Wait. You have a boat?" My voice reached something close to a screech. Mother and son stared at me as if I'd grown a second head.

"Of course," Rafe said dismissively.

I wanted to slap someone. I'd spent the last week assuming they were trapped unless the supply boat visited. "Why—"

Della interrupted me. "We cloak it." She wasn't quite as unconcerned as her son, but that did little to calm me.

"We leave in the morning, then." Rafe directed his words to Della, which made my urge to slap him all the stronger.

"Why wait? Show me your boat and I'll go after her alone. You can dig holes in the ground until All Souls for all I care."

Della put a quelling hand on my arm. "Vincent." One word, but she spoke volumes.

"Margaret came here to help you." My voice cracked.

Rafe's chin hit a particularly stubborn angle. "All her efforts, and yours, will be for naught if we don't find the amulet."

My hands were fisted so tight my nails cut into my palms. Maybe I wouldn't slap. Maybe I'd punch.

"We leave at first light."

"We can go now. It's just after noon."

Rafe all but growled. "First light."

"He has to reset the protection spell," Della said, "and if you wait till morning, I may be able to give you a better idea of where to search.

I was fighting a losing battle but couldn't bring myself to quit. "How many tunnels can the city have? We'll start asking questions, and someone will tell us."

Rafe's scowl grew even blacker than normal. I could imagine that diving into a crowd of strangers would be like asking him to fly to the moon.

"Tomorrow, Vincent," Della said with an air of conviction. "The Witches' Council took her because they want us to join. They must know killing our weatherwitch won't further their aim."

"So?" I sounded petulant but couldn't help myself. In reality, I did understand. Finding the amulet by Samhain had to be our priority. I'd defer just about anything in order to achieve that goal. Anything but Margaret.

If choosing one person over the rest made me selfish, then so be it.

"In the morning I'll do another search," Della said. "Hopefully you'll have more to go on."

I glanced at Rafe, who nodded, reinforcing his mother's words. "Come with me. You can help set the wards."

His gaze was directed at the window, but I recognized the concession for what it was. "Of course." I'd be little actual help, but his offer was an unexpected consolation.

Della watched us, her expression puzzled. She must find it notable for her son to make such an offer.

Without explaining ourselves, we put on our wet things and headed into the forest, stopping in the same clearing as before. This time, Rafe spoke harsher words, his voice threaded with fire. He raised another dome, but rather than milky white, this one had jagged streaks of blood red and black.

Oliver Stevenson might have found a way through the old spell, but this one would hold. Its potency was visible, its power thrummed in the air. The Seattle Council may have captured Margaret, but they would not be able to breach this spell.

And tomorrow, they'd learn the extent of their mistake.

Chapter Eighteen

Now we knew who had Margaret, but we still did not know where. I slept little, too worried to find a comfortable spot on that abysmal cot. Did I worry about losing a day when Samhain was so close? Of course, but Rafe had had weeks to find the amulet, with no luck. What would happen in the next three days to change that? Where else could he possibly look? I never asked those questions, so I never got the answers. Martin Gallagher had deliberately made the amulet impossible to find, and right now, Margaret took precedence.

I roused myself sometime after sunrise, washing and dressing in the frigid bedroom. Della worked her seeking spell again. Other than an image of tunnels, however, she had nothing to add. After that, things moved quickly, since we only had one day to search for Margaret. For this trip, Rafe left his fine overcoat and polished boots at home. Dressed in his black cloak and mud-stained trousers, he stood on the end of the dock, one hand held high in the air. "Come."

At his one-word command, the water at his feet shimmered and blurred. Something appeared, long and dark, and slowly became visible. A boat. A rowboat, to be more specific. I could do little but stand on the stony beach, arms crossed, shaking my head. Every time I thought I could trust Rafe and his mother, they did something else that showed me how little I truly knew them.

I could only hope my ignorance didn't end up getting anyone hurt.

The boat was a sturdy contraption, some ten feet long with two benches and a pair of paddles set lengthwise. Once the thing was fully visible, Rafe waved me in.

At the edge of the dock, I noticed something strange. A twisted bit of fabric stuck to the wood, as if someone had dropped it in the rain and many feet had trod on it. I picked it up.

A necktie. With an I Magnin label. "Is this yours?" I held it up in Rafe's direction, already knowing the answer. "It's a striped silk necktie."

His gaze directed over the ocean, he gave a single shake of his head.

"Thought so."

Tucking the tie into my pocket, I settled myself on the rear bench, taking hold of the paddles without asking. Rutger shopped at I Magnin, and he favored silk. Beyond that, the presence of the tie made no sense whatsoever. "You'll have to tell me where to go."

"The current may fight you, but head south along the shoreline." Rafe's level tone helped fix my mind on the task at hand.

I hadn't rowed a boat since our summers on Lake Michigan. I knew the basics, and went to work, though rowing on an ocean was a new experience. It wasn't long before Rafe's warning came to pass and I found myself wrestling the current as well as the waves.

To take my mind off the blisters forming on my palms, I started up a conversation. "What was the spell you tried, the one that changed your eyes?"

Rafe was quiet for so long I came to regret starting with something so difficult. I'd begun to ponder other topics when he spoke.

"The amulet."

Another silence had me biting my lip to keep from prompting him. Rafe would answer in his own time, or not at all.

"Martin kept the amulet in the room he and Mother shared. I was a curious child and, while I wasn't spying, I did see him with it. Even as a child, I knew it reeked of evil."

"They say curiosity killed the cat," I said, mostly to take my mind off the set of swells trying to beach our little craft on the nearby shore.

"In my case, it wasn't so dire."

His dry tone made me laugh.

"I asked Mother what it was, and she made the mistake of telling me that destroying the amulet would send the demon spirit back to hell. She never imagined I would find the thing, but I did. I only knew a simple destruction spell, but I gave it all the power I could muster. I don't know whether the protection spell was set by Martin or by the man who created the amulet in the first place, but my attempt backfired. I was knocked out, and when I woke, I could see the spirit world, but nothing else."

He paused and I made sympathetic noises, which he ignored. "Really, it was dumb luck that I wasn't killed. After that, Mother decided it was best if I didn't go to school in town…" He spoke calmly, as if any unhappiness had been washed clean by time. "…and Martin hid the amulet again."

Despite the cool, grey drizzle, the exertion had me sweating in my suit. A gust of wind tried to take my hat and I broke off mid-stroke to recapture it.

"What's wrong?" Rafe asked.

Squashing my hat firmly in place, I resumed my work. "Nothing. My hat." A new question came to me, and I posed it before I could censure myself. "Martin. Why don't you call him father?"

Rafe answered quickly. "Martin Gallagher wasn't my father. He took Mother in when she was with child, after she agreed to help him hide the Ferox Cor away."

"I see." Any number of possible situations presented themselves, though I settled on one. She must have traded the Baron name for the protection he could offer her. Since I had some experience with trading on a name, I offered no criticism.

"It was a false bargain, in the end," Rafe said, as if reading my mind. "He thought that with the Ferox Cor in hand and a Baron at his side, he'd rule the world. She convinced him to hide it away, and over time, he saw the wisdom of that choice. She came to love him, though, more than was good for her." He seemed to be waiting for me to say something, so I did.

"Seems to me that your mother saved us all from a fairly terrible fate."

"She did."

His voice had a finality that discouraged further questions. A bead of sweat rolled down the side of my face, though we seemed to be making progress. Picking through Rafe's words in search of any false notes, I stroked the oars. If nothing else, he'd explained why he didn't seem to mourn Martin's passing.

We were passed by fishing boats making their way into the harbor, larger passenger vessels that sailed between Seattle and other cities along the coast, and one large, steam-powered freighter that sent rolling waves in our direction. My arms and shoulders were long ready to give up before we reached our destination.

"Look for the place where dugouts tie up," Rafe said. "They call it Ballast Island."

"I think we're almost there." I hoped so, anyway. Saltwater splashed onto an open blister on my palm, making it sting.

The shoreline was as dark and drab as the clouds. Close ahead, many canoes were grounded on a rocky outcropping rising above the waves. Beyond that, piers jutted out into the water, proudly displaying their industry. The piers were crowded with fishing boats and freighters, brick buildings huddled in the mist, and the whole place crawled with men, mostly men, hollering, laughing, busy men.

There were people on the place he called Ballast Island, too, although plainly it wasn't an island. As a Midwest boy, I didn't know much about shipping, but during my time in San Francisco I'd learned that ballast was the material — rocks and sand and chunks of broken concrete — that was loaded on ships to keep them steady when their hulls were empty. So, the "island" really was just a pile of rocks dumped by cargo ships on their way in and out of Seattle's harbor.

The Lighthouse Keeper

We let the waves take us close to the rocks. When the hull scraped along something solid, Rafe jumped out and pulled us the rest of the way up the rocky shore. I followed, and soon both of us stood on solid ground, our boots and the hems of our trousers wet.

Unlike those on the piers, the few people here were engaged in the business of living. A cluster of tents stood between us and the street, and two women squatted in front of them, cooking something on an open fire. The scent of roasting meat had my stomach growling, and children played a game with small stones in front of another tent. At our approach, however, everyone stopped what they were doing and stared at us.

An older man approached, flanked by a pair of younger, but no less stern, companions. They all had straight dark hair and their clothing was worn.

"Who are you?" the old man asked.

Before I could answer, Rafe spoke up. "Rafe Gallagher, Martin's son."

The man nodded, as if he'd expected that answer. "What do you want?"

"Martin is dead, and some men from the city have taken our new weatherwitch."

Another nod, this one more considering.

"We ask your permission to leave the boat here while we look for her."

The old man pointed to one of the younger men. "See to it."

"Thank you." Rafe bowed, so I followed suit.

The old man laughed and said something in a language I didn't understand. The others responded, and after a moment, they waved us on. Rafe kept a hand on my arm as I led us around the bigger rocks and between the tents. I kept my mouth shut until we reached the street.

"What was all that?"

Rafe didn't answer until we were a good block away. "They lived here before any of us, but the mayor has made it illegal for them to be within the city limits. No one cares about that pile of rocks, though, so they camp there on their way to their winter home. I expect that group will soon move on."

"How do you know all this? I've read about people having trouble with Indians, but I've never really seen any."

"Sometimes they stop at the lighthouse, and we talk." He tilted his head, as if examining my question from many different angles. "I would say we've caused them more trouble than they've caused us."

I hadn't ever looked at it that way. Rafe's tone didn't invite questions, so I kept quiet. Those three children had been barefoot, which made my cold toes even colder. I had a few dollars in my wallet and was tempted to run back and give them the money for shoes.

Instead, I moved ahead with determination, Rafe's hand still on my arm. We walked up the muddy street without a true destination. Warehouses lined the block and a steady flow of men from the docks had me altering our path more than once.

We finally reached an open air market. Carts full of potatoes, carrots, and greens were set up beside a display of fresh fish on ice and another with cuts of beef. In between was a macabre rack of dead chickens hung by their feet, and a swarm of housewives bartered for the best price on all of it.

"We need to find a saloon," I said finally.

"Why?"

Rafe crowded close to me, as if the multitude of spirit energies made it even harder for him to see.

"So we can talk to people. Someone will know where there are tunnels, but we can't simply shout our questions in the middle of the street."

His grip tightened. "True."

Then, as if I'd commanded it to appear, I saw a sign across the street. "This way."

We had to wait a moment for the traffic to clear so we could cross. A gap between carriages and farm carts gave us a chance to squelch through the mix of mud and horse manure that covered the street. At the door of the saloon, I paused to scrape the muck off my boots.

"I wish we were here under more pleasant circumstances," I murmured.

Rafe, still standing close to me, said, "Me too."

Heat rose in my cheeks, likely because my heartbeat took off like a stallion at the starting gun. I'd been so focused on the task at hand — getting to the city and finding Margaret — that my attraction to Rafe Gallagher had been banked.

Those two words brought it all back.

Glad he couldn't see my idiot's smile, I led us into the saloon.

The room was dark and blessedly warm. I straightened, doffing my hat, before heading for the bar. The bartender, a grizzled man whose light blue eyes looked younger than his salt-and-pepper hair suggested, took our measure before coming over.

"What can I do for you?" he asked, his tone guarded.

"Whiskey, please, and lunch if you still have it." My blistered hand stung even more now that some blood was returning to it. Though we'd left early, it had taken most of the morning to row to Seattle, and my belly wanted lunch, whether or not it was time.

Rafe said nothing, which made the bartender raise a brow. "This one mute as well as blind?" he asked, staring pointedly at the cane Rafe had leant against the bar.

"Not at all." I put a hand on Rafe's arm, his tension thrumming through me. "He'll have what I'm having."

"All right. I just thought he might want to speak for himself."

The Lighthouse Keeper

I opened my wallet and put a five dollar bill on the table. "Two whiskeys and two of whatever you're serving for lunch."

"Kitchen's closed, but I'll send a boy to the market. There's a stand over there with meat pies."

"I'd be obliged if you would."

The bartender turned his back to us and reached for a bottle from the shelf behind the bar.

"I don't drink whiskey," Rafe murmured.

"Don't worry. I'll ask him for some water, too."

When the bartender brought our drinks, I got my handkerchief out, wet it with whiskey, and dabbed the blister. It made my eyes water, but I didn't want it to get inflamed.

"What is it?" Rafe asked.

I told him, and he gently took hold of my hand. I caught the bartender giving us a strange look, but then Rafe pulled something out of a pocket, a small vial. "Mother's salve."

He unscrewed the lid and rubbed a small amount on the blister. The lavender herbal scent cut cleanly through the saloon's funk and the sting faded.

"Is there anything you can't do?" I asked quietly.

His lips twitched like he might want to grin, but he didn't otherwise respond except to tuck the salve away.

A few minutes later, the bartender propped himself on the bar in front of us. "Your meat pies'll be along in a minute, and while we wait, why don't you tell ol' Uncle Dusty what you're really up to."

Chapter Nineteen

Pardon me?" Rafe's whole body tensed at the bartender's question.

I put a quelling hand on his arm. Getting kicked out of the saloon wouldn't serve anyone's purpose. "You're Dusty?" I asked with my smile at its most winning.

"I am."

"My name's Vincent Fairchild and this is Randolph Griffin, and we were hoping we could ask you a couple of questions."

"Strange fellows like you can ask, but I don't know as I'll be willing to answer."

I set a second five dollar bill on top of the first. "We need to find someone, and the only clue we have is that they're somewhere underground, in a place with tunnels."

"Who is this person, and why do you need to find them?" His grin said his question was aimed at annoying us rather than any need to know, so I just smiled wider.

"What would you say if I told you it was my runaway bride?"

"Nah," he waved away my words. "You don't look like the marrying kind."

"Maybe not, but I still need to find her."

"Who?"

"A very dear friend."

"Tell me again why you need to find her?"

Rafe clenched his fists. "Because," he said slowly, his anger simmering just under the surface, "our friend is trapped in some tunnels underground, and if you think that's a decent place for a lady, that makes you the strange one."

"All right, all right." Dusty held his hands up, showing us his palms. "I was just teasing you."

I might have guessed at his game, but Rafe clearly had not.

A boy of about ten ran through the front door of the saloon, carrying a paper bag. He set it on the bar and the bartender flipped a coin in his direction. The boy ran out and the bartender brought us the bag, along with a pair of small plates. "Here's your lunch," he said. "Now let me think for a minute. There's the mines over in Newcastle. Those have tunnels, for sure."

The smell set my mouth watering. I put a meat pie on each plate and passed one to Rafe. "That sounds promising. Can you think of any other places?"

"There's the old city."

"Old city?"

The bartender smiled. "You must not be from around here. See, back in '89, a fire burned most of the city right to the ground. When they rebuilt, they raised the streets one full story. There's buildings downtown that have a first floor underground. The old sidewalks and such are still in place, and there are ways to get down into the tunnels. Your friend could be waiting for you there."

I took a bite of the meat pie, grateful for the warmth and the savory flavor. Grateful I could feel my fingers and that the blister no longer stung. Grateful that we might be a step closer to finding Margaret. "How far is it to downtown?"

"About a mile south of here. Just stay on Front Street and you'll come to it. Look for the Dexter Horton buildings on the corner of Front and Washington. Take the stairs to the lower level and you'll find the tunnels."

It sounded almost too easy. "Where's the other place you mentioned? Newcastle?"

He palmed both five dollar bills. "It's on the other side of Lake Washington, southeast of here. There's a train, but it's mostly used to bring coal in so they can ship it away."

"We'd probably have to hire a team to get us there."

"You might."

Rafe's dark gaze weighed on me. He'd had a few bites of his meat pie, while I'd all but demolished mine. "You ready?" I asked him.

"Let's go."

With that, I wrapped the remains of his meat pie in the paper bag and downed what was left of my whiskey. I'd have drunk Rafe's, too, but wanted to keep my head clear. If we couldn't find Margaret downtown, we were going to be in an even bigger mess. We didn't have time to waste.

The crowds had thinned as more men went in search of their lunches, and we made good time. "Who in the world is Randolph Griffin?" Rafe asked when we were some blocks from the saloon, heading south on Front Street.

I chuckled, taking care to match my pace to Rafe's. "The bartender might recognize the Fairchild name without knowing me specifically, but the odds were greater that he'd know who Rafe Gallagher is."

He came close to smiling again. I liked this lighter version of Rafe, though I didn't fool myself into believing his darker self was gone for good. For the moment, however, I simply let myself enjoy the illusion that we were two ordinary men on an excursion, rather than desperate witches determined to rescue their companion.

Warehouses gave way to shops like Wallis & Nordstrom Shoes, a department store called the Bon Marché, Cooper & Levy, and other retailers who promised to outfit the hardy prospector for their trip to the Yukon. I might have been tempted to stop, but Rafe discouraged that simply by his presence.

Asking Rafe to accompany me to the Bon Marché would have been a waste of everyone's time.

Our steady pace increased when the rain began. My overcoat had barely dried from yesterday and my hat was going to be a sodden mess before too much longer. As moisture seeped down underneath my collar, I moved with greater determination. We had to reach Washington Street soon.

I noticed the placard on the front of the building before I saw the street sign. "Dexter Horton Building. This is where he said to stop."

"It is."

With Rafe a steadying presence at my shoulder, we entered the main lobby, an airy marble and brass affair with tall windows, wooden furnishings, and high standard for its visitors.

Rafe and I didn't quite meet those standards. "We'd best find the way down quickly," I murmured, nervous that the concierge was going to ask us nicely — or not so nicely — to leave.

Ahead and to my left, a sign stuck out from the wall. "Stairs." I tugged on Rafe's arm. "That must be it."

Almost too easily, we reached the stairwell, where the stairs went up, and, more importantly, where they went down. At the bottom, however, we found our way blocked by a locked door.

Without hesitation, I reached for the coin in my pocket.

It wasn't there.

"Damn it."

Rafe moved closer. "What?"

"The door is locked." I patted my other pockets. "I always carry a coin, because whenever I don't, I need it most desperately."

"Hmm." Rafe dug through the folds of his cloak. "Here."

I'm not sure what he handed me. It might have been a knotted bit of wood or a partly carved creature of some sort.

Or it might have been a finger bone.

Before I could spend too much time pondering the alternatives, I gave it a push of power and held a brass key.

It fit the lock perfectly and we were in.

But where were we? A dark, echoing space. I sent up a witchlight. My initial impression was confirmed. The room seemed larger than the lobby above, as if someone had only bothered to put in the bare minimum of walls. There was a row of windows across from us, in the right direction to look onto Front Street.

Where Front Street had been, anyway.

There were a few pieces of broken furniture; a picture frame with three sides and a wooden crate with the lid leaning against the wall. The floor was thick with dust, and, on closer inspection, we saw footprints in that dust.

Footprints that we hadn't made.

"Oh." Rafe stood some two feet in front of the door, his body tense.

I'd gone several steps deeper into the room and glanced at him over my shoulder. "Are you all right?"

He lifted his amber spectacles and rubbed his bare eyes. "I don't suppose you can see the flames, can you?"

"Lord." I hadn't thought of that. "Take my hand."

I reached for him and he grasped my fingers. His touch was warm and firm. "Keep your eyes shut or look straight down. I'll make sure you're safe."

"I'm not sure…" His voice trailed off.

"Do you want to stay on the stairs? I can look for Margaret on my own." The idea frankly terrified me, but I'd try. I couldn't bear the thought that Rafe would have to walk through the memories of the fire.

"No." He shook his head without letting go of my hand. "Let's go."

I got us through the empty room. The big double doors that opened onto the unused sidewalk were not locked, fortunately, so it wasn't long till we were through them. I still had some sense of direction, guessing that going right would take us where we'd come from and going left would take us further south.

The wooden planking that had once been a sidewalk was still in decent repair. Some four feet along the street side, a wall rose up, in effect creating a tunnel. The light was brighter here, because patches of glass brick interrupted the darkness overhead at regular intervals. Along with my witchlight, it was easy to move about.

I had no idea how far the tunnels extended in either direction, so picked left at random. The prevailing scent was damp stone with an undercurrent of sewage that was more of a warning than an actual threat.

Rafe relaxed once we started moving, even going so far as to release my fingers. I hoped that meant he could no longer see flames.

The tunnel was quiet, the rattle and clank of traffic on the street overhead dampened. As odd as it was to be traveling underneath the city's main street, it wasn't unpleasant.

Not unpleasant until I heard them, that is.

A chittering sound, tapping, whispering, heavier than the scratching of rats behind the walls. "Do you hear that?"

"Yes."

We reached another building and I sent the witchlight in to illuminate the main room. The space was empty except for an abandoned sewing machine in one corner. The floor was covered with dust, but there were no footprints. I glanced at Rafe. "Not here."

"Agreed."

We moved on, accompanied by that chattering sound. Pattering, like very heavy mice or — I heard an unmistakable giggle — children. I whirled around, nearly knocking Rafe off balance.

"What do you see?" I asked quietly.

"Behind us. Four of them."

"Are they living, or are they spirits?"

"Living."

They might be able to help us. I continued walking, with Rafe at my heels. We went into the next building because there was some disturbance in the dust on the floor. The padding footsteps followed us.

This room was entirely empty, with a single door across from where we'd entered. The door was unlocked, and as soon as I crossed the threshold, I ducked to my right, leaving the door open. Rafe followed suit, taking a position opposite me with his back to the wall.

We didn't wait long at all until the ringleader came sneaking in. Through the dirt and the rags I guessed he was a boy. The child right behind him wore a filthy dress. I grabbed the third by the arm, earning myself a sharp kick to the shins and very nearly the gash of a deadly little blade.

Rafe caught the child's wrist before he could stab me, which brought the others crowding around, punching and kicking. I caught another blade before it could cause real damage and barely avoided getting bit by the littlest one.

"Hang on now. Stop."

I spoke with as much authority as I could muster, but things didn't calm down until Rafe hollered, "Desist" in a tone of voice that had me quaking.

"Be still. All of you," he said. The four children faced us, showing various levels of disrespect and anger, but no fear.

They all looked like they could stab us in the back without losing a wink of sleep. The biggest boy wore trousers that were some six inches too short and a pair of shoes that had somehow been tied around his feet, with pieces of leather flapping off here and there. The girl was as dirty as the other three; only her dress hinted at her sex, though given how ragged they all were, she could possibly be a he who had nothing else to wear.

The third, the one I grabbed, was young enough to be missing his two front teeth. A crude scar bisected one of his eyebrows, giving him a cockeyed look. The smallest couldn't have been more than five, although the soul that stared fiercely from his eyes had seen too much for such a young age.

"So," I said, with a smile that aimed for a friendly authority. "I wonder who would like one of these." I held up a dollar bill. The intensity of their attention left me with a sense of relief that I had three other bills in my wallet, as I could easily see the losers ganging up on the winner in a most unpleasant way.

"I'm looking for someone, a woman, who might be down here, and I wonder if any of you could help me find her."

"What 'zat?" the littlest child pointed at the witchlight. "Are you a witch?"

"It's a witchlight, and yes. Now is it worth a dollar to you to help me find my friend?"

The largest boy spoke up. "Maybe. What you all think?" He looked at the other children.

"I didn't see nobody," the boy with the scarred brow said, lisping on the *s*.

"Don't lie, Hammond." The girl took a swipe at him, fixing me in her flat stare. "We can take you, but it's a ways away."

I gestured toward the door. "Lead on."

Rafe mumbled something I didn't catch, but the children had taken off at a fast clip. "Hey." I hollered after them. "Nobody gets paid if you leave without us."

The girl came back first. She pointed at Rafe. "He can't move that fast, right?"

Rafe muttered something sharper, making me glance his way. Cane in one hand, he sketched a sigil of some kind with the other. When he finished, something clicked and the girl gave a yelp.

"What kinda nasty spell did you set?" She glared at him, her dirty chin raised like she was ready to take a punch.

"It'll fade soon," Rafe said. "We just need to be able to find you in case we get left behind again. You want that dollar, don't you?"

"Come on," she said, her grimace more frightening than someone her size should have been able to manage.

We followed. The biggest boy seemed to have left us, and the smaller two watched carefully as we approached. The children seemed to be comfortable enough with the idea of witchcraft, but then they had certainly not lived sheltered young lives.

"How far away?" Rafe asked.

The children looked at each other before answering. "Up toward Jackson, I think," the one called Hammond lisped. "We can take 'em, Bettany."

"We'll all go." She started off, the younger two right behind her and Rafe and I bringing up the rear.

The patches of glass bricks overhead gave us sufficient light to walk by, so I let the witchlight go out. The children led us up and around, a twisting route that made me wish I'd left us a trail of breadcrumbs to find our way back.

Keeping track of others' footprints took whatever bit of attention wasn't keeping track of our route. Rafe kept close to me, periodically flinching as if he passed another patch of remembered fire. We'd been walking for some fifteen minutes when the largest boy came jogging up from the direction in which we were headed.

"They're gone," he said. "Now gimme the dollar."

Drawing himself up to his full height, he made a show of palming another sharp blade.

"No friend, no dollar." I kept my voice light, my smile amused.

"She ain't there no more." He raised the knife. "Now gimme the dollar."

Rafe stepped out from behind me. "You will take us there now."

"I could just tell you any ol' place and you'd believe me." The cocky little bastard crossed his arms, his grin smug.

Rafe removed his spectacles, giving the child his full, black-eyed glare. "I'll know if she was there or not."

"You're lying," the boy said, though his face turned pale and his grin faded.

"I'm not."

"Don't be a fool, Jim," the girl, Bettany, said. "Let's just take 'em and they'll let us be."

He snorted a laugh, pocketing his blade. Bettany waved us on, with Hammond and the smallest boy right behind her. Rafe and I waited until the big boy, Jim, had started after them before we moved.

This search for Margaret had become more complicated than I'd expected.

We followed the children through a series of turns, coming at last to an abandoned storefront that still had an old *Pharmacy* sign in the window. The children led us inside, and from the scuffmarks in the dust, the place had seen other visitors.

"See?" the big kid, Jim, said. "She was here but she ain't no more."

I turned to Rafe. "What do you think?"

He lowered his glasses and scanned the place. "He's right."

"Damn it."

"Okay. Gimme that dollar," Jim crowed.

Grimacing, I reached for my wallet. "Can we get to the street from here?"

Bettany answered. "If you want. That door goes to more stairs, but you wanna be careful because you'll end up in a tavern. The owner goes off his chump when he catches us sneaking in."

"Thank you." I gave her a small bow and handed over the dollar.

Jim snatched it right out of her hand. "Ha! It's mine!"

With a little push of power, I turned the bill into a razor.

"Oy." He dropped the blade before it could do more than scratch him.

"You'll wait your turn," I said, taking out another dollar. I gave one to each child but told Jim he'd have to hold onto the razor till the magic faded and it turned back into a bill. They took off running, leaving Rafe and me in the dusty, twilight room.

"At least I can't feel the Ferox Cor watching us down here," I said, shrugging deeper into my coat. "And we're not in the rain."

"Excellent points, both of them." Rafe drew in a deep breath. "I'm sorry, Vincent, but we need to go back."

"Not without Margaret." I answered just as firmly. "I cannot imagine a circumstance under which I'd leave her to Oliver Stevenson's will."

"We won't leave her."

"So there's no point in going back to the lighthouse, then."

He paused before answering. "There's too many ghosts down here. Let's go someplace else where we can talk."

"Maybe we can get ourselves a proper lunch upstairs."

"Assuming they actually serve food."

I shared Rafe's skepticism, but led the way to the stairs, anyway. We'd reach a compromise. We had to.

Chapter Twenty

There was a tavern, and though the barman looked askance when we came in through the rear instead of the front like everybody else, he didn't question us. Rather than the bar, I asked if we could have a table. We didn't need curious ears overhearing our conversation.

They had oyster stew on the menu, which was fine by me, and soon we had two steaming bowls, two mugs of beer, and slices of bread and butter to occupy us. Rafe's cane leaned against our table and a handful of businessmen worked on their own bowls of stew. None gave us more than a passing glance.

Rafe moved his hands carefully over the silverware, gently tracing the distance between the spoon and the edge of the bowl. For an awful moment, I flushed with embarrassment, imagining how those fingertips would feel tracing lines on my body.

"Um," I cleared my throat, desperate to shift my mind onto another subject. "I'm pondering our next steps."

Rafe paused with the spoon halfway to his mouth. "We go back to the lighthouse, where Mother can read the cards again."

I watched him take a bite, the way his shoulders relaxed and the muscles in his throat worked. My body warmed, my prick swelled. I clenched my fists to keep control of my baser impulses.

"*If* we return to the lighthouse…" He wouldn't leave again. He'd already said so. Rafe might hold Margaret in some regard but finding the amulet was his highest priority.

And if he wouldn't leave, I couldn't leave. "That's one possibility."

"What?"

I made a show of pulling out my pocket watch. "It's after two p.m. I don't think we have time to paddle back before it gets dark." I tucked my watch away. "If we stay till morning, we'll have a few more hours to search."

"We should leave right now." Despite his words, Rafe stirred his stew, making no other move.

"Are you worried about your mother?"

His hesitation hinted that the answer was yes. Perhaps he should have stayed behind. The demon spirit had already proved its desire to possess one of us. What would stop it while Della was there alone?

As if reading my mind, Rafe said, "I set another spell. As long as Mother keeps to the house and the tower, no one, corporeal or not, will be able to touch her."

"In that case," I said, barely able to stifle my lecherous grin, "that leaves us with finding a place to spend the night."

Rafe must have caught my change in tone because one eyebrow raised. "There are a few other places we could look. There's Stevenson's fishing boat. They could have moved her there. Or if they were feeling more generous, they could have brought her to those sisters."

"The Franklins?"

"Yes. I think I can find where they live if necessary."

He was right, of course. We shouldn't waste time in amorous activities when we could look for our friend. Admonishing myself, I tried to remember who else had been at the Seattle Council meeting. "Mrs. Morrison, the psychic. She and Stevenson were the only ones with any level of power. Maybe we should pay her a visit." I gave him a critical once-over. To say he looked shabby was an understatement. "We'll get in through the back door, and you let me do most of the talking."

He swallowed another mouthful of soup. "Of course, Vincent. She's far more likely to talk to you than she is to me."

I risked a grin. "But she's far more likely to do what you tell her, if it comes to that. I'll be the silk glove and you can be the steel hand."

Nodding, he returned to his stew. I went back to sopping up the dregs of mine with a slice of bread, wondering again why I found him so appealing. He wasn't charming, and though he didn't currently have bits of leaf in his hair, it was only a matter of time.

In general, I liked powerful men, and Rafe had power to spare. He might have a shell that could protect us both, but it was his softer side, the man who carved delicate hummingbirds from wood and who was so cagey with his smile, that truly intrigued me. I could spend a good long while getting to know that side of him, though whether he'd let me was an open question.

We were going to have to interview the psychic first.

Swallowing the last of my beer, I set my mug down firmly. "What we need," I said, "is a city directory."

Rafe's expression didn't change. Likely he had no idea what I meant.

"You finish," I said, "and I'll go ask the proprietor if he has one."

I left Rafe with a nearly empty bowl and half a beer and went off to talk to the barkeep. He produced a directory from behind the bar, and I brought it to the table. "Let's see." I flipped through the first few pages of advertisements, then reached the combined list of businesses and citizens. I skimmed the first few pages before finding the letter M. I ran a nail down the list, stopping at Morrison. "There's a Meredith Morrison, clairvoyant, keeping rooms at 119 W. Virginia Street."

"That's her."

"She's not very far from advertising her services as a witch."

"Do you blame her?"

In anyone but Rafe, I'd have said he was using sarcasm. As it was, I chuckled. "That makes a certain amount of sense. I wonder if there's a streetcar heading in her direction."

Returning the directory, I learned that there was, in fact, a streetcar. Rafe was still chewing his final bite when I dropped a few bills on the table and headed for the door.

While waiting for the streetcar, Rafe asked a pertinent question. "Do we just knock on the door and ask for Margaret?"

"That's the sticky part." I rubbed my hands together to try to hold onto some of the restaurant's warmth. "What we need is a spell to make one of us invisible, so we can get inside and look for her. I mean, I'd rather not speak to Mrs. Morrison at all if we can help it."

"Makes sense."

The streetcar rattled up and we climbed aboard, Rafe tapping each step with his cane before moving. There weren't many passengers on the long bench running down the center of the car. There were no exterior walls, and if there was a source of heat, I couldn't find it. We were traveling in the direction of Ballast Island, at least, so we'd be able to make a quick escape if necessary.

"Let's take a look around the boardinghouse from the outside and see if anything presents itself." I tucked my hands under my armpits, ready to trade this raw damp cold for the San Francisco fog. *At least the fog doesn't make me ache so.*

Rafe nodded, apparently lost in thought. The driver called out, "Virginia."

The coach stopped, we climbed out, and Rafe stayed me with a hand on my arm. "You can change objects into whatever you want, but have you ever tried to change a person? Could you change me into something small that could search the boardinghouse without being noticed?"

"I... I... have never tried something like that." The very idea made me sick to my stomach. "I mean, I turned a man into a weasel once" — *and maybe a dog, too* — "but with the intention of turning him right

251

back. What if you got stuck? Or I don't know, someone stepped on you."

His snort was more of a chuckle. "Let's see if there's a way for a mouse to get in."

"No." I stood still, my hands clenched in fists. "What if we upset the balance of power in China?"

"What are you talking about?"

I waved his question away. "I am not going to change you into a mouse so you can see if Margaret is in the house."

His expression turned flat. "So what are we going to do?"

I thought quickly. "I'm going to change my own appearance, and I'm going to knock on the front door and keep the proprietress entertained while you sneak in through the back door in your normal man-sized form."

"And what will I do when I'm inside? I'm not going to be able to search the place. They'll notice when my cane starts banging into things."

A gull swooped overhead, shrieking a curse into the sky. A flare of sunlight snuck out from under the clouds on the western horizon. Arguing on Front Street was only giving passersby something to watch. Not sure how to resolve things, I ducked into a dry goods shop, where at least my hands would be warm. "I don't know if I can do two things at once," I said in an undertone, "and I have no idea if I could do anything with your eyes, anyway. You might be a mouse with amber spectacles.

"And besides, we have no real reason to think Margaret is in there in the first place. Let me put on a disguise and go talk to Mrs. Morrison."

"So she can read your mind and realize you're in disguise?"

"Lord." We were at an impasse. "We should have just engaged a room."

We were surrounded by racks of fabric and the odd bits necessary for sewing a garment, the air heavy with the scent of cotton and starch.

"It'll be fully dark soon," I said, "and the keeper will be serving her boarders dinner." The single electric light in the center of the ceiling crackled, sending off odd shadows. "Let's watch the boardinghouse for a while and see if anything happens to make us think Margaret's in there." I shoved my hands deep into the pockets of my overcoat. "Maybe we'll get lucky. Besides, once it's dark, we may be able to find a way in."

Two things worked in our favor. We rounded the corner onto Virginia Street and found a small café across the street from the boardinghouse. And, shortly after the waitress had brought our coffees, a team of horses pulled to a stop out front. It was an ordinary cab, with the driver up front and curtains obscuring the windows. The door opened on our side and a man got out.

"He's here."

"Who?" Rafe said, stirring cream into his coffee.

"Oliver Stevenson just got out of a cab, and…" I waited to see if he was alone. He was not. "Margaret's with him. He's dragging her by the arm, and… No. Stop."

With that, I was off. I sprinted out of the café, reaching into my pocket for my coin. No coin, but I still had Rafe's weird stick, and by the time I hit the sidewalk I had a revolver aimed right at Stevenson.

"Stop. Margaret. Get down."

She lunged, but Stevenson was quicker. He grabbed her by the waist, with her back to him, a deadly blade at her throat.

"I take it you've decided to join us?" Stevenson asked, his voice ugly. His drab blond hair hung in his face and he had the beginnings of a black eye on one side.

"Let her go." To my credit, my hand did not shake. I kept the revolver aimed at Stevenson's head, and I was a handy shot, one of the only useful things I'd learned growing up a Fairchild.

"We'll all go inside, Gallagher can sign the contract, and then you can have your weatherwitch back."

"No." Rafe strode past me. By the time he reached Stevenson, the knife was on the ground and Stevenson was on his knees. The fisherman covered his head with his hands, huddled up as if he was in grave pain.

Rafe simply stood in front of him, cane in one hand, the other extended over Stevenson's prostrate form. "You will leave us alone. Mother and I will not join with you, no matter what."

Something caught my eye. A running form from the direction of Front Street. "Rafe, watch out."

The person, whoever it was, flung a ball of witchfire at Rafe, who ducked out of the way. I took a quick shot in the runner's direction. The blast knocked me back a step and caused the runner to scream. Grabbing Margaret's arm, I yelled, "Get to the cab."

Jerking the door open, I propelled Margaret in, then ran to the driver. "I've got twenty dollars if you can get us out of here fast."

More runners were coming and Rafe still stood over Stevenson.

"Rafe," I screamed. "Now."

He ran to the cab more quickly than I would have expected. More balls of witchfire flew, landing on the damp street and sizzling out. For the moment, I climbed up front with the driver. "Where do you want to go?" he said.

"Start moving before any more of them arrive and I'll tell you."

Fortunately, he was willing to follow such an incomplete set of instructions. He called the team of horses into action and found a gap in the Virginia

Street traffic. A pair of police officers appeared in front of us, possibly drawn by the flying witchfire, and I sunk down in the seat, hoping they wouldn't think it was unusual for the driver to have a companion.

"You really have twenty dollars, or were you just pulling my leg?" The driver kept his eyes on the team, but he grinned as he spoke.

I reached for my wallet. "Right here, Mr...."

"O'Sullivan, and you can keep it till we get where we're going."

I sat back. "Thank you."

"Where are we going, by the way?"

"Give me a moment," I said, wondering what he'd say if I asked him to stop the cab so I could consult with Rafe and Margaret. The horses were a fine pair, and they picked their way through the muck at a nice crisp pace. "I don't know your city well, and it's too late to go back to where we came from."

"Ay?"

"Never mind. Take us to your best hotel, or the best one that you think might have two rooms." We'd need one for Margaret and a second for Rafe and me to share. I was willing to bet the cost of the rooms that Stevenson and his cronies wouldn't think to look for us someplace extravagant. "And, if you wouldn't mind doing me one favor?"

"For twenty beans, I guess I owe you at least one."

"If the man who hired you before us comes sniffing around, you don't know who we are, and you don't remember where you took us."

"All right," he said, again without taking his eyes off the road in front of us. "Reckon we should go to the Butler. That's where all the nobs want to go."

I should have brought more ready cash. "That'll do just fine."

At the next intersection he headed us right, or south, and soon we were in the heart of downtown. He stopped us in front of a sturdy looking block of a building. "This is it?" I asked.

"Those who strike it rich up north all want to stay here. I never have, myself, but I've heard plenty."

I saluted him with a finger to the brim of my bowler, a twenty in my other hand. "Thank you very much, Mr. O'Sullivan."

"You're very welcome, Mr...."

"Fairchild." I stifled a sigh. His eyes widened just a touch, but his smile stayed put. I clambered down from the front seat, grateful I'd been able to pull the bill out of my wallet despite my frozen fingers.

On opening the door to the cab, I found Margaret sitting hunched over, with her hands over her eyes, and Rafe as far away from her as possible in the small space. "What?"

"It's too late," she wailed. I had no idea what she was talking about, but I took hold of her arm and pulled her gently from the cab. Wrapping my arms around her, I tried to ask Rafe what the hell was going on without actually saying the words.

"It's a storm," he muttered on his way by. "They've set off a storm and she says we'll never get there in time to stop it."

Chapter Twenty-One

Half-carrying a distraught Margaret into the hotel lobby, I deposited her with Rafe and went to the front desk. The lobby was spacious, with the small touches — gilding, marble, silk — that I recognized. The exterior might look like an office building, but the lobby was definitely the sort of place the nobs would choose, to borrow O'Sullivan's words.

"Pardon me." I hailed the front desk clerk, who moved with the supercilious slowness of fine hotel keepers everywhere.

"Yes?" His hair was slicked back, his narrow nose ended in a point, and his lips were pursed, as if we smelled bad.

We probably did, but he didn't need to be so obvious.

His eyes widened when I let my smile flare. "I'm wondering if you have a suite available. We need two bedrooms and it would be lovely to have a sitting room to share."

He surveyed the three of us before answering. "We… do."

"Thank you. If you could have the bellhop show us the way, I'd very much appreciate it."

"It's… ten dollars a night."

I laid my last twenty on the marble counter. "Fortunately, I have enough. Please have supper brought up, along with a bottle of wine. And…" I fingered another five. "There'll be a bit extra if you can scare up a pipe and some tobacco."

I half-expected him to hold the bill up to the light to make sure it wasn't counterfeit. "I'll have them bring your change with dinner."

"Oh no, keep it with my regards." I hoped the amount wasn't small enough to insult him. His expression didn't change and he rang a bell, which brought a young man in the hotel's dark green uniform running.

"He'll see to your bags, as well."

I didn't let my smile fade one whit. "It'll just be us, I'm afraid. Our overnight kit is… temporarily unavailable."

The Lighthouse Keeper

Ignoring the way his eyebrows rose, I followed the bellhop, herding Margaret and Rafe over to the elevator. Margaret's expression was mutinous and Rafe's jaw was clenched so tight it made his molars squeak. I was reasonably sure that neither liked my plan, but at that moment, I didn't care. My magic might not compare with theirs, but if I could buy us some respite, I surely would.

The elevator took us to the top floor. The hall was thickly carpeted, with the kind of hush that would be difficult to disturb. It had been years since I'd been in an atmosphere that so clearly spoke of wealth and I'm ashamed to say the scent of furniture polish and dollars relaxed something deep inside me. I could deal with my companions' protests as long as I was promised a meal, a smoke, and a good night's sleep.

The bellhop stopped in front of a door and handed me the key. He left with a dollar warming his palm, and I let us in.

We were in a comfortable room with a merry fire in the fireplace, deep carpet underfoot, and a dining table with enough space for four. A loveseat and a pair of comfortable chairs faced the fire, and there were doors on either side that must lead to the bedrooms. I exhaled slowly, waiting for...

"What are we doing here?" Margaret sounded exhausted, as if she'd been taken against her will, trapped in an underground room, then snatched back in a blaze of witchfire.

261

"We're getting a good night's sleep," I said briskly. "We're each going to have a bath, we're going to have a decent meal, and we're going to go to bed. In the morning, we'll row back to the lighthouse."

"Not if the storm hits first."

That would cause a problem. I crossed my arms, searching for a way around it. Rafe, meanwhile, had said nothing. He stood so still I wondered whether he'd shatter if I touched him.

A pair of electric lights glowed on either side of the fireplace, their reflection sparkling in the windows that lined two walls. The suite must occupy a corner of the building. The closest window overlooked city lights. I walked over to the windows on the other wall. They showed a narrow strip of downtown, then unending blackness.

"Which direction is the storm coming from? Because we're on a corner, and the windows look west and south."

"I'm not sure." She grimaced as she spoke. "Honestly, most times the weather here comes from the southwest."

That was encouraging. "Do you need to be at the lighthouse in order to affect the weather?"

"Of course not," she snapped. "I simply need to touch the air."

"Good. Take a bath and have a decent supper, then we'll open one of the windows and you can set a protection spell that'll slow the thing down until we can get to the lighthouse."

Hands clasped in front of her, she caught her lower lip between her teeth. Her thoughts whirred behind her eyes, though I couldn't be sure the direction they were headed.

"Okay," she said finally. "But let me start the spell now."

"Are you strong enough? You've had a challenging day."

She waved off my concern. "Just get a window open."

Reluctantly — because, Lord, I'd just started warming up — I raised the sash on one of the two windows closest to the corner. Margaret leaned out, one hand propped on the sill and the other tracing sigils in the air.

For his part, Rafe still stood frozen in the center of the room.

"Why don't you go bathe," I suggested. He blinked but did not otherwise respond.

"Rafe?" I approached, close enough to touch him, though I refrained.

"How do you stand it?" He forced the words out through clenched teeth.

"Stand what?"

"So far," he said. "From the earth, I mean."

"Hmm…" I scrambled for an idea that would help someone so grounded in earth magic. "When you came here for school, how did you manage?"

"Dirt."

"What?"

"I kept dirt in my pocket."

We'd passed a couple of planter boxes on our way through the front door. I put my hand on his arm, surprised to feel him trembling. "I'll bring you some. Hold on for a moment."

I hadn't yet removed my overcoat, so I put my hat back on and pocketed the key. The elevator moved much too slowly, but as soon as humanly possible I returned with…

"Dirt."

I'd filled my handkerchief with soil from the front planter box. Rafe took it from me, his cane tumbling to the floor so he could cup the parcel in both hands. His shoulders relaxed, and some of the tension left his jaw.

"This will help," he said. "Thank you."

He tied the corners of the handkerchief in a knot and tucked the whole thing away in a fold of his cloak.

"Go bathe. Dinner should be here soon."

He went to the bathroom, and in a moment I heard the tap run. We'd each have a turn in the bath, and everyone's mood should improve by then.

Dinner arrived while I was struggling to force my clean body into the same dirty clothes I'd been wearing. Food gave me the impetus I needed to get dressed, although I could not bear to shove my feet into my boots, despite having wiped off the muck from the streets. Soon the three of us were seated at the dining table, each with a plate laden with pork chops, apples, and creamy potatoes. Margaret poured water from the pitcher they'd provided, and I poured the wine.

Margaret's hair was down, her long braid trailing on the floor. Rafe wore all black, though he'd left the cloak in the closet. I felt shabby and poorly put together. I'd also need to visit the bank before heading to the lighthouse. Granted, there'd be no place to spend it when we got there, but I'd feel better with a full wallet.

For a while, none of us had much to say, too busy carving up the pork chops and downing the wine. Once the first blush of hunger abated I dared pose a question to Margaret. "We know they got into the house," — despite the wards that should have stopped them — "brought you here, and hid you in the Old City tunnels for a time."

She sighed, spearing a bit of pork with her fork and swirling it around on her plate. "It was Stevenson and two others. They didn't even use magic, just a bit of chloroform on a rag to knock me out." Another sigh, this one deeper than the first. "I'd rather not talk about it."

I covered her hand with mine. "I'm so sorry we couldn't protect you."

That earned me a raised eyebrow and a frown. "Oh, take off the hair shirt. I feel stupid for not doing more to protect myself. Stevenson's no more threat than a hound dog, but there was someone else…" She blinked and looked away. "Someone's directing their bad comedy, someone who's both very smart and very strong."

"Oliver Stevenson did seem to have more resources than our first meeting with him would have indicated."

Margaret stirred the potatoes on her plate, glancing at the window periodically, as if she expected a devastating storm to hit at any moment. Rafe paused between bites, his expression darkening behind those amber lenses. "That tells us we need to be prepared for anything."

"Should we be recruiting help? I could wire Madam Munro."

"No." His scowl should have made me cautious.

I've never been good at being cautious. "Hypothetically, when we get back to the lighthouse tomorrow and the storm hits, Margaret will be occupied. As it's almost Samhain, you'll be busy trying to prevent Martin from doing anything devastating. If Stevenson and his crew of unknown assailants show up, either Della and I face them alone or you have to stop looking for the amulet."

"Mother and I have managed all these weeks," he said. "If you don't want to help us, then please stay here where it's safe."

"That's not what I mean." His remark stung harder than I let on. "But you can't do it all. We need help."

No one thought that idea required any further discussion. The word "help" sat in the air, as flaccid and impossible as a fish out of water.

Rafe might not think he needed help, but he was wrong. A handful of men throwing witchfire could do untold amounts of damage. If they somehow disabled the light, our problems would worsen.

The solution was simple. Before we left in the morning, I'd tell the others that I needed to make a visit to the bank, and while there, I'd find a telegraph office and send a message to Madam Munro.

Rafe might not like it — in fact, I had to stop myself from imagining Rafe's reaction — but it was the only way.

With that settled in my mind, I went back to enjoying my wine. Margaret soon murmured that she'd be retiring for the night, leaving Rafe and me alone.

"How was your dinner?" I asked, an opening salvo to what I hoped would be a more personal conversation.

"Rich." He took a sip of wine that did little more than wet his lips. "I'm used to simpler fare."

I eased back in my chair, giving my full belly more room. "As am I, though every now and then it's nice to have something fancy."

He shrugged, and we both grew quiet. It was companionable enough, though curiosity and something like tension underlaid the silence. We would be sharing a room, sharing a bed. I wondered if Rafe had ever done that before.

I'd soon find out.

The fire gave a loud pop, making us both jump. Wine sloshed onto the linen tablecloth.

"How will we clean that?" he asked, sounding more concerned than the situation warranted.

"The hotel laundry will take care of it." I tossed off the rest of my wine. "I'm not sleepy enough for bed yet. Shall we read?"

The room had a small bookcase, and while I hadn't perused the titles yet, I imagined it would be full of the sort of morally important stuff that I'd read in my college English Literature classes.

"You may read. I'll just..." His voice trailed off.

I found the little twig he'd given me, the one I'd changed into a revolver. "Here. I imagine you don't have the tools, but maybe you can plan what you'd make out of this."

"You turned it into a gun." He rolled the thing in his hands, taking its measure. "And your magical gun shot real bullets."

The Lighthouse Keeper

I cocked my head, as usual both glad and disappointed he couldn't see my grin. "My magic gun looked real enough to Stevenson's friend, so he believed the bullets were real."

"So you didn't shoot a real bullet? He screamed as if he'd been hit."

"Mm-hmm. He must have a particularly strong imagination." I tried hard to disguise my gloating, because after all, my power paled in comparison to Rafe's. "Let's go sit close to the fire and I'll read to you."

"You don't have to—"

I covered his hand with mine. "I want to. Come sit closer to the fire."

A moment later, I crouched in front of the bookcase. Most of the books would have been at home in a classroom, but the end of the lowest shelf held a handful of paper dime novels. "Oh, here we go. Nicholas Carter."

Rafe settled into one of the chairs. The front desk clerk had sent a pipe and a bag of tobacco with dinner, and I took the time to fill the bowl and light it before I started reading. "This one is called *A Dead Man's Grip*. That sounds intriguing."

Sputtering into his wineglass, Rafe waved me on. I stayed on the floor, settling cross-legged, the book open in my lap. "Do you smoke?" I held the pipe out to him.

He took it from me, drawing a deep inhale. "Nice." He exhaled a stream of smoke, then handed the pipe back to me. I took another drag, exceptionally excited that my lips touched where his had been. After sharing another puff, I began to read. Nicholas Carter was a detective, and soon we were deep into his adventure.

At the end of a chapter, I paused to take a sip of wine.

"Mother never read stories like this." Rafe wasn't smiling, exactly, but for once he wasn't radiating tension. He'd taken charge of the pipe so I could juggle the book and my glass of wine. The rich scent of tobacco added the perfect grace note to the scene.

"There are quite a few of these. I'll have to bring some with us back to the lighthouse." My cheeks flared with heat as soon as the words left my mouth. It was unlikely we'd have time for dime novels between now and Samhain, and after that? Well, one way or the other we'd have solved the problem of the Ferox Cor, and I would have no other reason to stay.

The thought left me feeling hollow.

If Rafe noticed my faux pas, he did not let on. "The supply boat used to bring us new books every so often. They haven't lately."

"Why not? They should." I passed him the pipe, my attention fully on the way his lips wrapped around the stem.

The Lighthouse Keeper

He reclined in the chair, his body relaxed, his knees spread. "Maybe we'll ask if they can bring your Nicholas Carter books."

They weren't mine, but it didn't matter. He handed the pipe back and I opened the book, only to be interrupted.

"So, I wonder if I should sleep out here."

I glanced at Rafe, amused by the color in his cheeks. "I assumed we'd share the second bedroom."

"You... Oh."

"We don't need to" — I got caught on whether to say what I meant out loud — "we can just... sleep."

"Of course."

"Unless you want to do more."

There was a long pause, full of unsaid words. "I'm not... Understand... I..."

Could this gentle soul possibly be the surly man I'd first met? Laying the pipe on the hearth, I crawled in his direction. "Samhain is the day after tomorrow, and from what I can tell, the world might end at the stroke of midnight. Let us enjoy each other this evening." *Because we might not have another chance.*

He exhaled with something like relief. "I would like that."

I reached him, putting a hand on each knee. "Where shall I begin?"

"My... inexperience has me at a loss, so perhaps we should move to the bedroom."

271

My grin would have made a blind man blink. "Perhaps we should."

I scrambled to my feet and reached for his hand. Our fingers intertwined and together we went to the bedroom, leaving the fire to burn itself out.

It's possible I felt a twinge of guilt, not for seducing him, but for neglecting the considerable problems we faced. At the same time, I was heartily tired of feeling frightened. In one way or another, fear had been weighing on me since I left San Francisco, and for this island of time, I wanted to let everything go.

The door was locked, no one knew where we were, and the anonymous voice in my head had quieted.

I closed the bedroom door behind us and turned to face Rafe Gallagher.

The only light came from a triangle of grey where the thin moonlight snuck under the overlapping window curtains. We didn't need any more than that, and anyway, the darkness equalized things. The bed was a dark mass in the center of the floor, with what I assumed were very fine pieces of wooden furniture placed along the walls.

Truly, though, all my attention was on Rafe.

He was a mere shadow in the darkened room. First, I reached for his glasses, shushing him when he gasped in surprise. From there, I moved to his shirt, delicately undoing the buttons closest to his throat.

The Lighthouse Keeper

His smoky herbal scent intoxicated me, and my breath came faster.

"Where's the dirt?" I didn't want him to lose his composure while we were...

He brought it from a pocket.

"Will you be okay without it for a little while?"

Rafe put a hand on either side of my waist, holding me in place. "As long as you're here. Your touch, your taste, your glorious spirit will sustain me."

"So much to live up to," I murmured. If I met that black gaze, I'd come undone. Instead, I paid careful attention to the buttons on his shirt, sliding each through the fabric hole with trembling fingers. His breath came quicker and I paused for a moment to press a kiss at the base of his throat. His skin tasted of salt and he shivered in a most satisfying way.

"I never thought something like this could happen."

I grinned against his skin, his soft chest hair brushing my chin. "You've had other things on your mind." I moved lower, sinking to my knees and unbuttoning his fly. He wore nothing under his trousers.

"What are you—"

I cut off his words by taking his prick in my hands. "I'm going to show you something." *And make very sure you enjoy every single moment.*

He'd been firm when I reached him, but now he was stiff and hard. "You can't," he said, his voice more of a wheeze, though the grip he had on my shoulders made it impossible to move away.

I wrapped my lips around the head of his prick, running my tongue across the slit. *Oh yes, I most certainly can.*

I swallowed him further. He whimpered, one hand twisting my hair, as if he couldn't decide whether to hold me in place or pull me away. I held the base of his shaft, my other hand teasing his balls. From here, his scent was less smoke and more herbal. I inhaled deeply, trying to squirrel that memory away.

"This—"

Whatever he'd meant to say was lost when I pulled off, then swallowed him down again.

"Vincent," he gasped. "You undo me."

His words made me so hard it hurt. I couldn't unbutton my own trousers without taking my hands off him, so I stifled my own need. His prick was long and lean, like the rest of him. I couldn't take all of him in without gagging, but I sucked what I could, finding a steady pace.

A burst of sour salt hit my tongue and he gave a garbled cry. I froze, tightening my grip on his shaft. Slowly I allowed him to slide from my mouth. "Not yet, love."

Both of us breathing hard, I gave his thighs a little shove. He leaned back on his elbows, and for a moment I wanted more light. I wanted to clearly see his debauched expression, to trace the shadow of hair that covered his chest and trailed down to his cock and balls.

I sat back on my heels, unbuttoning my own shirt and tugging his trousers down around his boots.

"You glow," he whispered, which made me chuckle.

"Just wait, Rafe Gallagher." I rose to my feet, eager to lose the rest of my clothing. When I stood before him naked, I said, "Now, what do you see?"

"A gift, one I'd never hoped to receive." He growled the words. "Come here. I want more of you."

I could no more ignore his command than I could fly to the moon. I went to him, my knees between his thighs, my hands on his shoulders. He lay back, pulling me with him. My body fit perfectly against his, our pricks pressed between our bellies.

His hands were everywhere, stroking my back, my shoulders, gripping the curve of my ass. Brushing the hair away from his face, I looked into those dark eyes. I once thought a demon peered out through his eyes, but now I saw an old, old soul, one who'd been asked to see and do too much. With a sigh, I bent my head and met his lips in a sweet kiss.

Well, I'd meant it to be sweet, but as soon as our lips touched, he wrapped his arms around me, one hand holding my head, the other tight around my chest. He locked one leg across mine, truly trapping me.

Pinned against him, utterly safe, I gave him all I could, my tongue in his mouth, my hips thrusting hard against him. My spirit opening, allowing him in. He began to thrust, a little tentative for my taste, so I reached down, raising my hips so I could clasp both our cocks. My grip firmed and he followed my cue, thrusting harder.

With that, I let our bodies take over. I pushed free of his clasping arms, propping myself on one hand so I could change the angle. That allowed him to play with my nipples, to stroke my chest, as if he could memorize me by touch. *Those hands.* I'd never felt anything like his fingers on my skin.

His power swirled around us, and I wondered what would happen when he went over. Would he grimace? Cry out? Set us both on fire? My own pleasure was close to peaking. I gritted my teeth to hold it off, thrusting even faster.

It didn't take long.

He stiffened, head rocked back, his mouth open in a soundless cry. Power wrapped both of us in a shell of safety. His cock pulsed, his thick, warm spend running over the back of my hand. I stayed poised over him, thrusting gently, bringing him back from where he'd gone.

Only when he opened his eyes and smiled up at me did I let him go. *That smile! I would do anything to see that smile*. My need grew. I tightened my grip on my own cock, my thumb firm across the tip in the way that made me shiver, and began thrusting.

Two strokes. Four. Pleasure grabbed me and gave me a rough shove into the abyss. Almost immediately, my prick was too sensitive to touch, so I used both hands to brace myself over Rafe, my head hanging low against his.

As he relaxed, his power calmed, settling over us like an embrace. "You are a wonder, Vincent Fairchild," he said. "I thought I would always be alone until I saw your beautiful spirit."

His words made me feel as fragile as a butterfly's wing and I bravely met his gaze, tracing his brows with my fingertip. "We've barely scratched the surface, love." My voice cracked, some unnamed emotion getting the better of me. I paused to clear my throat. "I have a few more tricks before we're done."

"Hmm." His breathing deepened, and I gingerly rolled off to lay beside him. My skin tingled as his power faded away. I'd clean us up as soon as the strength returned to my legs. In the meantime, I let his words echo in my mind. You are a wonder. *You* are a *wonder*. When had anyone said that about me before?

Never.

It might just be sex talk, but I hung onto it anyway. My other lovers had been there for my last name or my pretty face. Rafe had no use for either. If I was a wonder to him, I'd hold onto that for all I was worth.

Chapter Twenty-Two

Rafe woke up with the sun, which meant I did, too. I could have slept longer, but decided he deserved another lesson in pleasure. Soon we were tangled and sweaty. I couldn't wipe the smile from my face, though when he drifted off to sleep, I did not.

Instead, I washed and dressed and scratched a note on the hotel stationery. No sound came from Margaret's room and I risked her unending ire by cracking open her door. I peeked inside long enough to determine that she was there and hadn't been stolen from us again, and with that reassurance, I let myself out of our rooms.

A different clerk had command of the front desk, an older man whose hairline had receded to near baldness. A fringe of grey circled his head, making him look like a very well-dressed monk.

The lobby was empty except for the two of us. I approached the desk but he didn't look up from his book. "Excuse me," I said.

Was he hard of hearing, too? I rang the bell. "Excuse me?"

Still he continued reading. If I'd been in a thieving mood, I would have gone for the cashbox, just to see if I could get a reaction. Instead, I went around the desk and put my hand on the center of the book.

"Excuse me."

"What?" He jerked the book away from me. "What the hell are you doing?"

"I'm asking you a question, though you're lucky I didn't snatch the cash box while I was at it."

He shot a glance in the box's direction. "What do you want?"

"Are you always so helpful?

His only response was a glare.

Brushing the hair from my face, I made an attempt at charm. "I'm so sorry to disturb you, but I'm wondering if you could point me to the nearest telegraph office."

"Won't be open yet."

The Lighthouse Keeper

I pulled my watch out of my vest pocket. Nearly eight o'clock. "If you could please tell me where to go, I can be there when it does open."

I had every intention of asking Madam Munro for more help and hang the consequences. Begrudgingly, the desk clerk gave me an address, and with even less enthusiasm, he gave me directions to find it. Ordinarily, I would have tipped someone for their help, but I was out of cash. He didn't deserve it, anyway.

I'd have asked for directions to the nearest bank, but given his surly attitude, I hoped I would just stumble over one. Walking quickly to dodge the exasperating rain, I accomplished my tasks.

A telegraph went off to Madam Munro and a signed bank note restocked my wallet. *Thank you, Grandma Fairchild.*

I returned to the hotel to find both Rafe and Margaret dressed and waiting for me. She sat at the dining table, tapping an annoyed little rhythm on the note I'd left.

He stood in the middle of the room, arms crossed, scowl as black as the charred remains of our fire. A bulge in one pocket was likely the bag of dirt he'd needed to calm down.

Neither of them spoke, which was its own accusation. "I had some errands to run."

My words had little effect. I gave a sigh and asked if they were ready to leave. They were, and it was a very disgruntled group that rode the elevator down to the lobby. I returned our room key to yet another clerk, this one younger and more civil.

"Shall we book a cab?" I eyed the rain with reluctance.

"We can walk," Rafe said at the same moment Margaret responded.

"If you wish."

I shrugged. "Two against one. We'll get a cab." I caught the bellhop's attention and set him on the task. We might have made a motley crew, but the dollar I'd flashed was real enough, and soon we were ensconced in a decent carriage. The driver might have looked askance when I told him our destination was Ballast Island, but again, the sight of green inspired him to the task.

We'd barely started rolling when Margaret asked, "So where did you go, exactly?"

"To the bank, for one thing. This little adventure made a dent in my wallet."

"We could have bunked in the rowboat," Rafe said, as if that idea had actual merit.

I bit back a sarcastic reply. "I figured Oliver Stevenson wouldn't look for us in the most expensive hotel in the city, and since we're all still together, I'd say it was a good call."

Also, I'd needed a few moments of peace, although I didn't admit that.

"He wouldn't have found us anyway."

The Lighthouse Keeper

Ignoring Rafe's muttered reply, I focused on Margaret. "I also found a telegraph office and sent a request for help to Madam Munro."

"You did what?" Rafe might have been annoyed to wake up alone, but now he was angry.

"Asked for help." I carefully articulated each word, and if I drew on my family heritage, no one would fault me. Rafe angry was impressive. Rafe angry in a small carriage was a threat to life and limb.

"You should not have done that." He thundered the words, his expression black.

I could not afford to back down. "Why not?"

"We don't need help."

"Lord knows we do." I glanced at Margaret. "You see it, don't you?"

She met my gaze for the briefest moment, then turned her attention to her hands clasped in her lap. "Let's just get back to the lighthouse."

Not the response I'd hoped for, but it would have to do. Rafe sulked in his corner. Margaret made herself very small next to him on the bench. Across from them, I watched the rain splatter against the carriage window.

I didn't have Rafe's ego and knew enough to ask for help when I needed it. I occupied myself with that self-righteous thought and others like them all the way to the island. Once there, we claimed our canoe — I gave the old man who'd watched it a five dollar bill — and headed for the lighthouse.

I rowed, Rafe brooded, and Margaret sketched sigils in the air.

Our return to the lighthouse was without fanfare. Della appeared on the lawn, likely summoned by the sound of our voices. Well, my voice, anyway. Rafe hadn't said a word the whole trip and Margaret had spent the time watching the sky as if expecting the Four Horsemen of the Apocalypse to descend at any moment.

After making the rowboat disappear, Rafe went straight to his workshop and with a sigh, I let him go. I wasn't surprised by the way he'd shut me out, in fact, I'd half expected it.

He'd fit my body better than any other man I'd been with, but he kept so much of himself walled off that I doubted I'd ever truly reach him.

Still, his rejection stung.

His rejection and the sudden reemergence of that sense that there was a pebble in my shoe. Not a real stone, but something in my mind that shouldn't be there.

You didn't really believe he cared, did you?

That voice. I bit back a curse. Della and Margaret had disappeared into the tower, Rafe had shut me out, and I stood in the rain at the edge of the beach.

He doesn't care about the only things you have that are of any value.

Somehow the voice turned my own words back on me, and it made me want to scream. I stifled the impulse to run into the woods, figuring that would be my biggest mistake.

Besides, I couldn't be sure if the impulse to run was my own, or if it had been planted by the voice. My own nature would have me get under cover as quickly as possible, so that's what I did.

I hung up my coat and hat and made my way to the kitchen, the only source of warmth in the house. Della came in a few moments later, her scowl nearly as black as her son's.

"You have no idea the trouble you've caused, do you."

She hadn't asked a question, so I didn't answer her.

"It was all I could do to keep Rafe from chasing you off, that first day, and now you've invited more strangers."

I smacked the table, a gesture so out of character I startled myself. "Della Gallagher, tomorrow is Samhain." I listed the dangers we faced: the storm, the Seattle Council, the Ferox Cor. "I'm not willing to risk losing any one of you." The rough edge to my voice shut me up before I said anything stupid.

"But the more strangers who come here, the higher the chance that they'll take him." Her distress matched my own; exceeded it, even.

"Take who?"

"Rafe," she all but shrieked. "How many witches do you know who possess his strength? And how long do you think he'll survive if they lock him up in a city? Rafe's earth magic is a precious thing. They'll take it and pervert it and put it to their own uses."

"Wait." I was sincerely confused. "You notified Madam Munro first."

Some emotion, anger or something fiercer, hardened her features, except for her eyes. Her eyes flared like blue fire. "I did, and now I see what a mistake I made."

Her words drove me back a step. "You really believe that?" I had to blink back some unexpected emotion. "I apologize for upsetting you."

"But not for telegraphing Munro?"

Her words burned but my conviction did not waver. "No, ma'am. Not for that."

Before either of us could find an appropriate response, we were distracted by the sound of yelling.

Margaret and Rafe stood on the lawn, embroiled in an argument for the ages.

"What have you done?" Margaret waved a hand in the air, gesturing at everything or nothing at all.

She did draw my attention to the waves, which were crashing violently against an unseen barrier some twenty feet or so offshore. The sky roiled overhead, though the air around us was calm. Rafe's scowl would have frightened a saint, but he otherwise ignored her question.

Margaret, though, was not one to back down from a fight. "You set a protection spell strong enough to hold off the storm. You must have."

Rafe crossed his arms, his gaze directed over her head. "I did."

"Well, you must undo it. I cannot fight the storm if I cannot feel it."

Della brushed passed me, stopping between the other two. "What do you mean?" she asked Margaret.

The weatherwitch ran a weary hand over her forehead. "Look around. The storm cannot reach us."

"That's good, isn't it?"

Margaret waved off my question. "We may be safe, but others..." Her voice trailed off. Shaking herself, she raised a finger at Rafe. "We have no way of knowing how large this storm is, and while the people in the city may be safe, there could be fishermen caught up in it, or householders along Salmon Bay. This thing is big enough to kill people, and someone needs to stop it. *I* must stop it."

"I had to make the spell strong enough so that no one could break through." Rafe's tone lacked conviction.

Margaret didn't immediately press her advantage. "Which made sense, when you knew you were leaving your mother here alone."

I stifled a laugh. His pride would have had him make the ward as strong as possible, whether or not we were leaving. I might not know Rafe Gallagher well, but I knew that much.

Rafe let his arms fall to his sides. "How long will you need?"

"To fight this?" Margaret threw her arms out wide. "I have no earthly idea."

"I can't leave the wards down indefinitely."

Lord, he was stubborn. "No one's going to be able to get through this monster." I found myself shouting, too. "You can restore them the minute the wind dies down."

Della came to stand beside me. "You could even help her, Rafe."

"How?" He imbued that word with so much suspicion I almost laughed.

"You can add to her magic with yours."

Della was a Baron, so I believed her, but still Margaret and I shared un uncertain glance. Margaret gave a slight shake of her head, then faced Della wearing an expression of sturdy common sense.

Or stubbornness. I wasn't sure.

"I don't know that I'll need help, as long as the ward comes down so I can touch the wind." She tipped her head, showing off her firm jaw, an obvious display of resolution.

Della crossed her arms, the same posture her son had adopted, though her words were conciliatory. "Break the spell, Rafe."

The Lighthouse Keeper

For a moment, his jaw worked as if he would argue. With a huff, he turned toward the tower. "I'll do it from up there."

Margaret followed him, her shoulders squared and her head held high. I would never doubt her capability, but this storm was obviously a monster. Perhaps she should have taken Rafe up on his offer.

Once the door closed behind them, Della and I exchanged uncertain glances. "Should we go?" she asked, waiting for my response.

Of all of them, I was the least necessary, but I couldn't have stayed away. "Come on."

Halfway to the tower, a gust of wind slammed into us. Doors and windows rattled and the rush of air screamed under the eaves. A torrent of rain had me and Della scuttling to reach the tower door.

Once inside, I paused to catch my breath. Thunder rumbled, so close to us I jumped. Lightning flashed almost immediately after, leaving me blind and surrounded by the smell of ozone. Since I wasn't likely to truly breathe until this was over, I followed Della up the steps.

Margaret was outside on the widow's walk. Rafe stood at the railing, close to her, but not close enough to interfere. Della waited in the doorway, where I joined her. The wind tore at our clothing and hair. Margaret leaned out, one hand gripping the rail, the other held high, gesturing, spelling, doing what she could to divert this monster.

A clap of thunder had me quaking. Lightning flashed, this time close enough to knock Margaret over. She fell, landing awkwardly against the wall, but just as quickly she got a hand on the railing and pulled herself up. She screamed, both hands raised.

The storm ignored her, pelting us with rain. I was chilled to the bone, my shivers a combination of cold and fear. Cold, because I was soaked to the skin.

Fear, because that voice was back, telling me we'd never survive.

Or were those doubts my own?

More thunder. Another bolt of lightning, this time so close it sent sparks along the railing. Margaret kept her feet, though her head was bowed, her hands wavering. She relaxed one arm, allowing it to drop to her side. She fought, but she was fading.

I grabbed Rafe's arm. If Della said he could channel his power, then he could, and if we waited for Margaret's permission, the voice might be right. She might not survive the fight. I took hold of her hand. So cold, as if even the memory of warmth had been driven from her body. Rafe took my other hand, and there, in the midst of the downpour, he released his power.

It spun through me, a golden band I could see plainly when I closed my eyes. It wrapped around one arm, looped across my shoulders, and raced along the other arm to get to Margaret.

That golden band restored her.

The Lighthouse Keeper

The wind lessened the slightest bit, giving me hope in their combined magic. The storm was right overhead. Nevertheless, they hung on, despite the lashing rain, the fearsome wind. Fueled by Rafe's magic, Margaret battled that storm, with me the conduit and Della the witness.

When the wind finally lost its lethal power, Margaret collapsed. I caught her on the way down, and I'm ashamed to admit that Rafe had to catch me. We got Margaret inside and worked to revive her. Rain still fell, but it was more of a shower and the wind had all but given up.

Rafe's face was grey with exhaustion, but as soon as Margaret roused, he went outside to reset the protection spell. He'd only been gone a minute or two when he burst through the door. "Vincent, come."

Chapter Twenty-Three

The sun had set sometime during the monster storm, and the leftover clouds obscured the moon. I flicked my fingers to make a witchlight. I was done with fumbling around in the dark.

Clenching my teeth to keep from shivering, I first surveyed the scene, wondering what Rafe wanted me to see. Waves crashed on our beach, as high a tide as I'd seen since we arrived. The breeze spattered us with saltwater spray and the forest murmured, branches swaying.

You'll never give Rafe the help he needs.

I choked back a protest, and again I came close to telling Rafe about the voice. He might know the source; I had my suspicions, terrible enough that I didn't want to speak them out loud.

"What do you see?" Rafe pointed toward the horizon.

I joined him at the railing, and sure enough, "A light, all on its own." I squinted, willing myself to distinguish something in the murk. "I can't see a boat, let alone someone holding the light."

"There's someone out there, though his spirit is faint. It looks like he's fighting the tide to reach us." He gripped the railing. "What the hell is he doing out there?"

"He needs our help."

He ignored me. "It could be anybody, friend or foe," he murmured.

"Still, we should help—"

"No. There's no way."

"We could get a rope and..." My voice faded as doubt overcame my best impulses.

"If we had a rope, what would we do with it?"

"Swim it out to him."

My evident sincerity made him laugh. "Neither of us is going to jump into storm-tossed waters to bring an unknown person a rope."

I dashed a hand across my face, wiping away salt spray. "Well, unless you also possess the power of flight, I don't see how else to get it to him."

Rafe was silent for a long moment. The light in the waves flickered. I feared we'd lost him, and I hated feeling so helpless. "Let's at least go down to the dock." I didn't beg, but it was close.

He turned and left before I could respond. Giving the flickering light a final glance, I followed.

Somehow, I reached the dock before him. He must have stopped in his workshop, because he came up behind me, his cane in one hand and a length of rope in the other.

"Do you still see him?"

I squinted into the darkness, sending hope to the stranger in the boat, afraid we were inviting trouble by bringing him to shore.

You always bring trouble. Always have. Always will.

The words landed like a punch to the gut, but I fought them off. They weren't true. They were lies conjured by an evil presence. My rational mind held firm, though deep down, I felt the truth. I did bring trouble. I didn't. *You do.* No.

Laughter echoed through my mind, so loud that I didn't notice the thing Rafe held out to me.

"Make this into a real bird." His tone of voice didn't invite argument.

I, of course, tried. "Why? I thought you didn't want to help whoever it is?"

Between the dark and the glasses, I couldn't read his expression. He turned away, making it even harder, and when he finally said something, it was too soft for me to hear.

"What?"

The Lighthouse Keeper

He took hold of my hand. "You're a better man than I am, so we should do what you say."

I blinked rapidly, my eyes wet with something besides rain. I had no idea how to respond, other than to admit I could be leading us both astray.

"Here," he said, releasing my hand. "Make this into a real bird."

I moved the witchlight closer. He shifted his cane from one hand to another and showed me one of his carvings, a bird, a gull most likely. I touched it and gave a push of power, and the thing blossomed into a full-grown gull, its white-grey feathers glowing in the darkness. Rafe whispered to it, words I couldn't understand, but when he picked up the end of the rope, the gull grabbed it in its beak.

He tossed the bird into the air and it took off, flying straight and true in the direction of the light. It cried out when it dropped the rope, and the sudden tension told us the man had caught it.

We ran to the end of the dock, and, working together, we drew the rope in. The rolling waves made keeping the tension steady a challenge but in time, we learned to adjust. The light came closer and, despite the darkness, the silhouette of man and boat became more obvious.

The rough, wet rope chapped my hands, opening up the blister that had healed so nicely. The saltwater stung and my shoulders ached, although I suspected Rafe did most of the work.

The little boat came close enough for us to see that the light we'd been watching was a witchlight. The man must be a witch, although I wasn't sure if that was a good thing or not.

Who would help you, really? No one. No one at all.

"Shut up," I snapped. If Rafe heard me, he gave no sign. An extraordinarily large wave broke over the dock, and for a moment the rope slackened. "We've lost him."

Sudden tension jerked the rope through my hands, tearing at my skin.

"He's still with us." Rafe gave a mighty tug and, with the help of another huge wave, the little boat came up to the dock.

Leaving me to hold the rope, Rafe raced toward the boat and grasped the prow. "Toss me a line."

The man in the boat did as he asked, giving me a momentary glimpse of his profile. My heart dropped, leaving only emptiness in my chest. That profile, the light hair. Rafe extended his hand and the man grasped it.

That must have taken the last of his strength, for when he hit the dock, he fell in a heap. I busied myself coiling the rope, as if I could put off the moment of awkwardness as long as possible.

Hoisting the man up, Rafe helped him from the dock. When they reached me, the man's smile confirmed my worst fear. "Vince? Is that you?"

The Lighthouse Keeper

Rutger Smit, my closest confidant and sometime lover, stood wavering on the dock. He reached for me and I clasped his hand with both of mine. "I can't believe you're here," I said.

As if deciding the man could stand on his own, Rafe stepped aside. Rutger stayed upright, his eyes light with amusement. "I wanted to surprise you."

His voice was hoarse, as if he'd been screaming at the waves.

"How did you survive the storm?"

His answering shrug was careless, maybe too careless. "Equal parts weather shields and prayer."

He sounded convincing enough and then I cottoned to the reason for his uncertainty. Rafe stood behind me, one hand on my shoulder.

Mine.

He didn't need to say the word out loud. I gave Rutger a sheepish grin. He squeezed my hand and let it drop.

"Let's get inside." I turned toward the house, which left me face-to-chest with Rafe. He stood so still it was like he'd been carved in stone. "To the house, Rafe," I murmured. His eyes were black pits, and salt scum spattered his glasses. When he still didn't move, I put a hand on his cheek. "We should go in."

He covered my hand with his, and while he didn't relax, he did turn toward the house. I'd have some explaining to do, but Rutger would understand.

At least I hoped he'd understand.

Five people made Della's little kitchen too crowded, but it was the only warm place in the house. The oil lamp didn't give off much light, so I added a pair of witchlights, floating them along the ceiling. After a round of introductions, I busied myself draping wet outer garments around the living room, where they'd either dry or freeze. Rutger's bag with a change of clothes had been lost at sea, so I showed him the bedroom and offered to let him wear some of mine.

Rafe's jaw tightened at that, and I had to remind myself that I was Rafe's first lover. And that he'd been raised in the woods. And that he was powerful enough to do real damage if pushed.

It didn't make me happy, but he subsided into a state of withdrawal. I'd talk to him later, too. First, though, we needed to figure out what the hell Rutger was doing here.

"I just telegraphed Madam Munro this morning. How did you get here so fast?"

We'd given Rutger a seat at the table in deference to his extreme exertion. Margaret had the other seat. Della had wanted her to stay in bed, but Margaret insisted on joining us.

"I left San Francisco two days ago," Rutger said. "Munro wanted me out of the way, and figured if I came here, I could keep you out of trouble."

The Lighthouse Keeper

Rafe's huff of annoyance was unmistakable. We stood side by side, leaning against the wall with me closest to the stove. I didn't respond, except to shift my weight closer to him. "Where were you? The last time I talked to her, Madam Munro said you were missing."

His expression sobered. "That's a story for another time. Suffice it to say that after finding me, she put the entire Council to work on figuring out what happened."

As much as I wanted to demand he tell me everything, I settled for an easy smile. Or, as easy a smile as I could manage with a growling lover at my side.

I would definitely have words with Rafe about his behavior, although part of me was secretly pleased that he cared about me so much.

Only a wild man brought up in the dirt could possibly care that much about you.

I closed my eyes, drawing in a deep breath. The voice lied. It had to be a lie. "Sounds like the telegraph I sent won't bring us the help we need."

Della tsked, her back to the rest of us. She stirred something on the stove, surrounded by the scent of a hearty stew.

Rutger gave an apologetic shrug. "Doubtful she'll send anyone, but, well, I'm here."

"And I'm very glad." I wasn't going to pretend Rutger and I weren't friends. Rafe would need to adapt.

Rafe spoke up, his voice rough and low. "What can you do?"

"I'm a ritual master." Rutger sat straighter in his chair. "I can do most anything, but it takes time to set things up."

I caught Rafe's wrist in my hand, spread my fingertips over his palm, and gave him an affectionate squeeze. "Aside from the storm tonight—"

"It's not over," Margaret said, interrupting me. "I've built a buffer around us and diverted some of its energy to both the north and the south, but it'll regroup and come at us again."

"Lord." Tension crawled up the back of my neck. "In addition to the storm, a group of witches are trying to form a Seattle Witches' Council. They want Della and Rafe to join, and they're quite troublesome about it. And—" I glanced at Rafe, inviting him to explain the Ferox Cor.

"Martin Gallagher may try to cross the veil at Samhain, to bind the spirit of the Ferox Cor and take it to the afterworld."

The implications of that made Rutger blink, and honestly, I blinked too. After Margaret and I had to fight for every bit of information, here Rafe was giving it away.

The Lighthouse Keeper

On the other hand, Samhain was tomorrow. Secrets were a luxury we no longer had time to keep.

"The Ferox Cor?" Rutger's confusion was short-lived. "And Martin? Isn't he your father?"

"He's not, and if he crosses the veil and fails to get back across, he'll be trapped here, bound to the Cor, a source of unending evil."

"Christ." Rutger fisted his hands on his knees. "How do we stop him?"

"The Ferox Cor is tied to an amulet. I must find that amulet and destroy it. That's the only way."

"I can see why you need help." Rutger might claim to be a ritual master, but his real skill was in organization. The wheels were turning in his head, and before long he'd be barking out orders. "Let me think. I can probably lay out a screen to prevent him from crossing, or even a small labyrinth to trap him in."

Della gave a grudging nod, though Rafe sat unmoved.

"Thank you, Rutger," I said. "I knew you could help us." Though we all needed rest before any of that happened. "Let's have dinner and bunk down for the night."

"Why?" Rutger protested. "We can't afford to wait."

I didn't raise my voice, but still I took control of the situation. "Why? We should eat because Della was kind enough to cook for us, and you should sleep because you've spent hours fighting a deadly storm, and so have Margaret and Rafe. Tomorrow we can start at first light." I didn't add that Rafe had been searching for the thing for weeks, if not longer, and the odds of finding it before dusk on Samhain were painfully low.

"He's right," Rafe said, his tone so definitive none of us argued with him.

Rutger looked from one face to another. He didn't agree, but he was adept at recognizing the common will. "All right. Whatever you're cooking smells delicious, Mrs. Gallagher."

Della served up five bowls of stew. None of them were overflowing, and she reminded us that the supply boat wouldn't arrive until tomorrow. "Didn't really expect two of you, let alone three."

I was in the process of thanking her when Margaret pointed out that the supply boat might not reach us due to the storm. That killed my appetite. When my offer to help clean up was rebuffed, I decided that sleep was my best option.

"You can have the small bedroom, Rutger. I'll bunk with Rafe."

In the moment of silence following that announcement, I had time to gauge everyone's reaction. Surprise from Della and Margaret, amusement from Rutger, and grumpy satisfaction from Rafe.

The Lighthouse Keeper

"The workshop's not as fancy as in here," he said, which had me biting back a sarcastic reply. I knew it would be uncomfortable, and I didn't care. One way or the other, my time here would be ending soon, and I wanted as much of Rafe Gallagher as I could possibly get.

Chapter Twenty-Four

We retired soon after that. Putting my wet overcoat back on took some self-discipline, but it was only a short distance between the house and the workshop. As soon as we were both inside, I stripped it off, shivering hard. Rather than fuss with an oil lamp, I sent two witchlights to the ceiling. Margaret might scold me for upsetting the atmosphere in China, or thereabouts, but these were exceptional times.

Rafe knelt in front of the small grate, clearing the ash from his last fire. Water droplets sparkled in his dark hair and his sodden black cloak hugged his frame. Despite the cold, I could admire the breadth of his shoulders and the way his muscles shifted as he stood.

"You need to get out of those wet things." I tugged on the edge of his cloak.

He smiled past me. "As soon as I dump this and bring in some coal."

There was a box of coal next to the ash pile, against the house's rear wall. "Be quick."

While he was gone, I struck a taper and started the fire with kindling, blowing on the crackling pile of dry branches. I'd never admit it to him, but I hoped Rafe and I would have some quiet time together, though sleeping here wouldn't be as luxurious as the bed at the hotel. There were still things I could show him. Many things…

I was smiling when Rafe returned with the coal. He knelt down next to me near the small grate. I eased onto my heels and he began setting chunks of coal on my merry little blaze.

"Mother scolded you good."

With his attention on the flames, his expression was impossible to read. I ran the day's events through my mind. "Oh, about the telegram? I didn't mean to cause you trouble."

"She gets more worked up than I do."

Behind their amber lenses, his dark eyes focused on me. "She seemed upset by the idea that the Council would try to make you move to the city," I said.

He turned back to the fire. "Maybe it's time I went."

"Well, if you do, I hope you'll let me be your guide." I responded to his somber tone with levity. Saying the words, however, proved to me how very much I meant them.

Embarrassed by the strength of my feelings, I put a hand on his shoulder and pushed myself up to my feet. "Where's the bedroll?" My voice had a husky edge, adding to my self-consciousness.

He rose, too, and by the light of witchfire and the grate, we spread out the sleeping mat and blanket. I did convince him to take off his cloak, and soon we were lying together in our underthings, covered by the quilt.

I rested my head on Rafe's shoulder, as if it were the most natural thing in the world. "We should sleep while we can," I murmured. "Tomorrow will ask more from us than we have to give."

"Your friend, Rutger…"

"My *friend* Rutger." I gave the word careful emphasis and took a measured breath. "We worked together in the liaison office."

"He called you Vince."

I winced. He'd noticed. "You could call me Vince, too. Some of my friends do."

He was silent for a while. "I prefer Vincent."

I nodded against his chest and he brought his arm around my shoulder, holding me tighter against his body. As if it had a mind of its own, my hand caressed his skin, my fingers teasing the sparse dark hair between his nipples.

"I still have moments when I think this isn't possible."

I nipped his skin. "It is. Granted, it's not as ordinary as if one of us were a woman, but so long as we keep private things private, we'll be all right."

Another silence, long enough for me to feel suspended in time. I'd let the witchlights go out, so the glowing coals were our only illumination. The wind threw an occasional spatter of rain at the windows, but without the terrifying force of this afternoon. My prick was at half mast, my desire simmering, content for now with closeness and quiet.

"Have you ever lain like this with Rutger?"

The question landed like a sour note. Not because I'd have to lie, but because it brought up memories of drunken fumbling in places I'd rather not remember. "No," I said, telling the absolute truth. "I've never lain like this with Rutger."

"Good." With no more warning than that, Rafe rolled over on top of me, bracketing me with his arms. "Assuming we make it through tomorrow, I'd like to do this again." He kissed me, hard. "And again." Another kiss, and this time he nipped my lower lip. "And again."

I found I had no argument for that, and my simmering desire boiled over. We clutched each other, forehead to forehead, grinding our cocks together. Our kisses had an element of attack, our shared passion burning hotter than the fire in the grate. Again, Rafe created a barrier between us and anything harmful, a shield against the outside world.

I held him as he grew rigid, his climax dragging a harsh cry from him, and he did the same for me. Yes, there was mess to clean up and the only water was not too many steps from ice, but later, lying in his arms with sleep closing in, I sent up a prayer to the Father or the Mother or whoever was listening, thanking them for this moment right here and right now.

It seemed we'd barely fallen asleep when Della raised a cry. "The light's off again. Rafe? Margaret? Someone come. The light's out."

Rafe was up and dressing before my sleep-fuddled mind comprehended Della's meaning. The coals had burned low and the windows were still dark. Setting off a witchlight, I followed Rafe's example. He slammed out the door before I'd managed to button my trousers. My pocket watch said it was nearly four, though it felt even earlier.

I'd promised Rafe this day would ask a lot from us, and it appeared I'd spoken the truth.

We found Della on the lawn. Overhead, the lighthouse tower was a darker shadow in the night. Any moonlight was blotted out by clouds and even the drag and rush of the waves sounded sullen.

"Margaret reset the winding mechanism before bed," Della said. "It shouldn't have stopped so soon."

Wordlessly, Rafe headed for the tower door, and all of us trooped up the stairs to the top level. There we found a smoking ruin where the winding mechanism had been.

"What on earth?" Della cried. We all stood and stared, as if transfixed by the damage.

"Impossible," Rafe murmured. "No one could have broken through the shielding spell."

Della reached toward the burned remnants of the mechanism. "Someone must have."

"Impossible." Rafe ran a hand over the scorch marks without touching anything. "There are remnants of magic." Fisting both hands, he all but shouted, "No one could have broken through that spell."

Because you distracted him. Somehow or other, you are at fault.

NO. My jaw clenched.

"Do you have a spare? Something we can replace this with?" Margaret's cool common sense brought us all to the task at hand.

Without speaking, Rafe went down the stairs more quickly than a man with a cane should have been able. I followed, and found him on the ground floor, kneeling in front of the only cabinet in the place.

"Gone." He sat back on his heels, hands clasped, shoulders slumped. "Whoever destroyed the mechanism must have taken it, too."

"You don't have spare parts?" I asked. Repairing the light took priority. We could figure out who disrupted Rafe's spell later. "I mean, they may have taken the replacement, but maybe we could build one. Do you have anything in your workshop that might help?"

To his credit, he shook himself and rose to his feet. "Yes, though there may still be pieces we're missing."

"If you can describe them, I should be able to create them. My magic's not strong enough to last for long, but it might give us time to come up with something more permanent."

He faced me, his expression terrifying. "First, I must repair the spell."

"But the light…" Della said weakly.

Rafe shook his head. "Give me a moment."

I was still struggling to come up with a reasonable counter-argument when he disappeared up the stairs.

He was back sooner than I expected. "The spell is unharmed. The wards are in place."

We all stopped, sorting through the implications of his words.

Margaret was the first to understand. "If they didn't break through the wards, then whoever destroyed the mechanism was here already."

Rafe nodded once. "And is still here."

The Lighthouse Keeper

I glanced around, as if expecting a gaggle of strangers to bust through the tower door.

"I should never have lowered the wards," Rafe snapped.

"You had no choice." Margaret raised her finger, her words sharp. "I could never have let that monstrous storm destroy everything around us while we stayed safe."

Rafe said nothing, his gaze on the floor. Della edged closer to Margaret, which gave me an idea. "We'll split up. You and I will repair the mechanism, and while we do that, your mother and Margaret can look for any clues as to whether there's someone else here."

"Someone else is most definitely here," Rafe said tersely.

"I agree, so the sooner we fix the mechanism, the sooner we can find them." I kept my tone calm, or as calm as possible, and as soon as I stopped speaking, Rutger came through the tower door.

"Everything all right?" he asked, blinking at us, as if his eyes were still fogged with sleep.

"Just a small problem," I said, speaking with more confidence than I really felt. "Someone destroyed the lighthouse's winding mechanism." I glanced at Margaret, not daring to look at Della or Rafe. Margaret's expression was a careful mask. "Despite the protection wards, which means it was someone inside."

"Della and I are going to take a look around, to see if we can find anyone." Margaret's tone was cold, direct. "Maybe you can help us."

"Happy to. Point me in the direction you want me to look."

For one awkward moment, we all paused, as if a large elephant had walked into the room along with my friend. Rutger looked like himself, the same man I'd worked with and spent time with after work. He could not have destroyed the mechanism. He couldn't have.

"Let's go." Margaret brushed Della's arm, her face hard with determination. "We'll get started."

She spoke with such assurance that even Della brightened. "We can also look for the spare mechanism. If our enemy is still here, then so is the part that they stole." They flanked Rutger and more or less marched him out of the tower.

"Wait here, Vincent," Rafe said. "I'll go to my workshop and see if I have any of the things we'll need."

"Bring a few pieces of wood that I can use to make the rest."

"I'll be right back."

Alone in the tower, I tried to imagine who could have done this. Had someone snuck in while we were aiding Rutger? No one should have survived that storm, yet since Rutger had, perhaps there was someone we missed.

Or perhaps Rutger…No. My mind refused to think so ill of my friend. There *must* have been someone we missed. Someone from the Witches' Council, who'd managed to both survive the storm and escape our notice. Oliver Stevenson was a waterwitch. He would have the power to navigate the waves, despite the storm.

But did he want to cause Rafe and Della trouble for neglecting to keep the lighthouse burning or was this an attempt to distract us from finding the amulet?

Neither thought was particularly comforting. We'd need to work quickly, before the interloper could cause any more trouble.

Rafe's return interrupted my train of thought. Sighing, I said, "We should get started."

"If you can make things that are the right shape," he said, "I'll add a spell to fix them in place."

"We'll get the light running and then we can all look for the interloper."

"And the amulet."

Rafe's reminder had me gritting my teeth. We were down to our last day.

"The system is really quite simple," Rafe began. "The winding mechanism draws a ten-foot weighted cable up the shaft and then releases it. The system is balanced like a clock, so that as the weight sinks, it rotates a clip that triggers the light every ten seconds or so."

"And it's the crank that was burned?"

313

"The crank and its connection to the light fixture." He opened a small box. "I didn't think to check for the weight at the bottom of the shaft. The cable is twisted metal, so it wouldn't burn, although the spell may have snapped it."

"Let me look." Leaving him to unpack his tools, I jogged up the stairs.

No one was in the tower, although the silence had a heavy, watching feel. As I climbed the steps, the hairs on the back of my neck rose, and I fully expected to see Martin Gallagher or some other apparition when I reached the top.

I did not.

"Hurry, Vincent," Rafe called from the stairwell.

His impatience tightened the tension in my shoulders. Gritting my teeth, I took stock of the situation as quickly as possible. The lamp itself appeared to be intact, the bulbs unbroken and their mirrored scrim in one piece. The base, however, was scorched, and the hand crank that wound the weighted cable was a pile of charred debris.

That actually helped me, because the top of the shaft was now open. At first all I saw was darkness, so I made a witchlight and sent it down.

The light moved alongside the cable, a thick metal rope maybe two inches in diameter. It reached the spot where the cable's fractured end splayed out. The weight must have fallen to the floor.

I ran back downstairs to find the base of the shaft. There was no opening. "I need a handsaw."

"Why?" Rafe sounded more distracted than truly argumentative.

"The weight is at the bottom of the shaft. I need to cut through the wood."

"I'm not sure…"

"A piece of wood will do."

He handed me a small piece of wood. "I'm going upstairs. We need to work faster."

"I'll do my best."

Your best is never good enough.

Closing my eyes, I forced that voice into a corner of my mind. I didn't have time for foolishness.

As I went about my task, Rafe's muttering hurried me along. I turned the wood Rafe gave me into a small saw and made an opening wide enough for me to slip my hand through. The weight was a heavy ball with a loop at one end for the cable. I took a minute to fix its dimensions in my mind, then enlarged the opening so it would fit.

"Got it." I carried the weight upstairs, the broken cable dragging on the floor.

"Damnation. We have no way of repairing the cable."

Lord. "I'll think of something."

He laid out a handful of metal cogs and another handle, while I glared at the two broken ends of the cable, trying to figure out a way to connect them. "If

315

we had some sort of glue… hmm… maybe rubber cement."

"Just make it work."

I bit my lip to keep from snapping back at Rafe. Yes, the situation was dire, but we couldn't afford to fight with each other. Wordlessly I went about my task, turning a piece of wood into a glob of rubber cement, smearing it over both ends, and sticking them together. The thing we didn't have was time to wait for it to dry.

"Can you make this solid?" I lifted the repaired section of cable and described what I'd done. His scowl never lifted, but, raising a hand, he sent a burst of power that rushed past me like a gust of wind. Just as fast, the rubber cement hardened.

Assembling the mechanism was a trial for both of us. Rafe spoke in terse phrases that landed like bullets, and I did my best to keep up. In a matter of moments, we were snarling at each other.

"No. Smaller." Rafe held a small cog in the flat of his palm.

I gritted my teeth and sent another push of power at the object.

He ran a fingertip along the teeth. "More of them."

Inhaling sharply, I readied myself for another try.

"Hurry."

"Lord, Rafe. I'm doing the best that I can."

"Well, do better."

I snatched the cog away from him. "Listen to me, Rafe Gallagher. I am not your enemy. Now calm down or we'll never get this done."

My tone of voice must have been more forceful than my words, because Rafe took a literal step back. "I… I apologize."

Swallowing my aggravation, I murmured, "Accepted." I gave the cog another push of power, increasing the number of teeth along its perimeter. "Is this better?"

"Yes, thank you." His voice gruff, he took the piece and fitted it into the replacement mechanism. "We need one more."

This time he wanted something the size of my palm and I transformed a small piece of wood into the thing he'd described.

"That's right," he said, running his finger along the teeth. "That will work."

I couldn't tell whether his restrained manner was due to true regret or if he was simply biding his time. Either way, we'd accomplished our task. The last time I'd stood up to Rafe, I'd ended up with a burned wrist. At least this time he'd apologized.

Once he tested the hand crank to make sure we had the balance right, he put a binding spell onto the entire mechanism, holding my spells in place.

"There," he said finally, the tower light flashing overhead. He ran a hand through his hair with a weak smile. "You did well."

"It was nothing."

He placed a heavy hand on my shoulder. "Don't disparage yourself. Not many could have done what we just did, and I am sorry for being an ass. I haven't had much chance to work with others."

Taking hold of his hand, I gave his fingers a squeeze. "I'm just glad we were successful."

Dawn had turned the clouds a sullen grey, reminding me of all we still needed to accomplish. "We should go," I said, although neither of us made a move to leave.

My stomach growled, and we both chuckled. "Must be time for breakfast."

He reached out and ran a fingertip down my cheek, an easy intimacy that made drawing a breath almost impossible. "We will find the one who did this and then we will find the amulet," he whispered. "And we will destroy them both."

I had no answer for that, so I pulled him down for a kiss. Madam Munro had made it very clear she wanted me to bring the Ferox Cor to her, but I knew full well why Rafe wanted to destroy it.

I also knew I couldn't please both of them.

Chapter Twenty-Five

R afe didn't want to wait for breakfast. He left me with the few tools and the extra wood he'd brought to the tower and went off to search the area for our uninvited guest. I promised to stow the stuff in his workshop, then join him in the search.

We'd come close to blows over rebuilding the winding mechanism, yet we'd avoided saying anything we couldn't take back. I was glad. Rafe and I might be brand new and terribly fragile, but I valued what we shared.

Do you value it enough to stay here forever? He will, you know. His spirit will be trapped here as sure as Martin Gallagher's.

"For pity's sake," I said aloud. "If you think you can distract me with your chatter, you're wrong."

Mostly wrong, anyway. The voice in my head, the one that wasn't my own, had taken on greater substance, a nearly-visible figure who sat right behind my eyes.

You'll do what I say when it's time. You won't have a choice.

Somehow that threat, along with the echo of laughter, upset me more than anything else. I might not be a powerful magician and most people might value my name over my person, but damnation. I rarely let anyone tell me what to do. Grappling with my determination, I strode along the gravel path to the workshop, the crashing waves an accurate counterpoint to the storm in my head.

The workshop door was unlocked and I didn't feel a spell's telltale pop when I stepped across the threshold. Rather than try to guess where to put the things I'd returned, I set the package of tools on the closest workbench.

A few coals still burned in the grate, warming the air somewhat. Rafe and Della said they'd searched everywhere for the amulet. But had they? At one point I'd thought the workshop was the most obvious place to hide the Ferox Cor. With that in mind, I surveyed the cluttered little room.

Might we have missed something?

The Lighthouse Keeper

Conscious of how little time we had left, I got to work. Over and under, in corners and on shelves. I had only a vague notion of what I was looking for; some kind of bejeweled box of a size to hold an amulet. Given that my image wasn't terribly specific, I opened every box I saw, as well as looking behind and under them.

Nothing.

Did you really expect to find something?

Ignoring the voice, I turned to Rafe's workbench. It had a set of drawers in the front, the kind that got increasingly large from top to bottom. The narrow top drawer held a selection of fine chisels. The second one seemed to be a repository for half-finished projects. A wolf emerged from a block of wood the size of my palm next to one wing and the long, narrow beak of a hummingbird half-carved from another cube.

The third drawer was stuck. No amount of tugging would open it. The lowest and deepest drawer held pieces of wood stacked neatly according to size. As the only one likely large enough to hold the amulet, I opened it fully to make sure there was nothing hiding in a back corner.

There was only wood.

The third drawer bothered me. Rafe must have searched it already, which tempted me to simply ignore it.

The man has a right to some privacy. What if it's holding such items as are useful for private acts of pleasure?

Those words might have been intended to upset me, but they only made me laugh. If it did hold such objects, I could hardly object. "I highly doubt that."

No one responded to my comment, which was just as well. After all, I'd been talking to a voice only I could hear.

There was no visible lock on the third drawer, though when I slid a narrow file along the top, something blocked the file at the halfway point. A peg? I tried from the opposite direction and hit the same obstruction.

Acting on a hunch, I opened the second drawer an inch or so and felt along the lip of wood beneath it. There, at the center, I found a button. Pressing it resulted in a click.

"Let's see…" I tugged on the third drawer. It still wouldn't open. I ran the file along the top, and this time it went the whole way, without getting stuck at the center.

"Okay." I sat back on my heels. "I could go get Rafe and see if he can open it. Or…" I stared at the offending wooden drawer front. My gift allowed me to change a thing into something else, but I'd only ever tried to change small things. "If the drawer front was made of glass, I could break it."

If.

A glance at the rack of tools showed me what I'd need — a large, heavy hammer. With it at my side, I put both palms flat on the surface of the drawer and gave a push of power.

Nothing happened.

I wasn't surprised. Rafe was right when he said my magic was a parlor trick. Besides, I didn't even know if the amulet was in the drawer. Maybe the voice was correct, and I'd find an assortment of dildoes.

That image was so unlikely it forced a chuckle from me. "You're a Fairchild." Father wouldn't quit, no matter what. "Act like it."

I closed my eyes and directed all of my attention to that flat piece of wood. My mind's eye held tight to an image of a glass drawer. I took a deep breath, and on the exhale, I channeled power to my palms. The wood heated. I continued to send power into it. Then, with a little give, as if I'd unclogged a pipe, the wood turned to glass.

Quickly, before it could change back, I grabbed a hammer and slammed it against the drawer face. The glass shattered.

I squatted down and gently tugged on the bottom of the drawer. It slid open, and near the back, I found it.

The ivory box was smaller than I'd anticipated, but the rubies and emeralds embedded in the surface shone through a layer of dust. I sat back on my heels and opened the lid, revealing the amulet inside, golden, beautiful, and deadly.

The shards of glass on the floor started shivering. I had no idea if they'd reform before they turned back into wood or if they'd end up a pile of splinters. The shivering increased, which fascinated me. Faster than my eyes could follow, the shards came together and I snatched my hands out of the way. The drawer slammed shut with enough force that I was glad I didn't get caught.

Take it and run. Now. To the woods.

The command came through so crystal clear I almost dropped the box. I locked my knees, refusing to even take a step. The command surged, stronger than I'd yet experienced, as if the amulet itself was giving the voice power.

Still, I held on. Breathing hard, sweat running down the side of my face, I refused the voice's command. When it finally released its grip, I was left doubled over, gasping for breath. I clutched the amulet to my side.

Slowly I regained my composure and slipped the box into the pocket of my overcoat. I had no idea what to do next. Madam Munro would want me to hide the box in my belongings, keeping it secret until I returned to San Francisco.

Though would she say the same, if she knew what the consequences would be? If Martin Gallagher crossed the veil, he could well find the amulet no matter where I'd hidden it. And if he crossed the veil and then couldn't get back, he'd be fated to eternity as a ghostly evil.

Surely Madam Munro wouldn't want that to happen.

Unhappy with making the obvious decision, I went to the house, hoping to find Margaret. She'd know what to do.

Instead of Margaret, I found Rutger. He sat at the small table, sipping a cup of coffee.

"Good morning, Vince." He raised his mug in toast.

"I thought you were helping Margaret and Della." I winced at his use of my nickname. It struck an off note, as sour as the note of suspicion in my voice.

"Since I don't know my way around, they decided I'd be better served by making coffee." He waved at the pot. "Pour yourself some and come talk with me. Last night was something of a jumble. Can you refresh my memory?"

I did as he asked, keeping to the facts. Even my short summary of the storm made Rutger give a low whistle.

"Thank you most sincerely," he said. "I knew I was in some kind of trouble, and if your friend hadn't called that thing off, I never would have made it."

"She's very good at what she does."

His smile took on a sly edge. "You and Rafe get some sleep last night?"

"We did," I said shortly, hoping to turn the conversation in another direction. "Now, while we have some time, tell me what happened after I left the city."

"That's just the thing." He fiddled with his spoon as if he needed to keep his hands busy to disguise his nerves. "I woke up in the corner of the big greenhouse over at Golden Gate Park. I was curled up, my hands and feet bound, soaking wet from the humidity. One of the gardeners found me."

He flipped the spoon onto the floor. We both reached for it and came damned close to knocking heads together. "Calm yourself," I murmured. "It's just me."

"Might be just you, but I still don't know what happened those three days."

"Three days?"

"When I wouldn't let the gardener contact the police, he insisted on calling someone, so I gave him the address for the Council. Madam Munro arrived in person, and she's the one who told me how long I'd been missing and that she'd sent you away. There's been some other things happen, weird things, though the Council is pretty tight-lipped about all that. To be honest, I'm not sure why she decided to send me here, but last Monday she sent me a message, and now here I am."

I clapped him on the shoulder. "And I'm glad of it."

That made him laugh. "Your minder doesn't think so."

"He'll be fine," I said lightly, waving off Rutger's concern. "He's preoccupied with finding the Ferox Cor. Wait. That's not quite right." I crossed my arms, trying to order my thoughts. "He wants the amulet because whoever holds the amulet controls the Cor." And right now, that was me. The thought made me shudder. "If the amulet is destroyed, the demon spirit will go back wherever it came from, and Martin won't have a reason to cross the veil."

If you'd only just leave here, go into the forest, things would be fine.

I shut my eyes, ignoring the voice's hurtful tone. Rutger said something, and I had to ask him to repeat himself.

"Madam Munro thinks Martin took the Cor to build himself some kind of kingdom way up here where no one can find him."

"Madam Munro also thinks Rafe is a child," I said, perhaps too tartly. "Look around, Rutger. Does this look like a kingdom to you?"

"For a very poor king."

"You see? I think Martin came here because it was isolated, so he could keep the rest of us safe from the Ferox Cor."

You'll never be safe. Never.

Grimly, I ignored the voice, though with each comment, it became a greater threat to my composure, my serenity, my very sanity. "I don't know how he came by it in the first place, but I believe that once he realized its power, he did what he could to keep it away from those it could harm. Or Della convinced him to keep it away."

"Vincent is correct," Rafe said. He leaned against the door jamb between the kitchen and the hall, his cane resting against the wall. "When Martin realized what he'd done by stealing the Cor, he and Mother felt obligated to protect people from it."

"Noble of them." Rutger's tone of voice raised the hairs on the back of my neck, my claims of friendship sounding hollow.

Before I could question him, Margaret and Della arrived. Margaret slipped past Rafe to come stand by me, while Della stayed near her son.

"We haven't found anyone." Margaret stood with her arms crossed, her frown a fearsome thing. "If there's someone else here, they're very well hidden."

Rafe snorted, taking hold of his cane. "There's most definitely someone here. Whoever destroyed the winding mechanism did not come through the wards I set."

"Oh, that." Rutger's smile terrified me. "I'm the one who set the spell on your light. It'd be a pity if a ship went aground on the spit because you all were lax in your duties."

While he spoke, he slipped a revolver from the inside pocket of his coat and rested it on the table. I jumped from my seat, horrified by what he'd said. "You're lying."

He stood, but more slowly. Rafe lunged at him, freezing in mid-stride as if Rutger had raised in invisible shield. "Don't come any closer." He lifted the revolver, rocking it from side to side as if daring the rest of us to move.

Rafe eased back a step. He flexed his fingers, as if powering them for a spell. Margaret clutched my arm. I pulled her closer, hoping to protect her.

"Now, Vince, my old friend, come here." He gestured with the gun. Rafe made a sound very much like a growl. When I didn't move, Rutger aimed the revolver at Rafe. "I said, come here, now. Do it before your *friend* here gets hurt."

I hated the emphasis he put on *friend*, but I hated even more that I'd been the cause of this situation. I'm the one who vouched for Rutger. I'm the one who brought disaster to us all.

Chapter Twenty-Six

I didn't move fast enough for Rutger.

Any trace of his affable character faded away, the gun he'd aimed at Rafe never faltering. "I *will* shoot."

I ignored him, still convinced he was bluffing. He fired and the bullet sent up a spray of splinters from the floor in front of Rafe's feet. The echo of the gun's report covered my inglorious move in his direction.

Laughing, Rutger grabbed me by the wrist, yanking me close. "Now, none of you want to see sweet Vincent injured, do you?" I pondered a sharp kick to his shin, but the press of the pistol behind my ear quieted my resistance. I could not reconcile the man who was my friend with the way he clutched my arm and the press of cold steel against my head.

"You all disgust me. You truly do. Living here in squalor when you've got all the power of the world at your fingertips."

Della's eyes were wide, her face pale. "You don't know anything."

"You're wrong." He pulled me tighter against his body. Evil seemed to seep from his pores. "After tonight, you'll realize your mistake."

I had to fight an inappropriate laugh. He sounded like the villain in some Nick Carter paperback.

"Now. Vince and I have some business to attend to. Remember, I will shoot him if you give me any reason whatsoever."

Quickly, before I could lose my nerve, I sent a push of power at the gun in Rutger's hand. In an instant he held a fistful of daisies. But only for an instant. Rutger snarled, the gun returned, and he flung me to the floor. He turned on me, his face a mask of fury. I knelt at his feet, hands raised, attention trained on the pistol he pointed at me.

No one else moved.

"Come." Rutger waved the gun in the direction of the door. "The rest of you stay here. My good friend Oliver Stevenson and some of his associates will be along momentarily. Since you've been unable to find the amulet, Ollie will keep you entertained while the others do what you should have done before now."

Who was this man? In two years of working together, he'd never been anything but jovial. I did as he directed, mainly so no one else would get hurt. Passing Rafe, I tried to stop. Rutger jabbed me with the barrel of the pistol. "Keep going."

"Where?" We only had a few steps before we'd reach the front door. The amulet bumped against my thigh. Whatever else happened, I couldn't let Rutger know I had it.

"Out. Keep moving."

I stepped outside into a world of gray.

Figures moved through a fog so thick it hid even the ocean. They came closer. Oliver Stevenson and three other men, likely those who'd flung witchfire at us the day we'd gone after Margaret.

"Good. You're here." Rutger gave me a shove in their direction. "Two of you take this one and get him out of the way. Search him first, or he'll turn a clod of dirt into a key to let himself out."

I could, in fact, turn dirt into a key. Now the question became whether I could turn the amulet into something they wouldn't notice.

I thought not, but I'd have to try.

Oliver's friends grabbed me by the elbows and frog-marched me to the dock. One was young, all angles and bones, with a mean scar tugging his lower lip out of line. He pointed a nasty snub-nosed pistol at me. The other, the one who had my elbow in a death grip, was both taller and broader than me, and he smelled strongly of fish.

Midway up the dock, they wrestled me aboard a skiff. The low moan of the foghorn sent us on our way, although our destination was hidden.

I wasn't the only one who thought so.

"Where's the damned boat?" The bony one barked at his companion.

"Hell if I know."

They each had a paddle and we moved along at a good clip. I'd begun to hope they'd give up and take us back to the dock when a dark shadow emerged off to our right.

"There," the big one said.

They adjusted their strokes and soon we came up alongside a fishing boat. It stayed quiet in the water, as if it knew better than to travel far in fog this thick. The bony one grabbed a rope, pulling us closer still, and shoved me toward the other boat.

"Better make a good leap or you'll need to know how to swim."

I did as I was told. They followed.

I stumbled and landed on my knees, immediately looking for a weapon — or something I could turn into a weapon. Both of them were more agile than I'd expected. Bony was up and over almost as soon as I was, and his bulky friend had my hands trapped behind my back before I could reach for anything.

"Get the mitts," the big man said and Bony left my line of sight. I tried to wrestle myself free, but my captor had the advantage in size and strength, if not determination.

I was very good at many things but fighting my way free of an evildoer was not one of my skills. I'd never be able to charm my way out of this debacle.

Bony returned and between the two of them, they shoved stiff mittens over my hands, tying them together in the process. As soon as they let go, I sent a push of power into one hand, intending to turn the mitt into a sharp dagger.

Nothing happened.

In fact, rather than turning the mitten into something I could fight with, my power doubled back on itself, singeing my fingertips as it dissipated.

I must have gasped, because the big man laughed. "Hurts, doesn't it? These are lined with lead, son. You won't be able to do anything with them on." He gave me a shove, sending me stumbling toward the prow of the boat. I managed to stay on my feet, if only because I couldn't bear to fall in whatever slimed the bottom.

"Let's go," the big man said.

"Should we search him?"

The man's chuckle was answer enough. "They wouldn't have trusted this pansy with anything important."

The Lighthouse Keeper

As if to emphasize that point, he caught me with a quick jab to the face. Something cracked, and with my hands bound, I had no way of regaining my balance. I hit the slimy deck hard while he and his companion made it over the side of the boat. The splash of their oars helped me track their direction. Back to the dock, from what I could tell, though I'd be lying if I said I didn't wish they'd headed the wrong way.

Up close, the deck smelled like kerosene and fish guts. I managed to sit, though my head spun and I thought I might puke. Breathing deep to calm myself only made it worse because of the stink.

"Damn it." I closed my eyes, trying hard not to give in to despair. "Hello?" I called weakly. "Is anybody here?"

No answer. I truly was alone.

I scooted over until I could lean against a box set in the ship's prow. While it felt good to rest my head, I had to get back to the lighthouse. Which meant I had to free my hands from these infernal mitts. Which likely meant I had to stand up.

I just had no idea where to begin.

For a long while, I rested with my eyes closed. I was numb to the cold. The boat rocked gently, the splash of water against its hull having a hypnotic effect. I didn't sleep, exactly, but my mind went blank.

When I finally roused, it was impossible to guess the time of day. If anything, the fog had thickened til

I was swathed in dreary grey. This couldn't be a natural weather event. Either Stevenson had hired a weatherwitch or Margaret had done something to protect us. The rotten fish smell from the deck had long since deadened my nostrils to any scent at all and the combination of cold, damp, and fear had me shivering.

There must be a way back.

Raise the anchor. The waves will push you to shore.

I ignored that evil voice. There'd be no raising of anything with these mitts on. Besides, though the waves might push me in, I'd likely get grounded before long. More probable, I'd drift until I caught a current, and then who knows where I'd land.

Bainbridge Island, if I was lucky. Otherwise, the Pacific Ocean.

No, I had to do whatever possible to return to shore.

I tried to use my power a second time, more of a cry for help than asking for a specific task. Both hands burned with unspent magic. I'd never realized that lead would prevent me from using my power. That seemed like something Madam Munro or one of her associates might have mentioned. I laughed, but it was a bitter sound.

Better laughter than tears.

A set of waves made the boat sway with enough momentum to send me lurching to my feet. "There must be some place that doesn't stink of fish." The dark and the fog made it hard to see what was what, and I didn't dare try to make a witchlight.

With the exception of a single mast near the prow, the boat itself wasn't much bigger than the rowboat we'd taken to the city. There were benches — I found at least one with my knee — and a pile of nets folded up in the stern.

I gave up and sat on the closest bench. My overcoat had already been ruined so I might as well be comfortable. The sail's rigging rattled softly, the sound of hopelessness.

They're not coming for you.

"Shut up." If I was ashamed for talking to the voice in my head, I'd gone past the point of caring. "Besides, I've got the amulet. They'll want that, if nothing else."

Because there'd be no other reason for them to come. Admitting that to myself cut deeper than anything the voice had ever said.

"I'll just wait, then."

The voice had nothing to add, so for a moment all was quiet. Just me and the jingling sail. Waves slopping against the hull. The foghorn crooning over the water, warning all to stay away.

The hawk's scream, so sudden in the quiet, made me yelp. "Lord." The steady beat of the bird's wings forced me into action. I was a Fairchild, for pity's sake. If I had to choose between sitting here helpless and doing something, anything, well, I wasn't going to wait for rescue. Wasn't going to sit here like a crab, waiting for that hawk to make me his next meal, either. I'd swim in, if I had to, but I was going back to shore.

Rubbing my hands together, I managed to loosen one of the mittens. That proved that while the mittens were tied together, my hands were not. I didn't know whether to thank Stevenson's bullies or mock them for their stupidity. "This little pansy may yet do more damage than you expect."

Laughing at my own joke, I wiggled my hands until one slid out of its mittened trap. The other mitten fell away. "That's better."

Flexing my fingers, I reached for the mitts. I pulled the cord through one of my belt loops and tied them so they hung on one hip. I had no idea if I'd need them, though I might. "Now how do I get to shore?"

What I needed was a path through the water, or a bridge over it.

Could I make a bridge?

I had no idea how long it would need to be, and truly, I'd never made anything larger than that drawer front. But I had turned the drawer front into glass, so...

You'll drown. You're too weak to do something like that. Too weak.

Doing my best to ignore the voice, I shut my eyes and pictured the beach. I had no idea if the tide was in or out. Really, though, the sandbar went out quite a way from the shore, which is why only row boats could approach the dock. If I could get close enough, I might get my boots wet, but I could slog my way in. Did I dare to try?

"Don't have much choice," I murmured. The hawk's scream made my decision easy. It still circled the boat without alighting, a threatening shadow in the night.

The fog continued to thicken, and for a moment I worried that my magic wouldn't be able to penetrate it. "Only one way to know for sure."

For this venture to be successful, I had to believe it was possible. Any doubts would send me splashing to a watery, well, if not grave, then a watery bath.

"A Fairchild never doubts." I heard my father's pompous words and as usual, they made me laugh. Still, in this circumstance, he had a point. Glancing around, my gaze landed on the piled-up nets. They'd be fairly long. I could fling one in the direction of the shore, picture a bridge, use more power than I ever thought possible, and run like the dickens.

The bridge I pictured was wooden and just wider than me. The slats were tied together, and while there was no railing, I wouldn't need one. I'd run. I brought my hands to my mouth and took a few deep breaths, letting my moist exhalation warm my fingers. Well aware that I might only get one attempt, I waited until my tremors stopped and a sense of calm washed over me.

Then, picking up the top net, I went as far forward as I dared. Clutching the mast with one hand, I held the net in the other. Without giving the voice time to threaten my sense of purpose, I channeled all the power I could grab and threw the net.

Nothing. The bit I held slipped through my fingers and the whole thing splashed down. Small buoys tied to the corners kept it from sinking completely, but one wave took it out of my reach.

I gulped. There was one more net. I had to try again.

This time the doubts were harder to fight down, the voice alternating between threat and mockery. I had to do this. Rafe needed the amulet. Rafe. Maybe I couldn't channel his power, but I could make use of my desire for him. With his image in my mind, I closed my eyes — the fog limited what I could see anyway — sank myself into the memory of his strength, and reached for what was left of my power. And then I threw the net.

Rather than splash and sink, a glowing wooden bridge stretched into the fog.

I ran.

The fog was so thick I could see only a few slats ahead of me, which is how I ran right off the bridge and into the water. Fortunately, I managed to stay upright, and the waves didn't reach my knees. I ruined my boots, but I made it.

The Lighthouse Keeper

Relief warred with cockiness, because yes, I'd made a bridge. Then a wave broke against the back of my legs, reminding me I still had some distance to travel. One hand on the box, to make sure it was still in my pocket, I slogged the rest of the way to the beach. There's no walking quietly when you're shin-deep in water. I just had to hope no one was near.

Splashing footsteps gave way to crunching on gravel. Figures moved in the fog ahead of me, so I stopped once I cleared the last wave. There were at least two, maybe three, and they were silent as they went about their mysterious task.

The hawk gave a fearsome screech and I stumbled toward Rafe's workshop. It was close to the water, and while there was no glow of light from the window, I'd feel safer under the eaves.

Now that I was here, I needed to plan my next steps.

Chapter Twenty-Seven

W here was Rafe? Margaret? Della? The hawk cried out again. One of the figures on the lawn answered. "Go away. You'll only cause trouble."

Rutger, although I was unsure whether I'd truly recognized his voice or if his pulp fiction dialogue was the clue.

"I told you how to lay them out. Why are you dawdling?" This was surely Rutger. He must be setting up a ritual of some kind. The thought saddened on me. Whatever he had planned would go beyond my power to stop.

Knowing I might have to fight against a friend weighed heavily on my heart. Before it could sap me of my will to act, I slipped around the corner of the workshop.

The door was unlocked. Rafe wouldn't be here but being in the presence of his creations calmed me. The foghorn sounded, reassuring me that at least some things were going as expected.

I debated my next move. Alone in a place of relative safety, I let exhaustion wash over me. Making a bridge had taxed me, and for a moment, all I could do was fall into Rafe's chair and breathe. I didn't have long, but before anything else, I needed to restore myself.

The tower was likely to be guarded, though likely the guard wouldn't know how to wind the light. That could cause other problems, big problems, so big my mind shied away from them. We'd deal with a shipwreck if it happened. Otherwise, I wouldn't borrow trouble.

That left the house and the woods. If Rutger hadn't figured out how to secure Rafe, he'd be in the trees. I straightened, rocking my shoulders to loosen them. *Lord*. There was no way in hell I would attempt to navigate the forest in this fog. If Rafe was there, he'd be able to take care of himself.

That left the house. I stood, my legs still shaky, and gently opened the door. No one was outside, and I was on the opposite side of the building from where Rutger and his cronies had been shuffling about. The front door, however, was quite near where they'd been working. That created a bigger challenge.

Keeping close to the wall of the house, I walked along, taking care to make no noise. The ground underfoot was soft dirt with patches of grass, which helped. There was a light in the first window — the bedroom Margaret and Della had been sharing. Della lay on the bed, a bandage across her forehead. I listened carefully, though the only noise was the steady roll of the waves.

Moving slowly, I came to the kitchen window. The lights were brighter, although with the fog shrouding me, there was no glare so I could see in quite plainly. Two things immediately struck me:

Rafe was not there, and Margaret was tied to one of the chairs. Stevenson stood across from her, a pistol pointing in her direction.

"Tell me where he went, or you'll wish you had."

His words were muffled, and if Margaret answered, her voice was too quiet for me to hear.

But really. *Or you'll wish you had?* With that faux-threatening tone of voice? Both Rutger and Stevenson had read too many dime novels.

Debating my next move, I didn't notice the man behind me until he grabbed me and got a hand over my mouth. I inhaled to scream, smelled burning herbs, and came close to collapsing on the spot.

Rafe.

He must have felt me relax because he released his grasp. "They're making a mistake."

His voice, so low and dark, sent chills down my spine. "Why?"

"Because that idiot thinks he's going to control the Cor. From what I can tell, if he doesn't find the amulet, he's going to try to work the same spell the necromancer did all those years ago, to bind the Cor to a new object."

That sank my spirits. "Rutger is a ritual master."

"Maybe, but according to Martin, the Cor doesn't respond well to demands, and it's had years to learn how to avoid them."

"What?"

"Martin was able to control it because he had the amulet and he asked in a way the Cor could understand. He offered the Cor something it wanted. No one likes to be a slave."

"Not even a demon spirit?" I might have had a hint of sarcasm in my voice.

"Come with me. We'll hide away until this idiot is ready to play his game."

"No." I pulled away from his grasp. "Margaret is in there with Stevenson and he's got a gun, and it looks like they injured your mother."

Rafe paused, barely a darkened silhouette in the fog. "You're right. Here."

He took my hand and put a stone in it. "Make me a weapon and we'll get rid of him."

"The others will hear."

I wasn't sure, but I could almost swear he smiled. "They will, won't they."

"You are not going after him with a fake gun." I clutched his arm, afraid he'd go running off without me. "I don't know how many more men there are. We can't fight all of them at once."

"I could."

"I'm very sure you could, but it would be better to allow Rutger to set up his ritual, then you can go in and take it over. I had the impression you weren't completely sure of the steps you'd need to take to stop Martin, so we might as well take advantage of his power."

Rafe nodded, but before we could discuss the point further, a dull thump interrupted us. A quick glance through the kitchen window showed me Stevenson on the floor. Margaret had vanished.

"What did she do?" I pulled on Rafe's arm. "Margaret, she's—"

I was again interrupted, this time by the squeak of wood against wood.

"There," Rafe said, pointing toward the next set of windows. I set a ball of witchlight floating ahead of us and ran.

Margaret was easing open the window in the room she'd shared with Della. "Vincent, here."

I reached her with Rafe right behind me. Both of us lifted the sash, while Margaret helped Della from the bed. "Where can we go?" she asked, pulling the room's only chair to the window.

"The forest." Rafe's tone brooked no discussion. That didn't stop his mother.

"No." Even leaning on Margaret's arm, Della spoke firmly. "Your workshop has more wards than anywhere else. We'll go there."

Rafe froze, clearly caught between the desire to argue and his concern for Della. His mother braced herself on the window ledge, as if she needed to catch her breath before climbing on the chair.

"Come on," he said, offering Della his hand. "We'll go to the workroom. Vincent, can you unlock the door for us?"

"It's unlocked."

Rafe snarled a curse, though he cut it off short because Della reached for him. Carefully lifting her out through the window, he lowered her to the grass. Margaret followed, one hand on his shoulder to help her scramble over the sill.

We left without bothering to close the window, moving in a silent cluster to the workroom's door. Rafe pushed it open, breathing another curse when the knob turned.

The sense that we were being watched settled over me. It could have been the Cor, or Martin's specter, or hell, maybe it was the shelf full of small carved creatures. Something knew we were here.

Something, or someone.

I didn't dare make a witchlight. A fire in the grate would also show us up, and although the room was chilly, it was warmer than the forest would have been.

Rafe's pallet was still unrolled in front of the grate, and Margaret helped Della over to it. Rafe stood at the door with his back to the room.

"Resetting the wards?" I said softly.

"Mmhmm." He left off his task, settling into the room's only chair. I took off my overcoat and draped it around Margaret and Della, who huddled together on the pallet. My feet were wet and cold, but those two were colder.

We needed to come up with a plan, one that didn't involve waiting until close to midnight.

"Do we know how many helpers Rutger has?" I asked.

"Stevenson's going to be out for a while." Margaret's voice held a note of pride, and I found I couldn't blame her for it.

"At least four others," Rafe said. "I saw them come out of the forest."

"So there is a way through?"

He waved off my moment of outrage that was really more annoyance. "More likely they did some kind of transport spell. Does your friend have the skills for that?"

"My friend," I said bitterly. "Possibly, if it can be done with a ritual. There wasn't much call for him to use his gifts in our work."

"Why'd he take that job, then?" Margaret asked.

"I've been wondering the same thing." Why would a ritual master have agreed to work for the liaison's office? "When we met, he told me about his gift, but until he got here, I never saw him use it."

Our conversation petered off, as if we were all busy cataloguing our complaints. It was cold, we'd missed breakfast, likely lunch, and even dinner. I'd so utterly lost track of time I couldn't tell. Mostly I debated with myself, unsure whether or not I should tell Rafe about the amulet. The thing sat in my pocket, heavier than an object so small should weigh.

If I told him about the amulet, he'd try to take it from me. That might be the best course, as he'd be the one most likely to destroy it.

But then I'd have nothing to give to Madam Munro.

I found that thought was less distressing than it had once been. Madam Munro wasn't here, she hadn't learned the things I'd learned. Bringing the Ferox Cor to San Francisco would cause more problems than it would ever solve.

"Rafe, I—"

The door rattled, hard, and someone began hollering when it wouldn't open.

"Damn it." Rafe went to the window closest to the door, touching the sash and murmuring. He crossed the small room, stepping around the women on the pallet, and performed the same spell at the other window.

"Now they know where we are." Della straightened her shoulders, her face pale but her expression resolute.

The sense of being watched grew stronger. "We should disrupt whatever it is he's trying to do."

"It would help if we knew what that was." Rafe's frown deepened. "He must have learned about the Ferox Cor somehow."

"Perhaps. I only knew about it because Madam Munro sent us here to find it. Margaret, are you creating the fog?"

"No, it's—"

"Pardon me," Rafe interrupted her. "You were sent here to find the Ferox Cor?"

Under different circumstances, his indignation would have made me laugh. "Does it matter now? If you still mistrust my motives, this is going to be a very long night."

He stood, looming over me in the small space. Then, after a long moment through which I held my breath, he relaxed. "I suppose if you were going to steal the Cor, you'd have already left with the amulet in your pocket."

Only a few minutes ago, I'd been ready to tell him, but now I said nothing, resting my hand on the box's solid weight. A solid weight that had me feeling like a traitor.

The Lighthouse Keeper

Whoever holds the amulet controls the Ferox Cor.

I could tell it to go after Rutger, to chase him and his friends away. Or could I? I had so little power of my own. I could see the Cor brushing me aside, the way a tiger would tumble an annoying kitten. Even so, it was an idea. Something I could try as a last resort.

Della and Margaret murmured together. "What is it?" I asked.

"The light," Margaret said. "No one has wound it, and by now it'll have gone out."

I didn't like the idea of splitting up, but it might be necessary. "You and I can go wind it and Rafe can stay with his mother."

"No." Rafe knocked his cane on the floor. "I'll go."

Margaret stood up, pausing to drape my overcoat more securely around Della's shoulders. "You mustn't always play the hero, Rafe Gallagher." She took hold of my arm. "You keep your mother safe. Vincent and I can manage this task."

"I don't like it." Rafe positioned himself in front of the door, as if daring us to get past him.

Margaret and I shared a glance. Clearly she wanted me to fix this, so I plastered on a charming smile. "It only makes sense. None of us should go off on our own right now, and your mother is injured. You're the best one to protect her."

His frown only deepened.

"You don't have to do it all. Let us help you."

Something of my desperation must have struck him because he eased away from the door. I didn't care so much about winding the light, but I did care about Rafe.

He didn't need to do it all.

The door to the tower was close to where Rutger and his cronies had been setting up for the ritual. Margaret and I slipped around the corner, closest to the beach, and stopped there.

The fog was so thick I couldn't judge how many men were helping Rutger. They'd started to light their candles, however, small spots of muddy orange in the darkness. Rutger snarled instructions, harsh enough to make me wonder how I'd ever believed him to be a friend.

Someone else piped up, a weak plea. Stevenson. I met Margaret's gaze, though I couldn't tell if she was relieved she hadn't killed him, or disappointed. She was made from some pretty stern stuff.

Fingering the coin in my pocket, I pondered our choices. "I could create some kind of shield, something that would make us harder to see."

Margaret pursed her lips.

"Or you can conjure up a sudden storm to distract them?"

She grinned. "One minute." She closed her eyes and after a breath, she sketched a sigil in the air. The fog thickened, becoming almost solid. Voices rose in confusion, Rutgers the loudest of all.

The Lighthouse Keeper

"Have you lost control of the spell?" he snapped.

We didn't wait to hear the answer. Keeping close to the building, we slipped to the tower door. The lock yielded to a quickly crafted key, and we were in.

Face to face with the specter of Martin Gallagher.

Chapter Twenty-Eight

W hat on earth?" Margaret stopped right behind me, her hand on my shoulder.

Martin's specter stood between us and the stairs, arms raised as if he wanted to look even more frightening than normal. The coins still covered his eyes but he'd lost the rag holding his mouth shut and now it flopped open like a great black maw.

"We need to wind the light, Martin. Let us pass." My voice sounded amazingly calm, given the circumstances. The box in my pocket grew heavier. I put my hand on it, almost comforted by its warm weight.

Martin lowered his arms and I found myself frightened of what might come out of his gaping mouth. A low groan sent chills down my back. Margaret clutched my arm.

"Come on, Martin, we're — "

He rushed toward us, slamming into my shoulder and knocking Margaret back a few steps.

A frigid ache spread out from the place he hit and I clenched my teeth to keep them from chattering. I still clutched the amulet, though it was no longer warm.

By the time I regained my bearings, the ghost was gone. He shouldn't have been able to run me down like a football tackle, a fact I planned to discuss with Rafe later.

"Are you all right?" I asked Margert.

Her eyes were wide in her pale face, but she nodded.

"Let's get the light wound."

We climbed the stairs together, as if by unspoken agreement. Neither of us wanted to be left alone. At the top of the stairs, Margaret reached for the mechanism, but I stopped her.

With the smallest push of power I could muster, I turned my coin into a pair of pliers. "Use these." For all we knew, someone had put another spell on the handle.

"Good." She took the pliers and gave the mechanism a tug. The cable whined as it wound on the spool, an eerie sound that only added to my nerves. The light flashed, blinding me. I blinked, grateful that Margaret's silhouette remained. The light moved on, and for a moment I had the sense of how much of the world could be seen from the top of the tower. So much water and so much space, and no time to honor either of them.

"Back to the workshop," I said, still holding the coin so I'd have it ready in case I needed a weapon. Despite the darkness, I didn't make a witchlight, picking my way slowly down the stairs instead.

We reached the lower level and the door swung open. Stevenson stood there, the dark muzzle of his pistol drawing most of my attention.

"Happy to see both of you," he said. "It's time to join the others." He waved the gun in our direction and three of his companions filed in through the door. "Tie their hands, and this time, make sure that little pansy can't get loose."

His companions were young, raw, and if they could cobble a spell between the three of them, I'd be surprised. Margaret and I shared a glance. If she had a plan, she wasn't sharing. Stevenson's pistol had six shots, and he'd be able to get off a couple before I could do anything with my coin. Enough to do both of us harm.

I hated to give up without a fight, but I wasn't sure what to do next. If we broke free of these four, where would we go? The forest held little appeal, and this sliver of land was too small to provide many places to hide. Besides, Stevenson had said we'd "join the others." Had they already captured Rafe and Della?

A pair of young men grabbed my arms. I tried to shake free, more for show than any real desire to fight. Clenching the coin, I allowed them to bind my hands, putting up enough resistance to make my anger clear.

Once the third man had Margaret bound, they marched us out onto the lawn. The fog had cleared, and they'd set out four large candles, likely matched to the four points on the compass. The flames glowed in the darkness, and rows of smaller candles marked the sides of the square.

At the center of the square, a pair of men held lanterns, illuminating a small area. Rutger stood between them, with Rafe facing him.

Della stood to the left, outside of the square, her back to the ocean. Her posture was passive, expressionless, as if she'd already given up.

Stevenson's assistants pushed us toward Della. Poor Margaret was unable to lift her skirts, but she managed to avoid setting herself on fire as we passed close to the candles. I stumbled, unable to maintain my balance with my arms behind my back.

"Welcome." Rutger spoke without looking toward us. Instead, his attention was focused on the golden basin he held. He wore a black cape trimmed in gold, like some kind of stage warlock. Lantern light flickered across the liquid in the bowl, and while it looked clear now, I'd guess it wouldn't once he started his ritual.

Margaret and I crowded close to Della. The tendons in Rafe's neck stood out, as if he was fighting some fierce internal battle. Clearly he'd allowed himself to be captured, although I had to wonder why. Maybe they'd managed to grab Della first and used her as bait.

Rutger began to talk, although after "with or without the amulet, I will do this," I stopped paying attention. Rafe's glasses had been lost at some point, his eyes pools of blackness. His tension heightened my fear, and even Margaret's breathing came fast. I could turn the coin into a small knife, but handing it to her would be difficult, unless we were standing back to back. Hard to know if anyone would notice unless we tried.

I nudged her with my elbow, then eased around so I was standing at an angle to the square. I stretched my hands until I could tug at her sleeve. She twitched, as if I'd surprised her, but she too shifted around. Neither of us had made a big move, but now I could brush her fingers with mine. I managed to make a knife without dropping the coin and slipped the blade between her wrists and the rope binding her.

It wasn't easy. Rutger rambled on, dressing his words in as much magical palaver as possible, making clear his basic intent was to claim the Ferox Cor. Lord only knows where he dug up the binding spell.

And he meant to kill Rafe to power his ritual.

A bright, clear anger burned away my fear. I'd claim the Cor myself if I had to, before I'd let Rutger harm Rafe Gallagher.

The rope fell away from Margaret's wrists. She fumbled for the handle of the knife and went to work on the ropes binding me. Rutger set the basin on the ground at Rafe's feet and produced a dagger from inside his robe.

His voice rose as if he was excited to be placing the dagger against Rafe's chest. "And with this sacrifice," he said, "I shall call upon the Ferox Cor and bind it to me."

He raised the dagger. My heart beat so hard I could hear it. I jerked my hands free of the rope. Plunged my hand into my pocket. Flipped open the box and grasped the amulet.

"I so declaim," Rutger screamed, but as he brought the dagger down, Rafe doubled over. The blade missed him, and Rutger screamed again. "What are you doing?"

Rafe straightened, his earlier tension replaced by something much colder. "I am the Ferox Cor, and your silly games have no power over me." Rafe raised a hand, pointing at Rutger.

"No. Stop." Rutger clutched at his own throat. "I call the Ferox Cor to me."

Rafe laughed, a sound that could have come from Hell itself. A faint beam of light passed from his fingertip to Rutger's face.

Rutger fell to his knees, still demanding the Cor do his bidding. Rafe didn't move until Rutger had collapsed altogether. Then, he turned toward us.

"I will kill them all," he said, his voice so low and threatening my mind went blank with terror.

"No," I whispered. Rational thought might have left me, but I knew in my bones Rafe would never forgive himself for that kind of destruction. I must do this. In this moment, the choice was no choice at all. Madam Munro would either understand or she would not. Rafe would either forgive me or he would not. Cold with certainty, I unlatched the box in my pocket.

Slowly, hoping that Margaret would plunge the knife into my heart before I could cause too much damage, I raised the amulet.

"He who holds the amulet controls the spirit." My lips were dry, my words a papery whisper. "I call the Ferox Cor to me."

The amulet was pretty, its gold and jewels flickering in the lantern light. Rafe gave a great cry, flinging his arms wide, and though I could not see it, I felt the Cor leave him.

Fear choked the breath from my lungs. The Cor would enter me, its voice a nonstop reminder of my own failings, and —

The Lighthouse Keeper

An unseen force knocked me to the ground, yanking the amulet from my hand.

Della Gallagher stood over me, the amulet raised high. "Come to me. Now."

The crack of a pistol broke through the scene. Della put her hands to her chest, blood running over the golden amulet. Oliver Stevenson strode through the square of candlelight, his pistol now pointed at Rafe.

Everyone moved at once. Margaret ran to Della and Rafe tackled Stevenson, knocking the gun from his hand. I grabbed it, waving it at Stevenson's young cronies. They looked like they were more likely to run for the dock than to trouble us further.

Another crack, louder than the gunshot, drew my gaze to the center of the candlelit square. A seam of darkness opened in the air, and the specter of Martin Gallagher stepped through. He walked toward Della, who lay sprawled on the grass. Reaching her, he bent down and touched her head. A momentary fog concealed them both, and when it cleared, Martin's specter had a companion: a ghostly Della, who still held the amulet.

She floated rather than walked, coming close to Rafe. I couldn't read his expression in the dark but I went to him anyway. His mother — or her specter — brushed a hand over his brow. She lacked the coins over her eyes, but still her expression was impossible to read. Rafe shrunk, reduced by the sudden onslaught of grief. I wrapped an arm around his waist, grateful that he allowed me the contact.

Della rejoined Martin, and a third, a being of darkness, drifted between them. Martin led his little party to the seam.

They stepped through and disappeared. The dark night was as it had been.

Rafe clutched at me. I would have pulled him closer, but Stevenson distracted me.

"You think you won this, but you're wrong. I'll —"

I raised the pistol and my shot went true. The bullet hit him in the belly with a dull thud, and he dropped to the gravel beach. His companions were gone, Rutger still lay in a heap, and I had no time to offer any of them aid. Instead, I dropped the gun and drew Rafe close.

I reached for Margaret with my other hand. Shuddering, she rested her forehead on my shoulder. The three of us stood together long enough for those who had come with Stevenson to make their escape.

I was too wrung out to care.

My old friend betrayed me and my new friends needed me. The rest could take care of themselves.

Chapter Twenty-Nine

While I would have stood with Rafe and Margaret as long as time itself, the reality of the situation soon intruded. Stevenson had stopped groaning, and when we finally moved apart, we found him in a large pool of blood. Dead.

I'd killed a man. That thought sat uneasily in my soul. Yes, he'd threatened those I held dear, but there might have been another way.

"I'm glad," Rafe said, as if he'd read my mind. He gave Stevenson's shoulder a nudging kick. "He killed my mother. If anything, a gunshot was too good for him."

Rafe and I stood side by side, arms still around each other. Margaret knelt beside Rutger, though she soon joined us. Her long skirts were stained with mud and tears streaked her cheeks. "He's dead, too. What should we do with them?"

"Find a boat and set them adrift." Rafe spoke with such ringing authority I did not argue the point.

"While you do that, I'm going to call up a rainstorm," Margaret said. "Wash this place clean."

First, though, we took care of Della's body. With more gentleness than I would have thought possible, Rafe lifted her in his arms. He stared out over the ocean as if caught in some internal debate.

"We could put her in the cave with Martin," I suggested, and he gave a sharp nod. With him leading the way, we went into the forest. Margaret kept a hand on my arm, which helped steady both of us. Rafe didn't appear to need his cane or the witchlight I floated over our heads. He cut an unerring path to the cave.

It took the two of us longer to cross the stream than it had taken Rafe, and by the time we reached the mouth of the cave, he'd gone inside. The darkness felt thick, a palpable substance that I hesitated to penetrate. "Rafe?"

His voice came from within that darkness. "Here."

"I'm not sure…" Margaret said softly, and I took her reluctance to heart.

"We'll wait." I called out without moving further than the entrance. I told myself we were giving Rafe time alone with his parents, but in all honesty, I'd reached my limit for horror.

Margaret was no more inclined to enter that dreadful darkness than I was, so we waited. Rafe came out after a while, moving with a weariness that tugged at my heart.

"She always did choose him first," he said. He stood with his arms crossed, his shoulders bowed as if he bore a great weight.

Margaret put a hand on his arm. "I'm sorry. Your mother was a good woman."

"She'll be happier now." He sounded stiff, but he covered Margaret's hand with his own.

I couldn't think of a thing to say, so I contented myself with standing close to him, lending support with my presence. He seemed to understand, shifting his weight to come even nearer to me.

"Let's go," he said finally. Again with him in the lead, we crossed the stream and wound through the trees. Breaking free of the forest, Margaret went down to the beach to call some rain, and Rafe sent me to the dock to see if Stevenson's companions had left a boat. Somehow they had, and although it was grim work, Rafe and I loaded the dead men onto it. I wiped off Stevenson's gun and laid it on top of him. He could take it to hell for all I cared.

"I'll push them out to catch the current."

Without giving me time to debate, Rafe jumped in, dragging the shallow boat behind him. When the water reached his shoulders, he gave the thing a final push and it floated out beyond the waves.

All the while Rafe was gone, I repeated what he'd said after I shot Stevenson. "I'm glad." I'm glad. *I'm glad*. I hadn't set out to kill someone, but I was man enough to own my actions. And Rafe was glad of it.

Still, I'd always used my looks to turn situations to my advantage and it would take time to reconcile the pretty boy with the man who shot to kill.

I'd save my grieving for Rutger until later.

Water pouring off his broad shoulders, Rafe strode up the beach without the aid of his cane, his cloak clinging to his form. A light sprinkling of rain fell. In time, it would wash away Stevenson's blood. It would clean the rest of us, too, and I tipped my face to the clouds, shivering deep in my core.

Rafe must be colder even than me. He approached, draping an arm over my shoulder in a surprisingly possessive way. Margaret joined us and we went slowly toward the house.

"You should go to the workshop," Margaret said. We stopped a few feet from the door.

"Will you be all right alone?" I hated the idea, but Rafe needed to get out of his wet clothes and all three of us couldn't very well strip in front of the stove.

Margaret grasped my hand and gave it a squeeze. "With luck the coals in the stove will still be warm. You two should stay together."

Though I was unsure what she meant — or afraid to imagine too many possibilities — I leaned over and placed a kiss on her cheek. "Before we settle down, I'll take a look around and make sure all of Stevenson's friends are gone."

I made a witchlight and handed it to her. "This'll last an hour or so."

"Thank you, Vincent." She returned my kiss and the light followed her into the house.

Once the door was closed tight behind her, I turned to Rafe. Rain had slicked his hair and without his glasses, those dark eyes pinned me in place. "If you go light the grate I can take a look —"

"Hush. No one is here except the three of us."

"You're sure?"

Without answering, he steered both of us toward his workshop. The rain began to fall more heavily, though the rhythmic surge and retreat of the waves soothed me. Once we were inside, he knelt to stir the coals in the grate. I made another witchlight, which cast shadows behind all the small creatures on the shelves.

I stood helplessly, unsure what to do. Yes, we'd rid ourselves of the Ferox Cor, but Rafe had just lost his mother. There was nothing I could say to take away that pain.

With a sharp pop, the fire in the grate burst into life. I took off my soggy overcoat and hung it on the back of Rafe's chair. He took off his cloak, too, hanging it on a peg by the door. We faced each other, neither sure what to do next.

"You should take off your wet clothes." I tracked the placket of his shirt. I didn't intend to seduce him. I simply liked the feel of him, of knowing he was still with me.

He shrugged out of his shirt, and I mirrored him. Soon we were both down to our drawers. Lifting the blanket from the pallet in front of the fire, he extended his hand to me. With that invitation, I sat next to him. He reclined and pulled the blanket over both of us.

We needed to make a few adjustments, but soon we were comfortable, Rafe on his back and my head on his shoulder. His breathing was deep and even, and while I wanted to ask him how he felt, I couldn't find the words. Instead, I allowed myself to drift.

"You're very brave," he murmured, his voice rumbling through his chest against my cheek.

I smiled, tilting my head so I could press a kiss to his skin. "As are you."

I would have gone on listing his various attributes, his strength, his artistry, his hidden sweetness, but he spoke up instead. "I hope we'll have some time together when we're not fighting an earthbound demon."

Snuggling in closer, I found another spot to kiss. "So do I."

That seemed to satisfy us both, and soon, we were asleep.

The Lighthouse Keeper

Only a few hours later, we woke to someone pounding on the workshop door.

"Rafe? Vincent?" Margaret's apprehension roused me. Rafe sat propped on one elbow, while I clambered to my feet.

My overcoat was still damp, so I pulled on a shirt and cracked the door open. "What is it?"

Margaret's braid still hung down over her shoulder and she wore the same muddy dress she'd had on the night before. "Madam Munro."

I blinked, not sure I'd heard her correctly. "It's… who?"

"Madam Munro," she hissed. "She arrived in Seattle late yesterday and paid a fisherman a great deal of money to bring her here first thing."

"Why?"

She made a disgusted sound. I rubbed my face, hoping I'd wake up enough to make sense of the situation.

"Just remember what Della said, that we mustn't tell her about Rafe."

"Yes, all right, I won't."

Rafe came up behind me, warm against my back. "Tell who about me?"

"Madam Munro." I reached for his hand, hoping Margaret wouldn't notice. "Your mother was afraid that if the Council found out the extent of your power, they'd make you work for them."

His laugh would have reassured me, but I was still too overwrought after last night.

"Get dressed, both of you." Margaret turned to go. "And Rafe, let Vincent talk to her. You'll only get yourself in trouble."

She left us with the door open just a crack. I closed it and turned. Rafe didn't move, which put us belly to belly. Strands of dark hair framed his face and those bottomless eyes seemed to see deep inside of me.

"Where are your glasses?" I asked, because otherwise I was going to drag him back to the pallet on the floor.

He sighed, resting his forehead against mine. "I'm not sure, nor can I remember where I dropped my cane. Goddamn them." He pushed away from me and stood with his fists on his hips. "Selfish bastards, the lot of them."

I approached slowly and put a hand on his shoulder. "Let's get dressed."

The only way out was through.

Margaret had dressed herself fully and was passing around cups of coffee when we came in. Without his cane, Rafe walked more slowly than normal, but his steps were sure. Margaret and I shared a quick and worried glance, and then I faced the woman who'd sent me here.

Madam Munro sat in the front room, taking up the window bench with her presence. Her regal cheekbones and stern expression looked even grander in this humble setting.

Grander, and more intimidating.

She hadn't come alone. A woman stood near the window, holding the edge of one of the curtains so she could peer outside. "Sometimes the clouds look like mother-of-pearl."

She turned and my jaw dropped. Mrs. Morrison smiled at us, her delicate lavender frock as out of place in these rustic surroundings as a jeweled brooch on a beggar.

"Why are you here?" Rafe asked, his tone freezing cold. I moved closer to him, to take advantage of his shields. He'd chosen his one decent frock coat and trousers that were very nearly clean. With his hair combed back from his face and dressed in respectable clothing, his dark eyes were somehow larger and blacker. The psychic, however, did not appear at all disturbed.

"Who are you to be asking any such questions of us?" Madam Munro's anger crackled through the room.

Rafe met her with frigid calm. "Rafe Gallagher. Who are you, and why have you brought a psychic into my home?"

"Agatha Munro. I'm the head of the San Francisco Witches' Council, and Mrs. Morrison is here on my order."

Her lack of etiquette made her ire plain. The way the two of them stared at each other, there'd be no need to tell Madam Munro about Rafe's power. It poured from him, and though her expression never changed, I could feel her surprise. She met his strength with her own, until the very air seemed to vibrate.

"Aunt Aggie?" Mrs. Morrison broke through their stand-off. "Please do introduce us."

How she'd managed to keep her lovely dress in pristine condition while traveling by fishing vessel was a mystery, though Madam Munro looked equally tidy. In comparison, I felt grimy and worn. I stood straight, however, and if I couldn't smile, at least I didn't scowl.

"We've met before," I said. Schooling my expression was a challenge, as I badly wanted to yell at them both. "If you've been working for Madam Munro, why was I sent to find the Ferox Cor?"

"It's been destroyed," Rafe said.

Madam Munro glared at him. "What?"

Rafe simply gazed in her direction.

"Last night, Madam Munro," I said, mainly to fill in the threatening silence. When no one else spoke up, I continued, describing the events of the last week, attempting to find a balance between brevity and adequate detail for understanding.

Madam Munro interrupted me only once, to ask, "You're sure it was Rutger Smit?"

"Yes." He'd known me and I'd known him. There was no doubt in my mind that my old workmate had come here to do us harm. She didn't question my assertion, so I continued my sorry tale. Only when I told her we'd sent Rutger and Stevenson to their watery grave did her expression change, becoming somehow sterner.

"I suppose it can't be helped now." She gave Mrs. Morrison an expectant look.

Mrs. Morrison shrugged, a subtle gesture of resignation. "He's telling the truth, and it appears they did what needed to be done. The Ferox Cor is beyond the reach of anyone who would put it to ill use, and we've found the final piece of the puzzle."

"What puzzle?" The words escaped me before I could frame them in a more politic way.

Madam Munro faced me fully. "We've been following young Smit since shortly after you left San Francisco. Something about the events of that Saturday night rang false, if you will, and with you safely off the playing field, our attention was drawn to his absence.

"We didn't realize you had a thaumaturge following you until too late." Madam Munro sounded more annoyed than sympathetic. "Meredith has been sending me regular updates, you see. Your telegraph came as we were almost out the door on our way here."

I was puzzled by her mention of a thaumaturge. "I thought Rutger was a ritual master."

"Thaumaturge." Her tone was definite. "We think he cloaked the source of his power in order to get close to the Council. It seems a short step to guess that's how he learned about the Cor."

The knowledge shocked something deep within me, shocked and caused me pain. Memories rushed through my mind; working together: visiting the saloon after work, Saturdays in Golden Gate Park. I'd sucked his cock, for pity's sake. How had I been so wrong?

Though if Rutger had been a thaumaturge, it explained where Stevenson got the spells he'd plagued us with. Rutger had supplied them. He'd broken through Rafe's protection spell, and set the nightmare curse on the winding mechanism, and half a dozen other things besides.

I gave myself several heartbeats to wallow, then pulled myself together. Rutger was dead. Now it was Rafe I needed to concern myself with. Madam Munro would almost certainly want him to come to San Francisco, but his mother was correct when she said he'd hate living in the city. I needed to protect Rafe, even if it meant leaving him.

Leaving him? Oh Lord. No.

"Meredith, could you please see to the whereabouts of the boat with the two bodies? We'd do well not to leave them behind." Madam Munro produced a small notebook from the satchel at her feet. "And Fairchild, I'd like a written report of these events, and do include as much detail as possible."

"Of course, Madam, though I'd still like to know why you sent me here if you already had an agent in place."

She gave me a look that could have frozen my marrow. "She's my niece and she was tasked with keeping an eye on the local witches. She couldn't get close to the Gallaghers without giving herself away."

Mrs. Morrison — Meredith — fluttered her fingers at me. "Seems you were expendable."

"Quiet," Madam Munro snapped at her. "Now see here, someone named Barnard will be here to retrieve us in" — she glanced at a small clock she wore on an Albertina chain around her neck — "an hour. Please be ready to travel with us."

"Are you certain, Madam? Margaret needs —"

"Meredith will stay with Margaret for the time being —"

"No, Aunt Aggie, I'm sure that's not —"

"You'll stay." If I'd thought Madam Munro was cold when she looked at me, now she was fairly frigid. "And yes, Mr. Fairchild, I am sure you'll be traveling with me. As will Mr. Gallagher, too, I do hope."

The back of Rafe's hand brushed mine. "No," I said, "Rafe should stay here —"

"Thank you, Madam Munro. I would be happy to travel with you."

I only just stopped myself from hitting him with my elbow. "Rafe, you don't—"

"At least part of the way. I'd like to look for my father."

"What?" I grabbed his elbow, jerking him around so we faced one another. "What are you talking about?"

"I told you Martin Gallagher wasn't my father." He spoke directly to me, as if the others had left the room. "I'd like to find the man who got Mother with me, and I'd like it very much if you would help."

Perhaps the others *had* left the room. I had eyes only for Rafe. "Of course." Was I smiling? I must have been, although for once I wasn't orchestrating it. Rafe would find traveling difficult, but if I could ease his way… "I'd be honored."

"As would I." Madam Munro's interruption was far more annoying than it should have been. "Your mother was a Barron, born and raised in San Francisco. It would make a great deal of sense to start your search there."

Rafe didn't take notice of her, but I murmured thanks. She'd set us a trap, as neat as that, but I tried not to let it worry me. She'd have us where she wanted us, ready to use Rafe's power and my name, but when it came down to it, we'd find a way out of her clutches. Besides, I had questions too, like how Rutger had managed to fool me so completely, and why I'd been able to turn a fishing net into a wooden bridge. Had someone blocked my real power, and if so, why?

These last few days had given me much to think about, me and Rafe together. We'd find our answers, and we'd do it together.

The End

...They come forth from the darkness, and their sails

Gleam for a moment only in the blaze,

And eager faces, as the light unveils,

Gaze at the tower, and vanish while they gaze...

From The Lighthouse by Henry Wadsworth Longfellow

Liv Rancourt

Acknowledgements

This book was a long time in coming....a looong time. I started its earliest incarnation in the summer of 2018. It was a Creepy Doll story, set in the 1940s, and I drafted most of it during CampNaNoWriMo that July. The story didn't quite work the way I wanted it to, but I liked pieces of it, mainly the setting and the characters, so I transplanted them into something new.

That version was my NaNoWriMo project in 2019. (NaNoWRiMo stands for National Novel Writing Month, a global challenge where you commit to writing 50,000 words in the month of November. There are also shorter challenges – CampNaNoWriMo – at other times in the year.)

The Lighthouse Keeper

This time the story was set in 1898 Seattle, with witches and fairies and all sorts of magical creatures. And…things still didn't quite click. I put it aside, figuring I'd pull out the good parts later.

(Lol…are you sensing a theme?)

Then in late '21/early '22, I grabbed hold of a new idea: a paranormal series set in Victorian San Francisco, centered around a rooming house with quirky characters, witches, and all kinds of magical goodness. (The fairies got the ax, as did the near-vampire creatures, but there was still plenty of magic to go around.) After a bunch of research, it was time to get drafting.

Right away, the characters from that old Creepy Doll story made themselves known and, with them in mind, I scribbled down some scenes. Still (still!) I couldn't find my way into the story.

I needed one final *thing* to pull all my ideas together.

I found that *thing* when my friend KB invited me out on her boat. We were noodling around Puget Sound when I saw the West Point Lighthouse. Voila!! I had my remote location, and everything else fell into place.

I drafted most of *The Lighthouse Keeper* during NaNoWriMo 2022. I'd hoped to publish it in early spring '23, however when I saw what my cover artist created, I knew the book had to be the very best I could make it. With that in mind, and with a new editor to help me, I've been living in this world for months.

And it's finally time for me to thank all the people who helped me get here. KB, thank you for taking me out on your boat! Dear Husband, thank you for your patience while I'm on this writing journey.

Irene and Kelly, thank you for your excellent beta-reading insights. Angela, your developmental and line edit notes were amazing, and Meg, your sharp eye cleaned up so many problems.

Nat, your cover…there are no words. I truly couldn't love it more.

Finally, I have to thank you readers, who have made all this possible. I hope you had fun with Rafe and Vincent, and yes, they'll have another book – and this one won't take me four years to write!

Happy reading!

About the Author

Liv Rancourt is a multi-published author of gay and m/m romance. Because love is love, even with fangs.

Liv is a huge fan of paranormal romance and urban fantasy and loves history just as much, so her stories often feature vampires or magic or they're set in the past...or all of the above. She also co-authors two m/m paranormal romance series with Irene Preston. Their partnership works because Liv is good at blowing things up and Irene is good at explaining why.

When Liv isn't writing she takes care of tiny premature babies in the NICU. Her husband is a soul of patience, her kids are her pride and joy, and her dog Burnsie is endlessly entertaining

More books by Liv!

Soulmates
Soulmates is fast-paced, sexy gay paranormal romance, the first book in the Soulmates series.

Tested
The Soulmates are back, and this time their bonds are being Tested...

Redeemed
The grand finale...or it is?

The Vampire's Pirate
Book 1 in the Immortal and Illicit Duology
Is death too great a risk when the reward is freedom?

The Lighthouse Keeper

The Pirate's Vampire
*(This is my current work in progress. Join my mailing list
so you don't miss it!)*

The Clockwork Monk
*(This one is a Steampunk-light novella that's perma-free
over on Prolificworks.)*
Trevor Chalmers tells himself he only believes in fine
suits, strong brandy,
and muscular men.
He's wrong.

Lost & Found
(Have you ever wanted to visit Paris in June…of 1920?)
A dancer who cannot dance and a physician who
cannot heal must find in each other the strength to
love.

Aqua Follies
(Stand-alone gay romance set in 1955 Seattle.)
Sometimes one smile does change everything.

Change of Heart
*(Stand-alone(ish) novella set in 1933 New Orleans, with a
side helping of a certain vampire who appears in the Hours
of the Night series.)*
Preacher always said New Orleans was a den of sin,
so of course Clarabelle had to see for herself.

Liv Rancourt

Paranormal romances co-written with Irene Preston

The Hours of the Night series

Vespers
If he follows his heart, he'll lose his soul.

Bonfire
Silent night, holy hell.

Nocturne
It's Mardi Gras, *cher,* and this time *le bon temps* kicks
off with murder.

Benedictus (Coming soon!)

The Haunts and Hoaxes series

Haunted
A reluctant psychic meets a skeptical historian.
Shenanigans ensue.

Harrowed
There's nothing scarier than the truth.

The Lighthouse Keeper

*

We also contributed a novella to the second season of the Royal Powers series. If a super-royal-romcom sounds like your thing, try…

The Frogman and the Spy

www.ingramcontent.com/pod-product-compliance
Lightning Source LLC
Chambersburg PA
CBHW021756190726
48290CB00005B/1289